MW01273854

SANDBOX SECRETS

JAYMEE LEE SCHWAB

Sandbox Secrets

tellwell

Tellwell Talent
www.tellwell.ca

ISBN
978-0-2288-6850-7 (Hardcover)
978-0-2288-6842-2 (Paperback)
978-0-2288-6843-9 (eBook)

PART 1

June 6, 1988

Chapter 1

Kathy Gibbons was in a loveless marriage. They hadn't slept together in the same bed for a couple of years. Her husband, Calvin, was always passed out in his chair when she got home from work. Kathy longed for the kisses they never shared. The flirting and love she had always wanted. The bills piled up, and the stress grew. He had been laid off his job at the Meat Packing Plant and stayed that way. He collected next-to-nothing paycheques while she worked full-time at the Diner and weekends at the Laundromat. It was so upsetting that she was worried about leaving her daughter alone with her dad. Those types of thoughts should never have to enter a woman's mind.

Kathy wouldn't let him touch her anymore. He disgusted her. She knew he watched pornography late at night and had found clippings of little girls and boys in a shoebox in the garage. She found them that day when she was looking for the gardening tools. Kathy had confronted her husband with them that evening. Tears in her eyes, she threw them on his lap.

"You're sick. How could I have ever married a man who enjoys looking at little children."

"Those aren't mine. Brian was in the garage with his friends one day. I saw them out there. Those boys are always fooling around. Maybe you should tell your sister to keep her damn kid out of our yard. Probably out there smoking pot and God knows what else."

Kathy breathed in disgust. Turning around and heading into the kitchen, she went up the stairs and into her daughter's room. Animal shadows cast about the walls and the ceiling as her night light turned the bedroom into a jungle safari. Kathy pulled the blankets over Jessica and kissed her on the cheek. She felt warm. 'Maybe I should call in sick tonight,' she wondered. Diane was out of town and Julie was home with the flu. There was no one she could call to take her shift. She closed the curtains on the two-pane window and left the room.

The volume rose on the TV, and she was out the door to work. The awful pains in her stomach that she had felt earlier returned. Seeing the clippings in her mind again made her nauseous. 'This is my last night shift,' she whispered to herself as she pulled into the parking lot and shut off the ignition.

She always had the closing shifts at work and felt uncomfortable leaving him alone with their daughter. Numerous times, Kathy had asked Jessica if her father had ever been inappropriate with her in any way or made her feel strange. The answer was always, "No, Mommy."

Kathy poured the last drip of coffee into the ceramic cup on the table. The chapped hands of a man wrapped his fingers around the mug.

"Slow night?" He looked at her with curious eyes. The Diner had been, but her mind raced. She couldn't shake the feeling that something wasn't right.

"Ya," she said, turning back to the counter. Kathy was in no mood for conversation. She rinsed the pot and set it on the counter. The till had been counted, and she was waiting patiently for the clock to tell her she could go home. It was 10:53 PM.

"I'm ready to close up if you're done, Sir."

"All right, all right, I get it. You want to leave. Well, don't let an old man like me keep you." He threw some change on the table and walked out. Kathy quickly grabbed his cup, ran a cloth over the ring of coffee left behind, and locked up the Diner.

She hurried out to her two-door Neon, unlocking the driver's door. She jumped into the seat and fired it up. The urge to get home plagued her. Her nausea returned as she pulled onto the Interstate. The rain was pelting down. The fog that hung in the air made the gloom she already felt intensify. She clicked off the radio and listened to the sound of the thunder and the storm as she sped home.

Chapter 2

As she pulled into the driveway, Kathy noticed there was no light coming from her daughter's bedroom window. The trees danced back and forth in the yard as the wind howled through the branches. She checked the other windows for light. Her daughter was afraid of the dark. Kathy always left the night light on in her room to help her sleep. There was no light now, and this alarmed her. She grabbed her purse and slammed the door. The rain was coming down even heavier now. She could see the reflection of a lightning strike and hear the thunder behind her. Kathy turned the knob and went inside.

The air felt damp against her face. The smell of booze lingered. Kathy set her purse on the side table and unzipped her coat. The house was silent. She peered into the living room. The chair where her husband always sat was empty, along with a twenty-six-ounce bottle on the TV tray. Her heart raced through the kitchen and up the back stairs, as she neared the top. Her mouth was dry, making it hard to swallow. Down the hall, she stopped in front of the second door. The coloured stickers JESSICA stared up at her. Kathy placed her hand on the door and slowly pushed it open. The smell of whiskey now filled her nostrils, hitting the back of her throat, making her gag. It was dark. Lightning lit up the room. She could see her husband on the edge of the bed. He wasn't moving, but she could hear him breathing heavy. Kathy rushed to the bed.

"What the fuck have you done?!?!"

She pushed her husband off the bed and cradled her daughter's lifeless body in her arms. She was screaming. Eyes wild, she reached for the lamp on the bedside table. The animals that danced around the room made her dizzy. She rocked back and forth, stroking the long blonde hair on Jessica's head. Her lips were already turning purple. There was blood on the sheets and her nightgown. Kathy gagged and threw up beside the bed. Calvin was still on the floor. His hands covered his face as he wept.

"I'm so sorry, Kathy. I'm so sorry," he kept repeating it. The more he said it, the madder she became. She laid Jessica's body back on the bed and lunged at her husband. Kathy was on top of him, arms flaying, and legs kicking. She was striking him hard in the face. She couldn't stop. The rage and adrenaline forced themselves out of her like someone had just poured gasoline on a fire and lit a match. Her heart ached as the thoughts of what he had done to their little girl played around in her mind. She was going to kill him. She wanted him to suffer a horrible death. Tears were pouring out of her, and her throat ached. Her whole body ached. Kathy got up and kicked the man who she had once loved. He was now the monster that took her baby from her, in the same fashion she had received her.

Her mind raced. She couldn't focus. Kathy knew that she had to be strong. The image of Jessica's face flashed through her memory. It was burned there. She wanted to run. She needed to escape the events that had taken place that night. She was so angry at herself for not listening to her intuition. She knew something was wrong. Why didn't she listen? Why didn't she leave him before it got to this? She suddenly blamed herself. If only she had left sooner, she would still have her little girl in her arms.

Kathy ran to her bedroom and grabbed a suitcase. She opened dresser drawers and rummaged through the closet. Panic set in. How am I going to live with this for the rest of my life? What will people think? Will they blame me for staying with a man who clearly showed signs of needing help long ago? Kathy flung her body on the bed. She cried until she threw up again. Devastation and guilt set in. As she lay there, she thought about going to the kitchen and getting a knife. She wanted to kill her husband. As much as she despised him, Kathy could never take his life. A part of her that had once loved him crept in.

The memory of their daughter's birth played in her mind like watching it on video. She was so happy and excited to start their family and live happily ever after. When did it all change? When did he become this sick predator who just murdered their daughter through sexual acts? The more she thought about it, the clearer it became. He had always been that monster. She thought of prom and the way he had forced himself on her. She had told herself that it happened because he was just young, and he couldn't control the testosterone flowing through his veins. He had been violent with her a couple of times in the bedroom over the years and made her believe that it was fun to pleasure each other with a bit of abuse. He said it was healthy for their relationship to let out their anger on each other in the bedroom.

Kathy sat on the edge of the bed and took a few deep breaths. She wiped the tears from her face and got up. A few more items were tossed into the suitcase. She zipped it up and left the room.

Calvin was still on the floor. Stepping over him, Kathy climbed onto her daughter's bed. She wrapped her arms around her baby girl and cried.

"I'm sorry, my angel, I should've known. I should've taken you away from here. Now he has taken you from me. I love you."

Kathy wrapped Jessica's favourite blanket around her shoulders and stood up. It was the same one she had brought her home from the hospital in. Kathy leaned down and kissed her on the lips. She left the room and lugged her suitcase down the stairs. Reaching the bottom, she stared at a picture on the wall. It was Jessica on her first day of kindergarten. Two pigtails braided on either side hung over her shoulders with a smile that could heal the world. Kathy pulled the picture off the wall and slid it into the front pocket of her suitcase. She turned and looked up the stairs. She had to get out of this house and away from the evil that engulfed it. Kathy opened the door. She walked to the driveway and opened the trunk. Her suitcase in, she climbed into the driver seat. Kathy pulled her cell phone out of her purse and dialed 911.

"911, is this an emergency?" the voice on the other end asked.

"Yes, my husband has raped and killed my daughter. The address is 53 Cottonwell Road. He is still inside. Please send someone to take that fucking bastard to jail."

Kathy hung up the phone and backed out of the driveway. The rain was still coming down, and a crack of thunder rumbled through her spine. Where was she going? She didn't know, but she couldn't stay there. She wanted to die and be in heaven with her little girl. She couldn't face anyone, the neighbours, reporters, family. She knew they would all blame her.

The ambulance pulled into the driveway, the red lights on top spinning, with a patrol car right behind it. The responders got out and followed the police officer inside. They looked around and went up the stairs. They entered Jessica's bedroom and flicked on the light. There was a man on the floor in the fetal position and a child on the bed. A medic checked her for a pulse, nothing. She was dead. He motioned for the second responder to get the stretcher. The officer radioed for backup. He knelt and grabbed Calvin's arm.

"Sir, are you awake? Do you know what has happened?"

Calvin groaned and uttered the words, "I'm sorry." The officer reached for his cuffs and fastened them around Calvin's wrists.

"You are under arrest for murder. You have the right to remain silent. Anything you say can and will be used against you in a court of law. You have the right to speak to an attorney. If you cannot afford an attorney, one will be appointed for you. Do you understand these rights as they have been read to you?"

Calvin nodded as the officer pulled him to his feet. The responder returned with the stretcher and the two medics carefully placed the child's body on it. Her face so pale, one reached down and closed her eyes. They strapped her down and continued to transport her outside.

The officer pushed Calvin into the backseat. Other officers were at the scene and taping off the property. Neighbours stood by and watched in horror as the stretcher was placed in the ambulance. Calvin was taken to the station and held in custody in a cell, waiting to be questioned. He was still intoxicated.

Kathy drove about twenty miles and pulled off the road. Her eyes were swollen, and her head was pounding. She was scared. The storm was clearing, and she could see the stars being uncovered in the sky as the clouds rolled on. She used to sit in the backyard with Jessica and swing under the stars on a calm, clear night. Pointing out for her different constellations and waiting patiently for a shooting star so her daughter could see it, get that surprised look on her face, like only children can, and make a wish.

Kathy wrapped her arms around the steering wheel and cried. She tilted her head and stared out the window. She would never look at this sky with her baby again. She didn't want to look at the moon shining its light down so bright and beautiful. Kathy wanted to be in the dark. Her mind wandered while sitting there. As she had packed her suitcase, the images of running and starting over engulfed her, the realization now that running wasn't the answer. All she wanted was to be with her child. The bridge now seemed like an easy option.

Kathy rummaged through the glove box and pulled out a piece of paper. Unfolding it, she laid it on the passenger seat. Hands in her purse, she found a pen at the bottom, pulled it out and clicked the end. The tears were streaming down her face and landing on the paper. It was blurry as she rubbed her eyes. Her hand was shaking. She was still trying to keep the nausea to the bottom of her stomach. Kathy breathed deep and began to write:

I cannot go on without her
I cannot live in the same world as him
I blame myself
I'm sorry

The words scrawled on the paper stared back at her. Pressing the button in the glove box, Kathy popped the trunk, opened the car door, and stepped outside. She leaned her head back and gazed into the night. She could hear water running. The river that ran along the outskirts of town was moving fast. There was an old, covered bridge where she had brought Jessica to see the graffiti and years of writing on the walls. She loved the sound of the water flowing underneath them. They would play make-believe and pretend that if you went out the other end of the bridge, you would end up in a magical place with fairies and rainbows. This made her cry again. She wanted so badly to walk through and be in that place with her daughter again.

She lifted the trunk door and unzipped the front compartment of her suitcase. The picture of Jessica stared up at her. She stood there for a minute and stared back. Picking it up, she held it to her chest and slammed the trunk door. Kathy could hear the river flowing and followed the sound of the water to the bridge.

Kathy pulled the receipt out of her pocket. She reread it, folded it, and shoved it between two planks on the bridge. She stepped around the entrance and stared at the river splashing below. Kathy took a deep breath, looked up at the clear night sky, and said a prayer asking for God's forgiveness.

Kathy's car was spotted by a patroller. Pulling up beside it, he got out of the cruiser. He unbuckled his flashlight from his belt and clicked it on. Shining the light into the backseat then the front. He walked around the car and back to his.

On the radio, he pressed the button. "I have located the Neon which belongs to Kathy Gibbons. Please send Forensics for further investigation." Giving the location, he replaced the handset back in the holster and waited.

Ten minutes later, a van pulled up, and the engine stopped. A burly man stepped out. His name was Alfred Coffy. Everyone called him 'Coffee,' and joked about how he was always wired up like someone on a caffeine buzz. He had been in the business for thirty years and had seen everything from homicide to suicide. Lifting his cap off his head, he ran his fingers through his hair, and then replaced it. Pulling out a pair of clear plastic gloves, he stretched them over his fingers, lifted the handle on the door and pulled it open. He stuck his head inside. Keys were in the ignition. A purse sat on the floor of the passenger seat. He pulled out a wallet and looked inside. Kathy's drivers licence stared back at him. Closing the wallet, he returned it to the purse. He opened the glove box and pressed the button for the trunk. It popped open. Around to the back of the car, Coffy lifted the trunk door. There was a suitcase inside. He unzipped it. There were a few items of clothing and a pair of shoes. He searched the other compartments and found nothing but an empty sanitary napkin wrapping.

"So, what do you think?" the officer asked as he looked him up and down.

"I don't know. It's hard to say with cases like these, a little girl dead, a man with blood on his hands, and a missing woman."

Coffy pulled out his flashlight, and both men walked down the path towards the bridge. They shone their light into the grass along the sides and looked for clues of the woman's whereabouts. They reached the old, covered bridge and stepped under its roof. Flashlights shone against the old wood panels holding the structure in place. Coffy stepped around the outside of the bridge and shone his flashlight down at the river. The current was strong. Water splashed against the rocks. He pulled the light toward himself along the ground and noticed something. He walked over to the pile on the ground. Coffy knelt and brushed it slightly with the flashlight. It was a red cotton cardigan. He picked it up and smelt it. It still smelled fresh. Smells of vanilla and deep fryer grease hung in the fabric.

"You better come take a look at this." The officer called to Coffy as he pointed the LED light coming from his wand toward something wedged between two panelling boards on the wall. Coffy folded up the sweater and stuck it in a plastic bag. He entered the bridge and pulled the paper out, unfolding it. Coffy read the few lines written on the note.

I cannot go on without her
I cannot live in the same world as him
I blame myself
I'm sorry

It was an oil change receipt from an auto body shop where Kathy had taken her car to be serviced. He pulled a brown paper envelope out of his pocket and placed it inside. There were no signs of a physical struggle on the bridge. Both officers assumed she had jumped from the bridge into the river, hit her head on the rocks below, and had been swept away.

They scoured the bank of the river, looking for any signs of her body.

"Classic case of suicide. Mother finds her daughter's death at the hands of her father. She would have been in shock and not thinking clearly. When something tragic like this happens, the parents who did nothing before it's too late are the ones to suffer truly. By the looks of the belongings in her car, Kathy must have had a plan to run away. Sometimes with a death as tragic as this, it is hard for the mother to cope or even think about it. She knows she will feel the looks from the people in the town, whispers, stories, rumors, lies, and guilt for not protecting her child. Kathy probably thought it would be better to end her own life than part of the drama that would arise. We can head back to the station now. I'll radio for the search team to come and do a good sweep of the riverbanks. It's flowing damn fast tonight, and if she did jump and did survive the impact, we may be too late."

Several hours had passed since Calvin had been brought in. His face was bruised and bloody. His hair had puke in it. He smelled of death, the death of his little girl. The officers wanted him to sober up a bit before the questioning. In situations like these, the accused usually break under the pressure more when they are sober.

Coffy entered the station and tossed his jacket on the chair behind his desk. He placed the envelope and the plastic bag in a box nearby. Pen on the paper, he made some notes and leaned back in his chair. It was a cut and dry case. The father is clearly to blame for the murder of the girl. If his wife's body shows up dead as well, the jury will not like this. Coffy pushed himself away from his desk. The wheel squeaked as he stood up. He made his way down the hall and motioned to one of the officers on duty.

"Bring Mr. Gibbons to Questioning Room C. Let's see what he has to say for himself. If it were up to me, that bastard would be in the chair. God damn pedophiles and rapists roaming the streets taking innocent children's lives."

He entered the room and sat at one of the two chairs placed on either side of a steel table. He pulled out a Virginia Slim from the half-wrapped pack in his shirt pocket and lit a match. Flinging it into the ashtray, he inhaled deeply. The smoke that he blew out created a haze that resembled people dancing and swaying in the night. He checked his watch and cleared his throat.

Calvin entered the interrogation room and was placed on the vacant chair.

"Can I please take these cuffs off?" He eyed Coffy.

With the flick of his wrist, the officer knew what Coffy meant. He unlocked the handcuffs that were bound around a killer. Calvin pulled his arms forward and rubbed his wrists. He wiped sweat and hair from his eyes with the back of his hand.

"Can I have one of those?" He eyed Coffy again.

"God damn it, you scum are all the same. You go around causing chaos, devastation, taking lives, and you all want something back as if we owe you for catching you and bringing you in."

He threw the pack of Slims on the table along with the matchbook.

"If it's going to get you to tell me what the fuck happened, then, by all means, smoke away."

Coffy placed a cassette recorder on the table. He stared at Calvin with disgust. The blood on his shirt was now dry and permanent. A little girl's absence from the world is now a permanent memory for the community. He wanted so badly to reach across the table and give him a beating.

He pressed record.

"State your name."

"Calvin Micheal Gibbons."

"Do you live in Willows Cove?"

"Yes."

"Did you grow up here?"

"I moved to Willows Cove when I was three years old with my father after my mother left. Dad thought it would be a good way for us to start somewhere new. He always blamed me for her leaving. Said the spark between them died when I came out of her with a penis. She wanted a girl."

"Where is your place of employment?"

"I used to work for Patty Packers, a meat packing plant. I was laid off three years ago during the e-coli outbreak. We all lost our jobs. The company didn't have enough money to clean the place up to health standards, so they shut the doors."

"Are you a happily married man, Mr. Gibbons?"

"Depends what you consider happy. If fucking your wife puts you in a happy marriage, then no, I ain't happy. I know she was out screwing around. Always off to work at all hours. She wouldn't let me touch her anymore. Probably too wore out from all the sex she was having around town."

Coffy cleared his throat. He envisioned the sick fuck in front of him molesting his daughter as a means of release because his wife wouldn't touch him. He lit another smoke.

"Do you know where your wife is, Mrs. Kathy Gibbons?"

His eyebrows raise, "No."

"We found her car parked at the Rally Covered Bridge. She left a suicide note. We believe she jumped into the river, Mr. Gibbons. We have a team on the riverbanks searching for her now. The storm that blew in earlier made the river more fierce than usual."

Calvin sat back in his chair and felt the eyes of Coffy burning into him. Tears welled up as he covered his face.

"How many children do you have, and state the ages."

"One," he choked out. "One daughter, she's five."

"You mean to say, you had a five-year-old girl Gibbons, and you took her very life by your own hands. You raped and penetrated that little girl so hard; you ruptured her insides."

"No... I..."

"No?? Mr. Gibbons. You are trying to tell me that you didn't enter your daughter's bedroom while she was asleep and have your way with her? You didn't squeeze her tiny arms with so much force holding her down that the blood vessels broke throughout? You didn't hold her against her will as she begged you to stop until you took her life?"

Coffy was furious. He stood up and faced the back wall. He could hear Calvin sobbing.

"Tell me in your words what you did to that innocent child." He sat back down and waited. Calvin started to speak and choke out the words while fidgeting in his chair.

"I was angry at my wife. She found some things in the garage. I wanted to tell her that I had them because she wouldn't satisfy me anymore. I'm a man. I have needs to, physical needs. She parades around the house half-naked and teases me with her body. I had a few drinks."

"A few drinks, Mr. Gibbons? What in your mind is a few?" Coffy slammed his hand on the table.

"I finished off a bottle of Jamaican Rum. There was nothing on TV. I was bored. I was horny. I was fed up with touching myself. I could smell my wife's perfume lingering in the air, taunting me. The clippings she found scattered on the carpet. The long hair of the girls turned me on. I went upstairs to the bedroom. I was going to pleasure myself in her underwear drawer. I wanted her to see what she was doing to me. Leaving me all the time." Calvin paused and looked at the floor.

"So, you went upstairs, and then what, Gibbons? You never made it to your bedroom, did you?"

Calvin gagged.

"Did you?"

Eyes still on the floor, he stammered, "No, I didn't. I could hear her breathing when I walked by. She was moaning, she must've been having a nightmare. I only went in to comfort her."

He could feel his blood begin to circulate faster through his veins. His heart picked up the pace as he replayed his actions in his mind.

"Continue Gibbons." Coffy stared at him with squinted eyes that could burn a hole in his soul.

"She was laying there so beautiful and pure. I sat on the bed and stroked her head. Her hair was so soft in my fingers. I put my head on her chest to listen to her breathing. She smelled good. I kissed her cheek and she moaned. Her body moved on the bed, and I wanted to keep kissing her. I never meant to hurt her."

Calvin's speech grew quiet as he spoke. The room was spinning, and he could still hear her voice inside his head. The smell of booze was so strong Coffy could taste it.

"I was drunk, and I wasn't thinking clear. I couldn't stop myself. She looked like her mother. I pulled her panties off and touched her. She woke up and looked at me. She kept saying, 'Daddy.' I wanted to stop, but it was too late. I was on top of her and inside her. It felt so good to be in a woman."

"A woman?? A woman??" Coffy yelled. "That was your five-year-old baby, not a fucking woman. I've heard enough." Coffy jumped to his feet, knocking over his chair. An officer opened the door. Coffy's eyes darted toward him. "Get him the fuck out of my sight."

Rushing into the bathroom, he leaned over a toilet in the stall and threw up. Coffy wiped his face as the sweat beads and tears rolled down his face and neck. The story he just heard played through his mind. Visions of the events made him throw up again. He splashed water on his face and went back to his desk.

Calvin was shoved into a six-foot by eight-foot cell in the police lock-up. His eyes were puffy and swollen. He could barely make out the men and the contents of the room. They were short on cells, so he had to sleep on a foam twin matt on the floor.

"You'll be lucky if you wake up tomorrow. They don't take lightly to your kind in here."

The officer slammed the barred gate closed behind him and winked at one of the inmates inside.

Calvin had been placed in a cell with two other men to await the hearing. The wink from the guard said it all. The men now knew the crime he had committed, and they were furious. Both men were in jail for theft and forgery. They each had children of their own. In a place where everyone has committed a crime, the ones who have molested, raped, and killed children get the worst treatment of all. This being a little bit of justice, knowing that the perpetrator will be subdued to unlawful things while behind bars made it easier for some to sleep at night.

"You fuckin' pedophile." One of the men whispered angrily through clenched teeth. Calvin sat on the matt and put his head in his hands. Closing his eyes, the remorse he felt over killing his daughter in such a horrific way set in. He knew that this feeling would be way worse than the beating he knew he would receive in that cell. The booze had worn off entirely, and Calvin was thirsty.

"I need water," Calvin muttered.

"What the fuck did you say, man?"

Calvin spoke softly again. "I need water."

The taller inmate stepped toward Calvin. He kicked him in the shin and spat on his head. "You need a drink, pig?"

Calvin looked up at him through a blurry gaze. Eyes squinting, he tried to focus.

"Don't look at me, you sick fuckin' baby killer. You want a drink? I'll give you a fuckin' drink." The inmate reached down and pulled Calvin to the floor. He shoved him toward the steel toilet against the wall. By the back of the neck, he forced Calvin's face into the bowl.

"You still thirsty, shit bag?" He pulled Calvin's head out and forced it down again just as fast. Calvin was sputtering and gasping for air. He had both hands on the toilet seat trying to stop the man from pushing him in. It was no use. The inmate did this a few more times before throwing Calvin in the corner. The other inmate laughed as he watched.

"Shut the fuck up, or you're next."

The guards walked the aisle and looked in on each cell.

"Lights Out!" could be heard throughout the halls. Some of the men hooted and hollered. One of the guards stopped at Calvin's cell.

"Sleep tight," he snickered as he dragged his wand along the metal bars.

Calvin laid on the matt and pulled his legs up into the fetal position. He put his back against the wall and watched the other men.

As the wood crackled in the fire pit beside the cabin, the men joked about their wives. The whiskey was flowing, and the flames licked higher. The smell of the campfire and their fresh meat lingered in the air. Cigarette butts littered the yard. A bag of sunflower seeds had been spilled, sprinkling the seeds across the ground. The dampness of the air was so humid and thick, the fog had set in. They were celebrating their kill. Ronnie was telling a story about an Urban Legend in the woods. The townspeople claimed that a family who had owned a cottage nearby haunted the land. The house had been struck by lightning and burned to the ground. The remains of the four bodies had never been recovered.

"Some nights when I was a boy, I would hear screams coming from the woods."

The howl of distant coyotes echoed in the valley, their cries piercing the silence. The Great Grey Owl hooted on the tree branch which shadowed the yard. Blinking its beady eyes, the plumaged neck of the bird rotated like that of a child out of an exorcism movie.

Calvin staggered as he stood up. The embers were glowing in the pit beside him. Two empty chairs cast shadows around him.

"Must have passed out," Calvin said aloud as he started toward the front door. The sound of twigs snapped behind him.

"Whose there?"

He swaggered back and forth. Staring into the trees, he looked for signs of life. Calvin reached for the shotgun leaning against the chopped woodpile. With the barrel raised, he waited. The forest cracked again, and Calvin pulled the trigger. The bullets sprayed the patch of wilderness that stood before him. The helpless yelp of his dog could be heard for miles. The realization of what he had done hit him hard. Calvin dropped to his knees. The shot woke his friends from their drunken stupor. When they found Calvin, he was on his knees. The weapon that ended Champ's life still hung in the grip of his fingers. Ronnie ran into the trees. The dog was dead. He scooped up the blood-soaked body and carried it towards his friends.

When he woke up, the memory he just relived ran over in his mind like a record with a needle stuck the way it did when his grandfather would fall asleep in his chair. His favourite song stuck on repeat as the vinyl spun round and round. Kathy never did ask what happened to Champ. She buried it deep down inside, forcing herself to let her pet go. She didn't want him to tell her, to lie.

It was the alcohol that had always done the most damage in his life. The withdrawals he was experiencing as he lay in his cell overwhelmed him. The sheets were soaked and ice cold. How did he get here? Who was this man so ruled by temptation? A lust was so overpowering it resulted in her loss, his loss, and Kathy's. The smell of sweat engulfed him. He felt claustrophobic, trapped with these strange men. Sentenced to a life behind bars, Calvin knew it was his fate and where he belonged. He now had to fight for a life he gave up.

He thought about when he was a boy. He was never certain when it started, but the uncontrollable need to fulfill his fantasies had him in a tight grip. He used to peep in town windows, spying on young girls and older women. He would watch them talk on the phone and brush their hair. Secretly being a part of women's lives as they would cheat on their husbands while they were out of town. The scandal invigorated him. His father, Stanley, caught him in the neighbour's yard when he was twelve years old. He got a few good lashings from the leather strap he would keep in the kitchen drawer.

"No son of mine is going to be known as the peeping tom. You better not embarrass me boy. I've raised you to have respect for women. If I catch you again, I'll cut it off. Do you understand?" Stanley was furious. Calvin was embarrassed. He couldn't even recall entering the yard.

He closed his eyes. The voices inside his head screamed at him, tormenting him. Calvin squeezed his lids tighter and forced his mind blank.

Chapter 3

"All rise." The courtroom went silent as the trial was about to begin. The jury consisted of twelve members. On this panel were eight men employed as follows: an electrician, janitor, journalist, dairy farmer, retail store manager, a chef, city bus driver, and a car salesman. A librarian, gymnastics teacher, pharmacist, and a waitress made up the four women. The judge entered and took his place at the front of the courtroom.

The prosecutor opened his briefcase, which sat on the table in front of him.

"Here we have the confession of Calvin Gibbons," he said as he removed the tape recorder from inside. He held it in the air so that the courtroom could see. He pressed play. As they listened to the words of a man tell the story of how he raped and murdered his daughter, the courtroom eyeballed Gibbons with disgust.

Nancy broke down in tears. She was becoming hysterical as the words entered her brain. She didn't want to listen, but she had to. The deaths of her sister and her niece were too much to handle. Her husband, Steve, put his arms around her and helped her out of the pew. They left the courtroom. The door slammed behind them and echoed off the walls. When the questioning ended, he turned off the tape and placed it back in the briefcase. His fingers shuffled through a few pages and picked one out.

"Here I have the Forensic report of Miss Jessica Dawn Gibbons. It states that the specimens taken for testing match the DNA of one, Calvin Micheal Gibbons, the victim's father."

Sliding the thin steel opener along the glued flap of the envelope, he pulled out the requested documents. The autopsy report came back as follows:

Willows Cove Coroner's Office	
DATE and HOUR AUTOPSY PERFORMED: 06/07/1988; 2:47 AM by Marilyn Smith, M.D. 963 Boathouse Way Willows Cove, NG 73957 555-836-XXXX (FAX 555-836-XXXX)	**Assistant:** Pauline Green, M.D. **Full Autopsy Performed**
SUMMARY REPORT OF AUTOPSY	
Name: GIBBONS, Jessica Dawn	**Coroner's Case #:** 1988-6534
Date of Birth: 2/14/1983	**Age:** 5
Race: Caucasian	**Sex:** Female
Date of Death: 06/06/1988	**Body Identified by:** Nancy Spencer, aunt of the deceased
Case # 053689-18-1988	**Investigative Agency:** Willows Cove Sheriff's Department

EXTERNAL EXAMINATION:

The autopsy was performed at 2:47 AM on June 07, 1988. The victim was brought into the room in a black body bag. Clothing consisted of white and purple striped nightgown. Pink nail polish covered the toenails.

The body when weighed, registered 38 lbs, measuring 43 inches tall. The eyelids were closed and swollen. Blonde hair at a length of 21 inches.

Nightgown was removed. Three bluish purple bruises present on outside of left bicep. Visible evidence of abuse around genitals and inner thighs. Brown hair was removed from underneath the fingernails on right hand. Hair placed in tube for testing.

A strawberry red birthmark measuring 4x11 cm on back of left calf.

INTERNAL EXAMINATION:

SKELETAL SYSTEM: Compressed disk in cervical region C4-C5.

RESPIRATORY SYSTEM--THROAT STRUCTURES: Throat clear of obstructions. No injuries to the lips, teeth, or gums.

CARDIOVASCULAR SYSTEM: The heart weighs 253 grams and has a normal size and configuration. No evidence of atherosclerosis is present.

FEMALE GENITAL SYSTEM: There is evidence of recent sexual activity. Ruptured membranes resulting in bruising on inner thighs. Indications that the sexual contact was forced. Vaginal fluid samples were removed for analysis. Hair was also removed from the lining of the vaginal wall for testing.

TOXICOLOGY: Blood and urine samples submitted.

LABORATORY DATA

Cerebrospinal fluid culture and sensitivity:
Nervous system intact at time of death

Drug Screen Results:

Urine screen {Immunoassay} was NEGATIVE.
Ethanol: 0 gm/dl, Blood (Heart)
Ethanol: 0 gm/dl, Vitreous
Marilyn Smith, M.D.
Chief Toxicologist
June 6, 1988

EVIDENCE COLLECTED:

1. One purple striped long sleeve nightgown, size Small.
2. Samples of Blood (type O+), Bile, and Tissue (heart, lung, brain, kidney, liver, spleen).
3. Ten swabs from various body locations, to be tested for the presence of semen.
4. Eleven autopsy photographs.
5. One post-mortem CT scan.
6. One post-mortem MRI.

OPINION

Time of Death: Body temperature, rigor and livor mortis, and stomach contents approximate the time of death between 8:30 and 9:30 PM on 6/6/1988.

Immediate Cause of Death: Asphyxia due to compression of internal organs. External pressure and force caused organs to rupture. Internal bleeding present.

Manner of Death: Homicide, Aggravated sexual assault

Willow's Cove Coroner's Office

June 7, 1988

The courtroom lit up with commotion. The evidence was enough to end all further questioning.

"We will take a short recess while the jury deliberates."

The members stood up and walked single file to the jury room.

Calvin could feel all the eyes on him. He placed his head down and started to cry. The door flew open, and Nancy ran down the aisle. She lunged at Calvin with extreme force. Hitting him with her fists, she screamed, "You piece of shit murderer. How could you do this? Why? Why would you do this to your own child? You sadistic fuck."

Members of the courtroom stood up to watch. Nancy's husband and one of the standing officers pulled Nancy off him. She was lit up like a bowl of firecrackers going off as they escorted her out of the room.

The jury had come to its conclusion. The judge returned to the Bench.

"All twelve members render the guilty verdict."

The judge sat forward. "Calvin Gibbons, you have been charged with the crime of aggravated sexual assault which resulted in the death of your five-year-old daughter, Jessica Gibbons. You are hereby sentenced to twenty years to life in a state penitentiary."

The judge pounded his gavel and left the Bench.

The Cove Times newspaper hosted the following excerpt on June 11, 1988:

Calvin Gibbons, an ex-employee of Patty Packers was sentenced to twenty years to life in a state penitentiary. He was found guilty of the death of his five-year-old daughter Jessica Gibbons. The injuries she sustained are too horrific to imagine. Gibbons' wife, Kathy, left a suicide note at the Rally Covered Bridge the night of the murder. Search teams and volunteers helped aid in the rescue of this woman. Funeral services for the late Jessica Gibbons will be held on Friday at the Willows Cove Cemetery. If anyone has any donations these can be directed to her Aunt, Nancy Spencer. Her contact information can be attained through The Cove Times.

The story was out, and the town bustled with the gossip. The family home was still under the yellow tape, and kids from the neighbourhood were breaking in to see if they could find anything worth talking about. A memorial had been set up for Kathy and Jessica, with hundreds of people crowding around pictures and flowers. Candles lit to honour them, signs in the air. People rioted with cardboard messages demanding that the court should have upheld the death penalty. The town news crew was on-site covering the gathering and taking statements from its members.

A man in his twenties grabbed the Reporter's microphone. "They put these kinds of sick men behind bars for a few years. Feed them and let them go outside. Then what, they let them out to do it again. It's an absolute outrage."

"He should be burned alive," a woman yelled at the camera.

The Reporter for Southside News, Paul Mason retrieved his microphone back.

"I am standing here in front of the home of the recently convicted killer, Calvin Gibbons. As you can see, the tragedy that has occurred has affected everyone in this community. When do we get to feel safe when your neighbours are cold-blooded killers? A little girl's life was taken in such a horrific way by a man who was to be her protector. The citizens are outraged at the sentencing he was given. They believe he should have been dealt the death penalty. All we can do now is say our prayers. This is Paul Mason reporting."

Chapter 4

The tiny church was filled with people coming to pay their respects and remember a child on Friday morning. The white casket with its beautiful arrangement of flowers sat at the front of the church awaiting its final resting place. The face of a carefree child stared at them. The innocent smile gave the reassurance that she had at least gotten the chance to enjoy life as a happy little girl, even if for a short period.

Once the pastor opened his bible and began to speak, the room went silent. “We will now read passages Mark: 13 – 16.”

“People were bringing little children to Jesus for him to place his hands on them, but the disciples rebuked them. When Jesus saw this, he was indignant. He said to them, “Let the children come to me, and do not hinder them, for the Kingdom of God belongs to such as these. Truly, I tell you, anyone who will not receive the Kingdom of God like a little child will never enter it. And he took the children in his arms, placed his hands on them and blessed them.”

“We must all remember to turn to God when something like this happens.”

With the bible closed, it was time for family and friends to say a few words. Nancy was the first to begin.

"In one of the stars, I shall be living. In one of them, I shall be laughing, and so it will be as if all the stars were laughing when you look at the sky at night. I heard this on '*The Little Prince*,' and it now makes me think of Jessica. She loved the way the stars lit up the sky. Kathy would check on her in the night and sometimes find her asleep on the floor in front of the window. They had slept on a blanket in the backyard one night, and I remember how excited she was telling me about her moonlight adventure. I am having a star named after Jessica, so I can find her when I need to be with her memory. I would be more than happy to share the stellar coordinates with anyone who would be interested."

Jessica's preschool teacher and a couple of others spoke before the service ended. '*Some Place Out There*' played through the tiny speakers as one-by-one a line formed to view the precious little girl. Teddy bears, skipping ropes, and yo-yos were placed all around her in the velvet lined box.

The church was emptied out as the town gathered at the Willows Cove Cemetery. Half the businesses closed their doors for the afternoon. Kathy had been well known in town. Her friendly nature made it easy for everyone to love her. The locals from the Diner came to the gravesite to pay their respects.

Her mother, Cheryl had passed away the year prior. She was diagnosed with cancer and refused treatment. She did not want to lose her hair from chemotherapy and had lost her will to live. This was difficult for Kathy to deal with. She begged her mother to treat the illness. Cheryl had given up on herself long before she had been diagnosed. When her husband left, a part of her went with him to. She had Kathy at a young age, and Jack had been the only man she had been intimate with. It was hard for her to be alone with no man in her life. She started sleeping around to find someone to fill that void, but no one ever stayed. When the tests came back positive for cancer, she was in a way relieved. Her time on earth would soon be ending, and this pleased her. She knew that no man would want to be with her in her condition, and refusing treatment seemed like an easy out. Kathy yelled at her, saying it was the coward's way, but Cheryl's response was always the same, "If you knew how much I was suffering, you wouldn't want me to go on."

Jack and Nancy had taken care of all the funeral arrangements for Jessica. She was placed next to her grandmother's plot. A tree was planted behind her headstone in memory of Kathy. Nancy had a couple of solar lights arranged. She knew that Jessica was scared of the dark and took comfort in the idea of the tiny lights illuminating at night.

The four-foot casket loomed above the hole dug for its final resting place. The roses piled up on top, spilling to the ground below. The sickness felt by everyone around could be seen on their faces, like that of a virus that had plagued a room full of quarantined people.

Nancy had written a poem that she wanted to read at the cemetery. Brian agreed to read it for her, and for his cousin. He pulled the folded-up piece of stationery paper out of his suit coat pocket and cleared his throat.

Your life was taken from this earth way too soon,

Your spirit will live on through the sun and the moon.

Your smile and laughter brought peace and harmony,

Your little footprints left imprints on the hearts of so many.

Your little beating heart now free to rest,

I love you Jessica Dawn, your life has made us truly blessed.

Brian wiped his tears and returned the poem to his pocket. Family and friends hung their heads and prayed for the little girl. One by one, they scooped up a handful of soil and tossed it on the casket as the cemetery staff lowered it to the ground.

Nancy knelt and cried. She clung to the rose and waited until the final movement was made. She released the grip on the stem and let it fall beneath the earth. The tree planted for Kathy swayed in the breeze. Cold air surrounded her as she got to her feet. With her hand in her pocket, her fingers played with the necklace she had brought. Three charms clung to the silver chain as she pulled it out, each one representing the lives of the three family members at her feet. Nancy hung the necklace on one of the branches close to the trunk. She said a silent prayer and turned to the street. Steve and Brian were waiting for her in the car. She climbed in as her husband started the ignition. Nancy cried as they drove away from the cemetery, leaving with it the members of her family she had loved so much.

PART 2

June 1982

Chapter 5

It was June of 1982 when Calvin had asked Kathy to be his date to the prom. Her initial response was no. She knew how the boys her age acted towards girls. Sex, sex, sex. That's all they thought about. It disgusted her to see some of her classmates get excited during sexual orientation classes. The teacher showed them how to put on a condom using a banana. Some of her girlfriends had started using the birth control pill. They were active with their boyfriends and wanted to be protected. Kathy didn't need the pill. She wasn't having relations with anyone, and she wanted to wait until marriage. Her father, Jack, walked out on her mother Cheryl, her older sister Nancy and Kathy, when she was in preschool. He had met another woman and moved in with her shortly after. Nancy had always been daddy's little girl, and she decided to go with her father. Kathy's mother despised him for this and forbade her from seeing him.

Cheryl changed after this. Always out on dates and bringing home strange men at all hours of the night. Kathy wondered if her mother was just lonely or horny or both. Maybe she had her own guilty reason for her husband leaving. They hadn't slept in the same bed for nine months before he left. Perhaps she had come to the conclusion that the only way to keep a man was to give him sex. Kathy realized young that if you give it to him so easy the only thing you'll get to keep is the notch in the headboard. Out of all the men she had seen her mother bring home, only two of them had been seen twice. Kathy didn't want this life. She dreamed of marrying her high school sweetheart and living happily ever after. She wanted to wait. She didn't want to just have sex. Like some kind of robot vagina that roamed the halls at school with all the other girls who had their hearts broken by boys who could feel no emotion aside from the flutter in their pants. She wanted to make love.

Cheryl had tried to convince Kathy to start using the pills. She had even booked an appointment with the gynecologist to receive a prescription. She had barely kissed a boy yet and had no intention of doing so anytime soon. The school year was ending. The classmates were finding their escorts and picking out clothes to wear.

When Cheryl heard at the coffee shop that Kathy had said no to Calvin, it bothered her. She approached Kathy that evening.

"Honey, I really think you should go. It will be a lot of fun. You can try on dresses, and we can get you a new pair of shoes. When a boy is interested in you, you shouldn't turn your back on him so easy Kathleen. You don't want to end up old and alone like your mother, do you?" Cheryl clasped Kathy's hands in her own.

Kathy pulled away. "I don't know, mom. Calvin is a little strange, and I would feel uncomfortable around the other girls in his class."

"Kathleen Crane, you have absolutely nothing to worry about those girls for. It's prom night, and they won't be worried about you. Please say yes."

Kathy sighed and looked at her mother. "Ok, mom, I'll go, but I'm only going to make you happy."

Cheryl put her arms in the air and hugged her daughter.

"Why are you so excited about Calvin Gibbons anyway? You don't even know him, mom."

"I know his father. He is a good man. He works hard to provide for himself and his son. Calvin's mother walked out on them when he was just a young boy. I have run into him a few times, and he has shown himself to be respectful to the ladies. He's not strange, Kathy; he's just a little shy. Being a bit reserved isn't always a bad trait to have in a man."

Kathy rolled her eyes. She threw her backpack on the couch and started fixing a snack in the kitchen. Cheryl followed behind her and opened the pantry.

"I made homemade salsa if you want me to melt some cheese on the nachos." Cheryl picked out a jar she had labelled sweet and mild and popped the top. She dumped half the bag of chips onto the plate.

"I can grate the cheese. You never put enough on." Kathy found the grater and shredded half the block from the fridge. Into the microwave for thirty-five seconds, the cheese snapped inside, and Kathy grabbed the plate out.

Cheryl spooned some salsa in a dish, and they gathered at the dining room table.

Cheryl dipped a chip. "So, what color do you want to wear? I know you love pink, but maybe you'll feel good in something red... and sleeveless?" She shoved the chip in her mouth and dipped one more.

"If I have to go to this thing, I'm wearing what I choose, mother."

They chatted about jewellery and what music the band would play. The plate was soon empty. Kathy slung her backpack over her shoulder and retired to her room to study. Calvin Gibbons wasn't the best-looking guy in school, but he did seem to have manners. Rumor was that his father had been strict with him growing up.

It was Saturday morning. Kathy made her bed and had a shower. Cheryl wanted to take her to the mall to pick out an outfit. After breakfast, Kathy found Calvin's number in the phone book. She dialed and listened to the ring on the other end.

"Hello," a voice answered.

"Hi, is Calvin home?"

"Speaking. Whose calling?"

Kathy paused for a moment. "It's Kathy Crane. I ...umm... I wanted to tell you that I will go with you to the prom if you haven't found another date."

"That's great. I'm excited that you want to go with me, Kathy. I will pick you up at seven o'clock on Friday."

"Ok." Kathy hung up the receiver. She felt an instant pain in her guts; a sudden uncertainty after agreeing to the date. When something wasn't right, she could usually sense it.

"Was that Calvin?" Her mother asked as she entered the kitchen.

"Yes, mom. I said yes. He will pick me up at seven. Feel free to give me an early curfew." She made a face at her mom and stuck out her tongue.

"Careful, you may need to use that soon." Kathy coughed at the idea.

They went down to the shops on Griswold Boulevard. Kathy liked the idea of window shopping. Doing this meant she didn't have to try anything on. Three hours had passed, and they still had no luck. Cheryl was pressuring her with anything that was backless or sleeveless. Kathy wanted something simple. They walked by a window, and she peered in. There was a manikin clothed with the perfect dress. It had shoulder straps and a flat white lace wrapped around the middle.

"There it is! I want that one!" Kathy entered the shop and approached the lifeless body showcasing her dress. A sales lady stepped beside her.

"Hi, can I help you find a size? It is a beautiful gown."

"I will try a size 2 if you have it."

The sales lady hurried to the back of the store. She came out carrying a box that contained the dress in her size. Into the dressing room, she tried it on. It fit like a glove in all the right places. Kathy had never been blessed with boobs, but the way the dress fit, it didn't seem to matter. She returned it to the box and walked towards the lady standing behind the check out counter.

"I am so excited you found something, Kathy." Cheryl dug around in her purse and pulled out her wallet.

"We take cash, credit or cheque," the cashier explained to her. She flipped open her wallet. There were no bills inside.

"I must have left my cheque book in the car. I will be right back," Cheryl explained as she hurried out the door. Crossing the street, she headed to the Main and High Branch.

Cheryl opened the door to the bank and proceeded toward the teller.

"Hi, I would like to get a cash advance on my credit card," she said, handing it to the lady behind the wicket.

The teller eyed Cheryl. She grabbed it from her and punched the numbers into the computer to bring up her account. A prompt popped up instructing her to retain the card.

"I'm sorry, Miss. It seems that you are overdrawn, and I can not return this card to you," the teller said as she pulled out a pair of scissors and proceeded to cut it up.

Cheryl cringed as she watched her destroy the tiny piece of plastic. Knowing Kathy was waiting for her to return with a payment, Cheryl fumbled through her wallet and found a blank cheque in the side pocket. 'This will have to do for now,' she thought to herself, knowing the cheque would bounce.

Out the door and across the street, she made her way back into the boutique.

"Here it is," she yelled to the cashier, waving the cheque in the air.

"Are you sure, mom? I know we can't really afford extra spending right now." Cheryl put her arm around Kathy and kissed her on the cheek. "It's not every day that your daughter gets to go to the prom. It's worth every cent spent."

"Thanks mom, and I'm sure I will have a memorable time."

Chapter 6

The week went by fast as all the students were busy cramming and studying for their exams. Kathy went straight home after school on Friday to start getting ready for the dance. Her mother was waiting impatiently to be a part of it. She had taken the afternoon off work just to be home and bought apple cider for Kathy and a bottle of Sparkling Peach Chardonnay for herself which they could enjoy during preparation. She knew she had a bottle at home, but there was a sale on, so thought may as well stock up. Knowing full well that she would want to indulge after Kathy left. Drink a bottle of wine with her memories as a young girl.

Cheryl curled Kathy's long brown hair and pinned it into a bun. Loose curls dangled around her face. She wrapped a white ribbon around her hair. Kathy worked on applying her make-up.

"You should wear ruby red lipstick. A man always notices a girl's mouth."

Kathy stared into the mirror. She was nothing like her mother. Always plastering her face and pushing up her breasts. She never wore much make-up. She didn't have to. Natural beauty meant more to her than posing as some high-maintenance Beauty Queen. A sweep of charcoal mascara and candy apple lip gloss was all she put on.

She had almost finished when they heard the doorbell.

"That must be Calvin. I'll go let him in." Cheryl looked back at Kathy, "You look stunning my dear." She went to the front door and opened it. He was standing on the front step dressed in a grey suede suit. His hair was combed to the side. She could tell he was holding his breath under the white dress shirt that hid behind the blue pin-striped tie.

Calvin stared at her and felt the blood rush from his face. "It's my fathers. I'm just borrowing. I have a corsage for Kathy. I didn't know what color she was wearing, but my dad said that white goes with everything."

Cheryl motioned him inside. "My, my, you look just like your father, so handsome," she brushed her hand down his sleeve, "and white will be perfect."

Kathy stood at the top of the staircase looking like an angel staring down at him. He couldn't wait to spend some time with her. She placed a hand on the rail and guided herself down the steps. The heels she was in were a bit big, so she had to walk carefully and still maintain grace. She reached the bottom and smiled at Calvin. He pinned the corsage onto her pink dress, being careful not to poke her as he did so. She smelled sweet like vanilla. Her hair was beautiful, her long dark lashes covering her big green eyes as she glanced at him and down to the floor. Calvin had been in love with Kathy since the third grade. So many nights, he lay in bed fantasising about her. When his father had brought Cheryl home a few times, he had heard them in the bedroom. To see her at the door excited him. He tried not to blush while looking at her, as the sounds of her moans rang through his ears.

With the corsage in place, Cheryl took the empty carton and grabbed her camera.

"Stand straight and beside each other," she directed as she focused the camera lens on the two of them. A couple of pictures were snapped.

"Ok, we're leaving now." Kathy grabbed her purse and yanked Calvin outside.

"Have a wonderful evening, you two. I won't wait up," Cheryl called after them as they walked down the driveway to Calvin's crew cab pickup truck. The passenger side door was tricky to open, so he pulled on it hard and let Kathy climb up. He closed it behind her and got in.

"Are you nervous?" he asked as he turned to Kathy.

"A little," Kathy replied in a quiet voice.

Calvin smiled at her. "Don't be. You'll be fine. You might be surprised with how much fun you do have."

The truck fired up, and the headlights shone down the street. The anxiety that Kathy had felt prior, returned. Her hands started to sweat. She pulled a tissue out of her purse and dried her now clammy hands.

They pulled into the school parking lot. Calvin opened her door and held out his hand for her to step down. The heels wobbled a bit across the gravel. Calvin placed his hand in hers. Her eyes grew big as he did this. She knew he was only trying to help her walk to the door, but it made her feel awkward. Not completely embarrassed though. She kind of enjoyed it. She felt proud having a man care so much for her and choose her before the other girls in school.

They went inside and followed the groups of students into the gymnasium. The music was loud. There was a disco ball in the middle of the room that cast beams of light around the gym.

"Do you want some punch?" Calvin asked as they made their way to the concession table.

"Sure, I could use something to drink."

He poured two glasses, and they mingled around the dance floor. Back to the punch bowl, they had a couple more. Kathy was starting to let loose. She thought maybe the sugar in the punch made her feel wound up. She was talking to a classmate when Calvin showed up with two more.

"I think I've had enough punch tonight, Calvin."

He looked disturbed. "Come on, just one more. It's going fast."

She took the plastic cup from him and gulped it down. Calvin took her cup and his own to the garbage can.

"May I have this dance?" He asked her while reaching out his hand. Kathy was nervous. She didn't know how to dance. Not with a boy at a prom. He pulled her close and wrapped her arms around him. His hands now on her waist, they swayed back and forth. Kathy watched all the couples kissing and dancing as if no one was watching. She wanted that one day, to marry the man of her dreams and live a fairy-tale lifestyle. They danced a few more songs, and Kathy's feet could barely go anymore. She sat down at a table with another glass of punch. Calvin followed her and sat next to her.

"My feet hurt, and I think they spiked the punch. I feel a little giddy and dizzy."

"Well, the best cure for that is fresh air. Why don't we go outside and get you some? You can sit out there and take your shoes off."

They walked outside and sat on a bench. Kathy kicked off her shoes. Calvin knelt and grabbed a foot. Starting to massage it, wanting so badly to cup her calf in his hand. The smell of vanilla filling his nostrils was so strong he could taste it.

"Does this bother you?" he questioned.

"No, it feels really good. Thank you."

"Well, I've had enough of the band's music tonight, and your feet hurt. What do you say we take a drive to Potter's Crossing? The night is still young, and the stars look awesome from up there. We could chat for a bit and enjoy this beautiful night."

He sounded so charismatic. She found it hard to say no to him. The spiked punch had hit Kathy a little harder. Inhibitions down, she looked at him and smiled. "Why not?"

"Sweet, I'll get the truck. You stay right there, ok. Don't go running off on me."

Kathy giggled as he bolted for the truck. She heard the engine fire up and could see his lights coming toward her. Calvin lifted the handle and pushed the passenger door open for her. She put on her seatbelt and adjusted it.

Calvin noticed. "I'm a good driver."

"I feel safe when I wear it." She felt slightly annoyed with his remark.

They drove a few miles to the landing and turned off the lights. The city was glowing. All the homes and businesses lit up, the stars reflecting on the river below. The moon was full and the air still.

"It's a really nice night," Calvin stated as he pulled Kathy closer across the seat. She restrained a bit. She had wanted to kiss someone; to feel that butterfly feeling her friends talked about. The air through the window felt cool on her face. It was almost soothing. Calvin tried again, and this time, she let him. She snuggled up close and laid her head on his shoulder. They both stared out the window. His hands slowly caressed her side and down to her leg. She felt her hair stand on end. Calvin couldn't help but become aroused. He thought of her mother and the noises he had heard her make. He placed her hand on the crotch of his pants. She quickly jerked it back.

"What's wrong?" he asked.

"Umm … I'm just nervous. I've never done anything like this before." Kathy tucked both of her hands under her thighs.

"We don't have to do anything you're not ready for," Calvin snapped and rolled his eyes.

Kathy felt stupid. She was with an older boy who seemed to like her. 'All my friends are doing it,' she thought to herself.

"Ok, I'm sorry."

She leaned toward Calvin and waited for his lips. He forced his mouth on hers, kissing her hard. Kathy felt uncomfortable and pulled away.

"Are you fucking kidding me?" he lashed out at her. "I knew you were a virgin, but I didn't realize you were a nun."

Kathy's face went hot. She knew she would be the laughingstock at school if she didn't put out. She didn't want to be called a virgin and tease.

"It's ok, I'm sorry, we can have some fun," Kathy whispered as she kissed him on the cheek. "But only on the outside, ok?"

"Sweet!" Calvin tore off his shirt and unbuttoned his pants.

"Why don't you sit on top of me, and we can just make out a bit."

Kathy looked at his chest. He had solid arms and a tan. She never realized Calvin had such a nice body. He was a great kisser, which made her want a little more. She climbed over and perched herself on top of him with the steering wheel pressing against her back. He put his hands on her boobs and rubbed the nipples. They perked up right away, and this aroused Calvin. He wanted to suck on them hard. He knew she could feel his bulge between her legs. He tilted her head and kissed her neck. He nibbled her ear and put his tongue in her mouth. He grabbed her by the back of her hair and kissed her harder, using one hand to push her onto his erection. It was throbbing, and he wanted to put it inside her. He had to. He waited so long for this moment, his fantasy of her coming true.

Kathy was starting to get turned on herself. The way he kissed her neck made her tingle. She unbuttoned the rest of the dress. He slid it off her. There she was, naked in his lap. He pulled her close and sucked on her perfect breasts. Kathy felt his boner through his shorts. She touched it. She wanted to see it. She was curious and ashamed. Things were moving way too fast. Her mother flashed in her mind. The sound of the front door closing and the vehicle backing out of the driveway and down the street was all too familiar. It either meant that he was leaving the house after being in the bedroom, or it was her mother coming in after being in his car. Kathy didn't want this.

"Lick it for me," he breathed out deeply.

"I don't know how. Maybe this is going too fast," Kathy blushed.

"I will show you how to perform oral sex, but we need to get into the back seat. So, go ahead, crawl back there, and lay on the seat. I'll go slow."

Kathy did as he instructed. Her heart was beating, and she felt dizzy. She was getting cold, and the vinyl on the seat clung to her skin like saran wrap. She wanted to put her dress back on. Calvin opened the back door and looked down at her beautiful untouched body.

"Scoot your bum on the seat towards me. Now put your legs over my shoulders."

Kathy did. She was embarrassed. She wondered how many he had seen and done this with before. Her legs started shaking. Her whole body was shaking. She wanted to stop. The back seat of anything on wheels isn't where she pictured her first physical moment. Her mouth was dry, and she was nauseous.

Face between her legs; he started to lick her. He rubbed her vagina with two fingers, as he did this, inserting one. She was tight. It made his blood rush.

"Ouch, that hurts a bit," she complained as she tried to squirm free.

"It'll only hurt for a minute, sweetie. I'm going to get you nice and wet first." Calvin proceeded to pleasure her. He could feel she liked it by the way she moved. Her juices were starting to moisten her insides as she moaned on the seat. Calvin pulled down his shorts and stroked himself a couple of times. He spread her legs open and forced himself inside her.

Her head shot up as she screamed in pain. "What are you doing?"

"This is what you wanted, babe. Just lean back and relax."

"No, we can't be doing this," Kathy cried as she tried to squirm her way around him. She was instantly sober and scared. How did she let things get so far? Tears started to form as the realization of what was happening hit her hard. He held her down and rammed it into her once more. He couldn't stop. He had to pleasure himself inside her. She was a virgin, and he loved it. It wasn't long before he came inside her and pulled up his pants. Kathy covered herself with her hands and cried. She felt violated and dirty. Calvin slammed the back door and got in the truck. He looked at Kathy and grinned. He threw her dress at her, "Get dressed."

She slid the gown that she and her mother had been so excited about over her head. The nausea was creeping up so bad she could taste it. Kathy pulled the few bobby pins from her hair that had come loose and were dangling. She wiped her eyes and crawled over the seat. Calvin cranked the stereo. A song about boys playing girls blasted through the speakers, loud and proud. All she wanted was to be home safe in her bed.

It was shortly after midnight when Kathy got home. Her mother was asleep in the recliner. The TV was still on. She clicked the power off and covered her with the yellow afghan her grandmother had made years ago. Tiptoeing her way up the stairs and into the bathroom, Kathy locked the door, and slipped off her dress. She pulled the pins out of her hair and looked in the mirror. Black smears of make-up ran down her cheeks and surrounded her eyes. Her nose was red, and her lips were dry. She reached into the tub and turned on the shower. She cranked the heat and let the water run, steaming up the tiny room. Kathy pulled the curtain back and stepped in. The water felt good against her skin. With her head back, she looked up and started to cry. As the water washed away her tears, she wished it would be so easy to wash away the incident that had just occurred. Kathy knew she couldn't tell her mother who would be so disappointed. Knowing she would feel guilty for making her go with him. She couldn't tell anyone. It was bad enough that she blamed herself. Kathy knew that it was her fault for letting it go so far. She was angry with herself for believing he wanted more from her than sex. Scrubbing every inch of her body until it was red, that was the first and last time she would let a man make her feel so dirty.

Chapter 7

It had been two months since she had spoken to Calvin. The way he looked at her when they crossed paths made her cringe. Kathy was torn between a love-hate relationship with him. A part of her wanted him to approach her. To tell her he was sorry, to say something. He took her virginity that night along with her dreams of a happy, normal life. During the summer, she had seen him driving around with his friends in the truck that staged her future. Laughing and enjoying their lives as they knew they didn't have to go back to high school. Free of teachers and studies. More time to party and bang chicks. All the while, she was left with having to face the worst night of her life, and he didn't even care. Kathy was trapped in a battle within herself. Kathy was pregnant. After missing her period for the second time, she decided to buy a test. Scared of anyone seeing her, she had borrowed her mother's car to drive to Carsdale to purchase one. Kathy told her mom that there was a workshop she had wanted to attend. She drove down on Saturday morning and had lunch. She window-shopped and went for ice cream. Knowing she may be pregnant lingered in her mind. Kathy took a few deep breaths and entered the pharmacy. Finding the feminine products aisle and staring at the little blue boxes on the shelf, she closed her eyes and picked one. With the little box under her arm, she proceeded to the till. Her heart was beating and her stomach in knots. The cashier rang the test through and eyed her while placing it in the plastic shopping bag along with the receipt. Kathy knew what the woman was thinking. Babies having babies. Kathy put her head down, grabbed her purchase, and left the store.

She was almost running across the parking lot to her car. Keys ready, she got in and started to cry. Paranoia and shame set in. She looked in the rear-view mirror and smiled. 'Ok, if it says positive, I'll have to be strong and deal with it.' Kathy dried her eyes with a napkin from the ice cream parlour shop that she had shoved in her purse. In the bottom corner, it said ENJOY! This made her smile. She laughed out loud and started the engine. Kathy drove to the gas station and found a parking spot out back. She took the test out of the packaging and slid it in her purse.

Into the store, she asked for the women's washroom. A chubby guy with curly red hair handed her a key on a silver baton. His name tag read, 'Roger.' He pointed her to the store's back entrance.

"You may have to jiggle it. Sometimes it sticks."

Kathy thanked him and closed the door. She clicked the lock and looked around. It smelled moist, and the light buzzed. Not exactly her choice for a life experience like this, but Kathy was too scared to do it at home. The test strip out, she read the directions on the back. One line=negative. Two lines=positive. She lined the toilet seat with paper and sat down. Stick between her legs; she urinated on the tip. Setting it on the sink with the cap replaced, she watched the time. She wanted to look at the stick, but she made herself wait. Two minutes passed. Her eyes flew to the piece of plastic that would foretell her fate. Two lines... 'Oh my god,' she thought, 'it's true.' Kathy immediately broke down. She cried in the stall until her eyes were puffy and her nose was plugged.

She returned the key to Roger and left the store. When she got in the front seat, all she wanted to do was cry, run away or wake up from this bad dream. It was getting late, and she knew her mom would be wondering where she was. Kathy took a few minutes to process her situation, calmed herself down, and drove home. There was no way she could tell her mother. Kathy was terrified.

As she pulled in the driveway, Kathy saw Cheryl was waiting on the step with a mug of tea in her hands and a shawl around her shoulders. It was starting to get cooler as fall set in. The colored leaves speckled the front porch and surrounded her mother, making her look like something out of a romance movie.

"How was the workshop? What did you learn? Did you have a good time?" Cheryl gazed up at Kathy. She could see the emptiness in her eyes and the paleness of her face.

"What's wrong, Kathleen?"

"Nothing, mom. The Workshop was fine. I learned how to make a candle using beeswax. I had pasta for lunch and put gas in the car. I'm not feeling very well. I'm going to go to bed. We can chat more in the morning." Kathy walked up the steps and opened the front door.

"I'll make pancakes for breakfast. I picked up some blueberries at the market."

"Sounds good mom. Good night."

Kathy threw the car keys on the table, poured herself a glass of milk, and went to her bedroom. She threw herself on her bed and wept. She crawled under the covers and cried herself to sleep.

In the morning, she got up and had breakfast with her mom. Kathy found her library card and went downtown. She opened the card catalogue, and with the paper and tiny pencils they supplied, she wrote down the location of the pregnancy literature. Her eyes examined the words on the spines of the books lined on the shelves until she stopped on one. 'Everything You Need to Know Before and During Pregnancy.'

She found a table and sat in the back in a corner booth and skimmed the pages. She didn't have much time to consider an abortion if she was two months along. She had always been against it. The thought of having the baby and giving it up for adoption was not an option either. There was no way she could go to term and hand her child to someone else.

Kathy read the pages and looked at the pictures. She had a life growing inside her. The more she thought about it, it excited her in a way. It excited her until her mind moved to Calvin. How was she going to tell him? Should she really? What will he say? Will he reject her and abandon her as her father did? She wanted to tell him. She had to. Kathy used her card to check out two books. Into her backpack, they went as she left the library. She needed to know more. Kathy locked the knob to her bedroom and pulled out a book, stopping on certain pages to read further. She had to tell someone. Kathy placed the books back into the plastic bag and shoved them into a suitcase in her closet. She was exhausted and wanted to lie down. With a couple of candles lit, she crawled into bed and daydreamed about the conversation she needed to have with the boy who impregnated her.

The next day, Kathy woke up with determination and acceptance. She did her hair and make-up and put on leggings with the boots she had recently bought. Looking amazing, she was out the door with confidence as she went to find Calvin. It was Sunday, and she knew he would be at the gym. She walked to the recreation centre and scoped out his truck in the parking lot. Kathy sat on a bench and waited. The butterflies and anxiety rose. There was no way she could predict the outcome of the situation she was about to have.

Kathy heard Calvin's voice yelling to one of his buddies on the way to his truck.

"Here goes." Kathy sighed and stood up.

She stared at him with every step. Calvin threw his gym bag in the box and unlocked the driver's door.

"Hi Calvin," Kathy said as she rounded the hood towards him.

"Kathy, hi, umm ... what are you doing here? Are you stalking me?" he chuckled.

"No, I'm not stalking you Calvin, but we really need to talk about something?" Kathy could feel her face grow hot.

"What is it? Is it going to take long cause I have somewhere I need to be?"

Jealousy creeping in, Kathy started to cry. She couldn't help it.

"I'm sorry ... I," she stammered as she turned away.

"Hey, hey, are you ok? I know I haven't been around much since prom, and I am sorry for that, Kathy. I was scared to talk to you after what happened. I assumed you never wanted to see me again." Calvin put his arm around her and gave her a squeeze.

Kathy wiped her eyes and placed her hand on his.

"I'm pregnant."

Calvin paused. His face went pale. He stared at her.

"Are you fucking serious? This isn't an attempt to try to trap me, is it Kathy?? Is it??"

Kathy fought back the tears. "No, not at all. Do you think I want this? To be carrying a child planted in me by a guy who hasn't spoken to me since it happened? I'm scared, Calvin. I haven't even told my mom. I needed to talk to you. I'm considering an abortion. I'm against it, but in a situation like this, it may be the best thing. I'm in high school. We aren't even dating, let alone married. I can't afford the procedure. I would need you to pay for it. I'm so angry at you for doing this to me." Kathy broke down and knelt on the cement.

"Come here, get up, get in the truck. Let's talk about this." Calvin put his arm around her and helped her into the truck. Kathy was trying to calm down.

"I think you should go to the doctor and find out for sure and how far along you may be, Kathy. If you are pregnant and I am the father, I want you to go through with the pregnancy. We will make it work. I just got a job at the meat packing plant. You can stay with your mom until I find us a home. It will be a lot of work and sacrifice, but I believe we can do this. I've always loved you, Kathy Crane, and if we are going to have a baby, I would like to ask your hand in marriage. My mother left me when I was young, and I know your father did the same. This can be a new beginning for us."

Kathy was in disbelief. She couldn't believe what she was hearing. The man who took her innocence wanted to help her with their future. They kissed long and hard in the truck. His hands were placed on her belly. The baby was his, and so was she. He had won her now. He owned her. He knew that Kathy would do whatever he asked from now on.

When she got home that night, she lay in bed and thought about the baby and Calvin. As happy as she was that he was so willing to be a part of this, she almost felt uncertain. She remembered the night in the truck when he had held her down and forced himself inside her.

His personality had changed. He acted like two different people. Did he plan this all along? Regardless of the reason or intention of the acts that night, they happened, and now Kathy had to endure the consequences.

Chapter 8

They got married in October. Kathy wanted to have the wedding before the snow fell and before she had the baby. If anything were to happen like she dreamed, then she would be sharing a last name with her child when it was born.

It was a small wedding. Thirty guests, most of them on Kathy's side, gathered in Calvin's grandpa's farmyard after the ceremony at the Church. The only family Calvin had that showed up was his dad. A couple of teachers from school went to give their blessings. They knew that it would be difficult for Kathy to attend and finish her schooling with a baby on the way. Mrs. Goldman had pulled her aside and told her very sternly that she would do whatever she could to help her finish her classes.

Nancy was a bridesmaid for the wedding. Kathy was so happy that she had come. They had never seen much of each other over the years. Nancy didn't care for Calvin. She didn't trust him. He looked to her like a snake in the grass. She knew what kinds of things he got into with his friends. She gave Kathy her opinion and tried to talk her out of it.

"Kathy, you don't have to marry him just because you are pregnant. I'm sure there are lots of men out there who would be more than happy to take care of you and the baby. Nice men with real jobs who could provide for you better than him. You're so young, and I'd hate to see you build yourself up for future heartache. You can always stay with mom. Steve and I would help you out as well."

"I appreciate your concern, Nancy, but I'm doing the right thing. Calvin loves me, and he would be lost without me. He needs me, and I need him now," Kathy had told her sister before the ceremony.

There were tables of sandwiches and sweets. The cake they had cut together stood in the middle of the table. It had rained that day, and the clouds still loomed. Buddies of Calvin's had formed a band and offered to play for the dance. All they wanted for payment was free liquor. This pleased the newlyweds as they couldn't afford to hire a band. They set up their equipment in the Quonset, where picnic tables were lined for seating. Everyone gathered to watch their first dance. Guests joined them on the floor and-one-by one, went home for the evening. Calvin spent most of the night pounding drinks with his buddies between songs. He had rented a hotel room in town for the night and had promised Kathy he would find a way to save up to take her on a lovely honeymoon.

Cheryl drove them to the motel on the East side of town. The room was far from wedding night material, but it was all Calvin could afford. He was too drunk to drive, and Kathy didn't know how to operate a stick shift.

Calvin promised he would teach her, this being another one of many things that he had promised her.

When they pulled up, Calvin opened the door and threw up. He was wasted. Cheryl and Kathy helped him into the room.

"Kathy, honey, are you sure you're going to be ok?" Cheryl was concerned about her.

"Yes, mom, we'll be fine. I'm sure he will sober up soon."

"You know you can call me anytime, and I will come get you."

"I know, mom. It's my wedding night, and I'm going to stay with my husband." Kathy pushed her mom out the door, "Good night."

Calvin was sitting on the corner of the bed, trying to take his shoes off. Kathy bent down to help him.

"What are you doing, woman?" He swatted at her.

"I'm just trying to help you."

Calvin grabbed her hand and looked at the ring. "You're my wife now. You're mine. You see that ring. That means I own you."

Kathy jerked her hand away. "I wish you wouldn't drink so much. You act differently. This is our wedding night."

"So, it is," Calvin grinned. He tore off his shirt, sending a couple of buttons to the floor.

Calvin stood up and pushed Kathy onto the bed. "Take off that dress. Whores shouldn't wear white."

Kathy's mouth dropped open. She couldn't believe what she was hearing. Tears formed in her eyes.

"Stop crying like a little baby. I didn't hurt you." Calvin was yelling now. His voice scared her.

"Please don't do this, Calvin. This is supposed to be our special night," Kathy begged him.

"I said take off that dress. You're going to learn how to satisfy your husband."

Kathy was crying now as she undressed. The emotions she felt the night of prom came rushing back to her. What had she done? How could she have gone through with this marriage? How could she have led herself into thinking this would ever work?

He flipped her over and held her down. Kathy closed her eyes and held her breath. She counted to herself until it was over. With his pants still around his knees, Calvin flopped on the bed beside her and passed out.

Chapter 9

Christmas came and went along with the start of a new year. According to the Chinese calendar, it was the year of the Snake, and this meant change. Kathy prayed that this would be so. She wanted so badly for her marriage to be a happy one. Calvin began drinking more and missing work. She was still living with Cheryl and thought it was best until the baby was born. Her mother wanted her to stay, to divorce Calvin, and raise the baby on her own. Kathy wouldn't hear it. She was going to make her new family work.

It was just after midnight when Kathy sat up in bed. She was soaked.

"Mom, Mom," Kathy yelled. "My water broke."

She could hear her mother stumble out of bed and race down the hall. Cheryl flicked on the light and ran towards her.

"Ok, ok, just relax. Remember to breathe slowly, sweetie. Let's get you to the hospital."

Cheryl was so excited. Her heart was racing as she gathered up the pre-packed bag for Kathy and found her keys. Kathy quickly changed her clothes and put on her coat. They were out the door and on their way in minutes.

"We have to call Calvin. He has to be there, mom."

"I'll phone him once we get you admitted. Just focus on you and your breathing now, Kathleen."

Cheryl grabbed her daughter's hand and squeezed it a little. Kathy braced herself in the passenger seat and practiced her breathing while staring at her mother. She couldn't believe it was happening. Her daughter was ready to enter the world. She was scared and eager.

The car pulled up to the Emergency entrance and squealed to a stop. Cheryl flung open the driver's door and ran to help Kathy out. Two paramedics were on their way out with a wheelchair. They assisted her into it and took her inside.

"I'm just going to park the car, Kathleen. Mama will be right behind you, ok," Cheryl yelled as she climbed in.

Into the parking stall and up to Admitting, she ran. Cheryl was sweating now, her emotions running wild. They had taken Kathy to the Maternity Ward. She was already in a gown and being prepped when Cheryl arrived. Her cervix was almost fully dilated, and the baby was going to be coming fast.

"Where's Calvin, mom. Did you phone him?" Kathy questioned her mother as she moaned in pain.

"I'll go right now."

Cheryl ran down the hall to the payphone. Quarter in the slot, she dialed the number. It rang with no answer. She hung up the receiver and ran back to the room.

"There was no answer, honey. I'll try again soon, ok."

"He has to be here, mom," Kathy cried.

"Shhh, don't get yourself upset. Everything will be fine."

The nurses wheeled Kathy into the delivery room. The baby girl weighing seven pounds was born on February 14, Valentine's Day. She was Kathy's gift of love. Calvin never made it to the hospital until that afternoon. He was hung over, and the smell he admitted was overwhelming. Kathy was so angry at him for missing the birth of their child. She was angry, but she wasn't surprised.

Chapter 10

They moved into a low-rental house a few blocks from Cheryl. The landlord agreed to let her paint one of the bedrooms pink. Kathy was excited about the plot for a garden in the backyard. Calvin promised her he would till it up for her in the spring. She couldn't wait until Jessica was older, so she could teach her how to plant and care for a garden. Making the rows and planting the seeds, learning to wait patiently for the signs of life. They had furnished their home with hand-me-downs, and Cheryl gave Kathy the crib she had used as a baby. She started to believe that her life might not be that bad.

The screen door swung open. The furball that followed Calvin into the kitchen tap-danced across the linoleum.

"I found him in the woods while we were hunting. Little fellow almost got himself killed."

"Can we keep him? I always wanted a dog," Kathy explained as the puppy jumped at her, licking her face.

"If no one claims him. I'll ask around."

Kathy's excitement grew. "He needs a name. What should we call him?" She asked her husband while scratching the dog's belly.

"I called him Champ in the truck, and he seemed to like that."

A couple of weeks had passed, and no one had come for Champ. Kathy had posted his picture in businesses around town, and not one call came back. She was so excited to have a pet. Kathy booked an appointment with the Vet to administer his shots. That same day, she stopped at the Pet Mart and bought a bag of chew toys and a leather leash. He was her protection now. Calvin spent most of his evenings down at the pub with his buddies after work. Watching sports on the big screen, gambling, and who knows what else.

Morgan's Den had been bought by a young couple, Scarlett and Jasper Winwood, who had recently moved to town. They renovated the inside and hired new staff. Scarlett was your average Barbie Doll type. Her husband Jasper was handsome and charming. He would flirt with the waitresses, tickling them and whispering behind the bar. There had been rumors that he had a side business offering customers sexual pleasure out of one of the hotel rooms above. Calvin was rarely even home for dinner. Kathy would leave his plate in the oven and lay awake in bed, listening for the sounds of him coming in the door stumbling drunk. She would pretend to sleep as he banged around the house. Champ was great company for her. He would follow her to bed and stay with her through the night.

"I wish you wouldn't feed him from the table like that. It's a bad habit to be teaching him," Kathy said while scooping another bite of potatoes.

Calvin grabbed her plate from underneath her and threw it across the room. "There, how about we don't feed you from the table either."

The shattering of the dish woke the baby. Kathy forcefully pushed herself away from the table and glared at him with hatred in her eyes.

She gathered Jessica in her arms and soothed her back down. Kathy turned on the electric swing and buckled the baby in. Champ was licking at the food on the floor. Kathy grabbed him by the collar and put him out the back door, so she could clean up the mess.

Calvin was going hunting for the weekend. He had stopped at the bank and took money out of Jessica's account for the trip. Money that Kathy had been putting away for her college fund. He bought beer and bullets. With his cooler full, he loaded up his pick-up and took Champ along.

"I'm gonna teach you how to hunt, dog," Calvin said while opening the passenger door for Champ to hop in. They backed out of the driveway. Kathy waved out the front window as they turned down the street. Craig and Ronnie were sitting in the driveway on lawn chairs, waiting for Calvin. They finished their beers and loaded their gear.

"We better stop and grab another bottle boys, it can get cold up there at night," Ronnie said while lighting a joint.

They made a quick stop at the liquor store and headed towards the woods. Hunting season had just started, and they were anxious for the kill. Craig's uncle owned a cabin. The log shack was built in the valley on the embankment of the river.

They unloaded their gear and got set up for the night. The wood stove was half full. Ronnie crumpled up a few sheets of newspaper and lit the end. He threw it in the chamber along with some more wood chunks and closed the metal door.

Craig spun the top off a bottle of rum and mixed three glasses. Shortly after, the fire died out along with the men.

The following morning, the three were up before the sun rose. Craig lit the stove and fried up a pan of bacon and eggs. The smell of grease saturated the cabin. A shot of rum in the coffee always helped make the blood warm up a little faster. Calvin fed Champ. With their bellies full and guns loaded, the men headed into the woods to catch their kill.

Chapter 11

He tossed the dog's lifeless body in the back of the truck. He wiped his hands on his jeans which were already covered in blood. His friends were waiting in the cab. Calvin opened the driver's door and climbed in. He glanced at Ronnie in the passenger seat. The wet path of a tear glistened on his cheek. He fired it up and drove to the highway.

He shut off the lights and pulled into the back alley behind the house when he got to town. Beer cans spilled onto the ground as he climbed out. Calvin grabbed the shovel out of the box and opened the back gate. He chugged back his beer and tossed the can towards the house. He laughed to himself with each shovel dug. The soil that Kathy had been so excited for a garden was soon to be the resting place of her beloved pet.

As he dug the hole, it started to rain. Calvin dropped the shovel and stumbled to the tailgate. The lightning lit up the sky, forcing a series of rumbled thunder to follow. He pulled the dog to the ground and dragged him to his grave. The rain was picking up and saturating the soil. Calvin shovelled the dirt over the animal as fast as he could. His boots were beginning to stick in the mud. He raked the last of the soil over the pile and packed it with the back of the shovel. He made his way to the back steps and went inside. Calvin crossed the kitchen and approached the sofa. He laid down and passed out with his muddy boots leaving a trail behind him.

The mess that Kathy found the next day was horrifying. Beer cans scattered, and blood spewed across the backyard. There was no sign of Champ, and Kathy already knew in her gut that the blood belonged to him. She fell to her knees beside the mound in the garden. The sickness rose and forced its way out. Kathy wiped her mouth and bawled.

The sound of the screen door slamming behind her startled her. Her head shot back with rage in her eyes. Calvin stood on the back porch. "I knew that dog was gonna get himself killed."

PART 3

June 2, 2005

Chapter 12

It was June 2nd, 2005, on a Friday night. Bruno was to be playing a gig with the band Death Star at The Nectar. It was an old Victorian building down on 3rd St. The locals really enjoyed the place and kept it busy. It served as a second home for him. He spent most of his nights there, drumming or helping with the maintenance of the building. He made enough to get by. He shared a house with another member of the band, Keith Shaffer. They grew up together. They were more like brothers. Bruno took music lessons through school and decided to expand playing in a garage to drum for a career. He had made quite an impression last year and had a full schedule doing what he loved best.

Shortly after eight o'clock the lead singer called to cancel the show. He had gotten strep throat and knew that he wouldn't be able to perform. He was on his way to the emergency room, realizing that a bottle of water wasn't going to cut it.

Bruno sat at the bar and finished his beer. He had not had a night off in months. He flipped open his cell phone and scrolled through the contact list. He eliminated those who would be out of town working, home with a kid, or out partying. Snapping it shut, he placed it back in his pocket. Bruno pushed the empty beer bottle across the bar. He wanted to do something different. He was craving something sweet. The Cheese Cake Castle was open until ten on the weekend. Bruno fumbled the change in his pocket and tossed a couple of bucks in the plastic jug on the counter. Throwing his jacket over his shoulder, he waved to the bartender and went outside. The clouds had rolled in, and the humidity rose.

"Looks like a storm," he said aloud.

Making his way down the street, he breathed in deep. It smelled damp. The air filled his lungs and felt good. He had given up smoking six months prior and couldn't believe how much better he felt. Cheesecake flavours filled his mind as he tried to let his taste buds decide. He reached the corner and waited at the red light. He could see across the street into the cafe and was pleased to find the place was empty. The cashier was behind the counter, and a girl sat alone at a table beside the window. He couldn't see her face, just her long dark curls. Her head was resting in her hand. She was reading a magazine. She intrigued him. He wanted to know what she was reading. He wanted to know her. She sat back in her chair and took a bite of the cheesecake. He could see the cherry toppings covering the last of the slice. She turned the page and glanced out the window. Bruno jumped back. He saw the green walk light flashing at him to cross.

'Did she see me?' He wondered.

Before the light turned red, he ran to the other side with seconds left. He couldn't help but stare at her. She looked like a painting in a museum, captivating his gaze. When he reached the front door, the raindrops began to fall. Pushing it open, he stepped in out of the rain. It smelled delicious. His taste buds lit up as he approached the counter. Scanning the menu on the wall, he made his decision.

"I'll have a slice of the blueberry cheesecake with extra whipped cream," he said to the clerk.

She entered his order into the till. He turned around and stared at her again.

"That will be $6.50," she said while wiping her hands on her apron.

Bruno pulled out his wallet and paid for the dessert. He stood there impatiently and waited. The girl behind the counter placed the plate in front of him. He picked it up and spun around, knocking the fork on the floor. He heard laughter and blushed as he made eye contact with the beautiful girl by the window. He picked it up and blew on it.

"Ten-second rule," he said to her with a smile that could melt butter on his face.

Bruno approached her and sat at the table next to her. He could feel her eyes on him. He looked up as she looked at the magazine on the table.

"What are you reading?"

She uncrossed her legs and sat up straight. "Umm, how to eat cheesecake 101," she giggled.

"Sounds interesting; I bet step 2 is to keep the fork on the plate."

They both smiled and blushed.

"My name is Brett, but everyone calls me Bruno," he said while sticking out his hand to shake hers.

"I'm Nina, and everyone calls me Nina," she said back while placing her hand in his.

Bruno lifted his plate and moved to the empty chair across from her.

"Mind if I sit with you?"

"Not at all."

She watched him pull his jacket off and hang it on the chair. It was denim with band logos plastered all over it.

"My dad used to listen to all of those bands," she began to tell him.

"Used to?" Bruno watched for her reply.

"Ya, I haven't seen him in six years. He left after my mother passed. I noticed the patch on your jacket. It always makes me think of him jamming out in the basement."

"Your father is a musician?"

"No, but he liked to think so. He always said that music was his soul, and without it he may as well be dead."

"Well, Nina, I would have to agree with him. I play the drums, and music really is my life. It helps a person not feel so alone sometimes."

"I know all about being alone," she whispered under her breath.

He placed his hand on hers. "A girl as pretty as you should never have to be alone."

Their eyes met and stayed that way for what felt like an eternity. The touch of his skin on hers gave her goosebumps up her arm. She wanted to pull away, but she couldn't. Bruno took another bite of the cake.

"It's really starting to come down out there," he pointed out the window.

"I love the rain. It's a cleanse for the world, washing away the old to make way for the new," Nina said as she took her last bite. She licked the fork and set it on the plate.

Bruno checked his watch. It was 8:45.

"Would you like to go to the movie with me?" he eyed her while his heart beat in his chest.

Nina's eyes lit up. "Yes, I would like that," she smiled.

"I know that 'Winter Alley' is playing at the Monarch. It's about a pack of wolves in the arctic. I think it's based on true events."

"I'm in. I could use a bit of action/adventure tonight," Nina said as she closed the pages of the magazine and shoved it into her backpack.

"The Monarch it is."

Bruno stood up and offered his hand to her. "Right this way, my lady."

Nina felt warm. Her stomach was full of butterflies, and she could tell her cheeks looked hot. He felt familiar. He felt safe. She knew nothing about him but craved to know more. She hadn't smiled that way in years. She pushed her chair in and let him lead her to the door. The rain was pouring down now, collecting at the curb and flowing down the street. Bruno took off his coat and held it over her head.

"Ok, on the count of three, we are running."

Nina smiled back at him. The excitement she felt as he counted down grew inside of her.

"Three!!"

Bruno pushed open the door, and the two ran down the street. They were laughing as he tried to keep his jacket steadied over her like an umbrella. Nina ran ahead and spun around with her arms in the air.

"Isn't it beautiful!!?"

The drops of rain that had dampened her hair made it shine in the streetlight. He was in awe. She looked so amazing, spinning and laughing on the street. He couldn't help but watch her. Bruno was happy. Happy that the gig was cancelled, and he got to meet what he thought looked like a beautiful angel sent down for him.

The billboard lights of the cinema lit up the street. People were buying tickets and popcorn. Bruno purchased two and ordered one large iced-tea and a box of chocolate almonds. He handed them to Nina as he pushed two straws into the slot of the plastic drink lid. She followed him into the theatre and down the third row from the back. They pulled down two seats halfway in and sat down.

"Thank you," she said as she opened the box of almonds.

"You are very welcome, and thank you for joining me this evening. I like you."

Nina stared up at the screen and tried to hold in her smile. She wanted to burst. The last half hour of her life made her feel good again. The movie began to play, and the room went silent. She looked at him out of the corner of her eye and wished the film would never end.

When the credits rolled up the screen, and the lights came on, everyone made their way from the theatre's front to the back in a single file fashion. The two strangers sat in their seats and waited. They were both waiting. Neither knew what for, but it seemed like the right thing to do. An already unspoken bond that made it feel right.

The audience dissipated, and they were left alone. Bruno put his hand on Nina's leg and gently squeezed his fingers. She had her head down. When she felt his touch, she turned her head. A curl fell across her face that made Bruno's heart skip a beat. Without thinking, he bent his head down and kissed her. With his eyes closed, he felt her kiss back and couldn't help but smile. They opened their eyes and laughed. The butterflies had kicked in. The two got out of their seats and made their way outside. It had stopped raining. The smell of wet soil was pungent. Bruno grabbed Nina's hand and pulled her in close. He put his face in her neck and breathed in deep.

"Mmmm, that smells so much better," he said while standing up straight.

Nina was speechless. She wanted to stand there and stare at him forever. He was beautiful and charismatic.

BrrRing!! BrrRing!!

Nina jumped. The phone in her pocket chimed again. She knew it was her grandmother. She knew she was late. She quickly pulled it out and spun around.

"Hi grandma, yes, I know what time it is. I am on my way right now."

She closed the phone and put it away.

"I have to go," she said, looking up at him.

"Can I see you again?" Bruno asked just to hear the answer.

"Yes, I hope so," Nina said with excitement in her voice. She fumbled in her bag and ripped a sheet of looseleaf from her binder.

She uncapped the pen from the side pocket and scribbled on the paper.

"Here is my number."

Nina stuffed it in his hand and turned away.

"I had a really great time with you tonight," she yelled back at him squeezing her backpack tight.

"I had the best time," Bruno yelled back.

Nina Gallaway wondered if she had schizophrenia. She thought she heard voices a couple of times and found herself feeling confused lately. This was the reason Nina had started avoiding her friends and withdrawing from the world. When she wasn't in school, she would walk along the edge of the forest or sit by Plymouth Pond. A lot of the kids from school hung out there after dark. It was a place away from their parents to drink beer or smoke pot. Nina hated how they treated the area. Bottles smashed, leaving shards of glass in the sand and aluminum cans piled up by the trees.

The pond was a sanctuary for her. Nina had grown very fond of photography and always carried her camera with her. It was her mother's camera. Nina had found it in a box in the attic. She took it in to have the film developed. The idea of seeing what her mother saw before she took her own life made Nina ecstatic. Her mother, Rose, was manic-depressive and overdosed on a combination of medications when Nina was eight years old. Her father abandoned her shortly after this, leaving her in the care of her grandmother, Lorraine Mayfield.

The roll was half full. There were twelve pictures of nature. Trees, rocks, the sky, and one housed a man in the distance with his fishing rod. She had stared at each of them and imagined herself being there, being with her mom. The last photo was of the two of them. She remembered when it had been taken. They were in the backyard at the picnic table. Nina's mom spent half the day braiding her hair. It was the town festival, and her dad was taking her for a ride on the Ferris wheel after supper. He was standing at the BBQ when he took the shot.

Nina thought of that day and the happiness that she felt. She missed them both, but also hated them, hate which grew more over the years. She was so angry with her father for abandoning her when she needed him the most. She always wondered how it was that he didn't need her to. Nina had never been daddy's little girl before her mom died, and his absence made the sting even more intense. It was hard for her to believe, but sometimes she would tell herself that he was happier without them in his life. Free from a marriage and a child to do whatever he wanted, a second option in life. Her grandmother had told her that he just couldn't handle the pain and was scared that she might do the same if he stayed in her life.

Nina always felt that her grandmother disapproved of her, and when she moved in, it was apparent. She was always respectful and polite. She would help with the cleaning and tried to have conversations with her grandmother, but it was always the cold shoulder. After awhile, Nina rebelled. She turned cold inside, cold and numb. She would not allow herself to feel pain or rejection again.

Lorraine Mayfield was a very prim and proper woman. She had been raised to be a lady. She couldn't stand the way Nina carried herself. She was raised to be strong when she was a child. Her mother would always tell her that women don't show emotion. A year after the loss of Rose, Lorraine felt that it was time for Nina to let go. It annoyed her to listen to her grandchild cry in the night. She soon resented her. She was intruding on her home and forcing her to raise another child at her age. When Nina began to distance herself, Lorraine could feel it. The thought of what teenagers did nowadays, repulsed her. They were always drinking and doing drugs, hanging with an older crowd, and roaming the streets at all hours.

Upon entering the house, her grandmother was waiting for her. The door was already swinging open as she climbed the steps.

"Get in this house right now," Lorraine demanded as her eyes grew big and her chin pulled down.

Nina swept past her and stood on the mat. Lorraine leaned in and smelled her hair as she kicked off her sneakers.

"I smell popcorn ...and cologne!! You were with a boy. I know it. You were sitting in a theatre in the dark doing

God knows what. Touching hands and...and what else, Nina?"

Nina wondered how it was that she always knew exactly where she had been or what she was doing. Senses like a trained police dog. She could smell peppermint on her breath that had been eaten twelve hours prior. She was usually right, and Nina hated this. But she was wrong this time. She hadn't been with a boy; she was with a man.

"I went to the movie grandma. Is that really such a sin?"

Lorraine scoffed at her as she started up the stairs to her bedroom.

"I will not have you talking to me like that in my house. You are grounded. I hope you enjoyed your evening out gallivanting because it will be your last for a while. And, I want your cell phone."

Nina froze mid step. She turned to her grandma at the bottom of the stairs.

"That's not fair. I didn't do anything wrong. I need it for emergencies, Grandma. How will you get a hold of me if something happens?"

She tapped her foot on the carpeted step and held her phone tight in her pocket.

"I won't need to try to get a hold of you, Nina. I will know exactly where you are. That is school and home. Do you understand?"

"Uhhgg," Nina gasped as she headed up the stairs.

"I will have that cell phone tomorrow before you go to school," Lorraine yelled after her.

Nina slammed her bedroom door and threw her pack on the bed. She hated how her grandmother treated her and constantly accused her of getting into trouble. She flopped on the bed and stared up at the ceiling. Bruno popped into her mind like a ray of sunshine through an open window. The way it does when the rain clouds part and the light shines down. She smiled to herself and drifted off to sleep.

When Nina awoke the next day, she couldn't believe the happiness she felt inside.

"Bruno," she said aloud as she smiled.

She rolled over in her bed and hugged her pillow. She replayed in her mind the night she had just had. He was so gentle. She would have given anything to make it last a little bit longer. She was grounded and losing her cell phone, but it had all been worth it.

"Shit," Nina cried as she sat up in bed.

Her mind raced as she imagined him calling her. He would call, and there would be no answer. What would he think when she doesn't reply? Would he stop trying and give up, give up on her? This frightened Nina in many ways. The unusual fear of losing someone she didn't know and the fear of the emotions she felt for someone she didn't know.

Nina stood up and looked out the window. The clouds had returned, and the gloom of the sky forecasted rain. A shiver ran down her spine as she crossed her arms and rubbed them repeatedly. A yawn forced its way out as she bent down and pulled her soon to be vacant cell phone out of her pocket. She checked the time. It was 7:04

AM. Flipping it open, she noticed a small envelope in the left-hand corner, a missed message. Nina clicked on the icon, and a message popped up. She didn't recognize the number and knew that it was from him before she read it. Her heart started to beat fast. She was jumping slightly in one spot.

With eyes full of excitement, she read.

'I couldn't wait until tomorrow to talk to you, Sweetie! I am working at The Nectar tonight, but I would love to hear from you ...'

Nina heard footsteps nearing down the hall. Lorraine opened the door and looked in.

"You awake in here?"

"Yes, Grandma," Nina answered as she turned her back and lifted the phone in front of herself swiftly. She quickly reread the message and hit delete.

"I want that cell phone now, missy. You don't need it while you get ready for school. Hand it over."

Nina sighed and stepped towards her. She held out her hand while her grandmother took it.

"Good," Lorraine snapped. "Breakfast in twenty minutes. You had better get a move on."

Nina stood still as her bedroom door closed. She tried to picture the phone number, Bruno's number, the only thing that mattered to her right now. How she wished she had gotten a chance to write it down. 'I'll be at The Nectar.' She thought about this for a minute. At least she could still reach him. Nina threw on a pair of blue jeans and rolled the cuffs up at the bottom. Half-buttoning a flannel shirt, she looked in the mirror. Flipping her head upside down, the hair was gathered into a ponytail and twisted into a bun. She curled her eyelashes with her fingers, pushing them up as she looked at the ceiling. She threw a tube of cherry red lip balm into her backpack and went to the kitchen to eat. Nina had no appetite but knew she had to force herself to get some down to bypass an argument with Lorraine.

The bell rang, alerting the students that it was time for the afternoon recess. Nina didn't need the bell. She had been staring at the clock all day, wanting to phone Bruno. She needed to tell him that her grandmother had taken her phone away, and to hear his voice. She had gotten lost deep in her thoughts, daydreaming about her first kiss.

She pushed her way through the other kids, bumping into Valerie Thiessen.

"Freak!" the blonde-haired drama queen said while glaring in her direction.

Nina hurried down the hall to the student payphone. She prayed that the phone book was still attached. Rounding the corner and speeding down the hall, she could see it now, dangling from the booth on a metal cord. Nina dropped her pack, lifted the book, and fumbled through the pages.

"Nectar, Nectar," she whispered to herself while scanning the N's on the page.

There it was, halfway down, The Nectar Night Club, 757 3rd St, 555-8375. Nina took a deep breath. Her fingers felt for a quarter in her inside pocket. Pulling one out, she plunked it in the slot. Her heart was beating fast, and she could feel her face grow hot.

'What should I say?' she thought.

Without thinking about it anymore, she pressed the seven numbered keys and waited. It rang three times.

"Hey there, you've reached The Nectar. How may I assist you this fine day?"

The voice on the other end made Nina smile, so happy and full of life.

"I … Umm … I'm looking for Bruno," she stuttered.

"Ahhh, Bruno, my man won't be in till later this evening. Can I help you with something?"

"No, that's ok, thank you." Nina hung up the receiver. Her heart had slowed its pace. As much as she had wanted to talk to him, she was slightly relieved he wasn't there. She slung her pack over her shoulder and exited the side entrance door. There was still time to spare before her next class. As she stepped outside, the noise around her seemed to intensify. Everything was so loud. She covered her ears and looked around. Kids were lounging on the lawn, some tossing a football around and others just grouped in packs giggling and gossiping. Her head began to pound. The pain intensified, making her squeeze her eyes shut. She stood there silent and still.

"Get outta the way!" a guy yelled at her, tripping around her as he bolted through the doors.

Nina jumped back. She looked around again and realized she had been standing there like a statue.

"Sorry," she muttered.

Nina shook her head. She could hear sounds, but nothing made sense. Her eyes were blurry. She made her way to a wooden bench and sat down. She felt nauseous and anxious. The screams and laughter filled her head. Nina began to panic. She was breathing heavy. The laughter seemed to get louder with every breath. She could hear voices calling to her. She clenched her chest and leaned forward.

"Are you ok?"

A voice called to her. She wanted to speak, but she couldn't. The words were there, but no sound came out. She stared at the girl standing over her as her face appeared to change shape.

Nina lunged at her, knocking her to the ground. She was on top of her and screaming. The sounds that came from her teenage frame resembled a mythical monster after its prey. Students began to gather and crowd around the scene.

"Get her off," someone yelled.

The girl on the ground was flailing her arms, trying to protect herself from the violent blows.

"Stop it! What are you doing? What's wrong with you?"

Mr. Harrison, the Gym Teacher, pushed his way through the teenagers and pulled Nina off the helpless girl.

"She attacked me; she's crazy!" the girl screamed.

Nina was panting. She stared at Mr. Harrison with wild eyes.

"Nina, Nina Gallaway, are you alright? Can you hear me?"

Mr. Harrison grabbed her by the shoulders and shook her hard.

"Get back to class! All of you!" he ordered at the students.

"She should be suspended. She doesn't belong here," the girl cried to him as she stood up.

"Nina, are you ok?"

He directed his attention to the girl she had just attacked. "I want you to go to the nurse's station. You have my permission to go home for the rest of the day. Have Principal Seymour call your mom to come and get you."

She brushed the dirt off her pants and glared at Nina. Mr. Harrison sat on the bench.

"What happened?" he asked her with urgency in his voice.

"I ... I ... don't know. It was so loud, the laughter and the screams. I was scared. She scared me."

Nina was shaking. "I don't know what happened," she started to cry.

Mr. Harrison placed his arm around her shoulder.

"Was someone picking on you? Is that what started this? You know we don't tolerate bullies at this school, Nina. You can talk to me."

Nina sat there silent.

"I have to report this incident to Principal Seymour. You do understand, right? Let's go inside and phone your grandmother."

Panic rose again. She knew how upset her grandma would be. She knew she would punish her. She tried hard to remember the event that had just taken place. The look on that girl's face terrified her.

"It's happening again," she mumbled.

"What's happening, Nina? I think you should speak to Miss Lauren, the school counsellor. She is very good at helping teen girls with their problems, and I'm sure she could assist you in figuring out whatever it is you feel is going on. Come on now, let's get you inside. We can stop at your locker and grab your things on the way to the office."

He picked her bag up off the ground and led her inside. There were still students whispering in the hallways.

"Get to class, I mean it," Mr. Harrison snapped at them.

Down the hall and to her locker, they went. Fumbling with the combination, Nina heard a click and released the lock. The tiny metal door opened, showcasing a variety of subject textbooks. She grabbed two and shoved them into her pack.

Slamming the door, she hooked the lock and spun the dial.

"All set then," he said to her while leading her down to the office.

"Mrs. Daniels, can you find Nina Gallaway's file and bring it into Mrs. Seymour's office. We need to fill out an incident report. And get Lorraine Mayfield down here to the school to pick her up."

Nina felt his hand in the small of her back as he gently pushed her through the open door. He pointed at the chair on the left. She rolled her eyes and plopped down.

"What seems to be going on here?" Seymour asked while clasping her hands on the desk. "I heard you started quite the commotion on the grounds, Nina. Why don't you start from the beginning?"

She stared at the woman on the other side of the desk, a woman who pretended to care to get her paycheck. She didn't want to talk to her about it, to anyone. She didn't even know herself how or why it began.

"I'm not exactly sure. I guess I got confused. I didn't feel good," Nina said, while rocking back on her hands in the oversized chair.

"Have you had episodes like this before? Have you seen a doctor?"

"No, I haven't been to the doctor."

"Well, I'm going to schedule you in with Miss Lauren three times a week after school."

Nina cut her off. "I can't stay after school."

"Why is that?" Seymour eyed her.

"My grandmother wouldn't approve."

"I will speak to Lorraine when she gets here, Nina. I have known her for a lot of years, and I'm sure she will understand. I know that you have been through some serious traumas in your life, and maybe you never got the help you needed. Sometimes we oppress things that we can't handle, but you know they always find a way of resurfacing until you truly deal, Nina. It's ok to ask for help."

When Lorraine arrived, Nina could feel it. She could almost hear her slamming the door on the 1953 true Anniversary Cadillac. The special edition car, also known as 'The Eldorado' was still in mint condition. The car mirrored Lorraine's identity of excellence. The paint glistened in the sun as if it had just been applied. The new car smell still invaded you upon entering to sit on the ivory leather seats that remained seemingly untouched aside from the rip in the back of the passenger seat, the rip that Nina had created. Lorraine was furious at her for this. She was six when it happened. They had been at the Greenhouse collecting bulbs to plant in the garden. Nina was excited to get home and help her grandmother put them in the ground. She leapt into the backseat. The strap on her right sandal had come undone and the metal clasp slid along the back of the front seat. Her heart stopped just as fast as her tiny leg as it pierced the leather. Lorraine heard the sound of the tear and lost control. Yelling at Nina all the way home, she insisted she spend the rest of the evening in her room.

Her stomach turned as she envisioned her forcefully stepping across the parking lot. Her purse tucked up under her arm so tight you could see the tiny bicep through her blouse. Nina knew she would be infuriated as she sat there waiting.

The door opened behind her, and in she walked. Eyes fixed on Nina. She stopped abruptly and crossed her arms.

"Thank you for coming down, Lorraine. It seems that Nina had an altercation with another classmate, and we feel it is for the best if she is excused for the day. I also feel it is in her best interest to see the school counsellor after school for a little while. She gave us quite the scare, and I am concerned that this may happen again if we don't seek treatment."

"Nina is not available after school. We have made previous arrangements, and what would I be teaching her if I excused her from that?"

Feeling the tension, Mrs. Seymour stood up from her desk. "Well, Lorraine, I guess you know what is best for your granddaughter. I will be keeping an eye on her."

"Yes, do that." Lorraine sneered as she grabbed Nina's sweater and pulled her from the chair.

Not a word was spoken on the way to the car or the house, the house that waited for her to be trapped in. The silence was deadly, and it engulfed her before she even entered. There were no happy voices or radio on playing oldies, just the tick of the grandfather clock and the creaks of the foundation. Being without her phone as well, her little device that allowed her to still be a part of the outside world, was taken from her. Nina could feel the panic returning as she thought about Bruno again.

'Do it.'

'What was that? Who was that?' she wondered as she shot her gaze at Lorraine.

Her hand was already placed and ready on the stainless-steel handle that would allow her to escape. The car came to a stop in the driveway, and Nina barreled out as fast as she could.

"Slow down!! Do you want to do some more damage to my car?" Lorraine yelled after her, waving her fists through the windshield.

Nina unlocked the front door and ran inside. She was scared and perplexed. She knew that she heard a voice in the car, and it did not come from the front seat or from anyone in the car. She shuffled up the stairs and retired to her bedroom.

She had woken in the night and got undressed. She didn't remember getting to her room or falling asleep. It was dark when she opened her eyes, and it scared her. Flicking on the light, she climbed back into bed and stared across the room.

Lorraine came in to wake her in the morning. Nina didn't feel good. She had a fever and spent most of the night awake.

"You feel warm," Lorraine stated as she placed her hand on her forehead. "I'm going to keep you home today, but that does not mean it's a play day. You will stay in bed and rest."

Bruno waited on the sidewalk across from Waterton High School. He watched the students pile out of the building in anticipation of being set free for the day. His eyes scanned the long dark-haired girls in the mix. A couple of them resembled the girl of his dreams, but she was nowhere in sight. He stood there with his hands in his pockets and gazed at the ground. Bruno kicked an over-sized stone sending it bouncing off the curb. How he craved a cigarette right now. The hope of seeing her again faded once again. Why hadn't she called? He got the nerve to try her once more. It went straight to voice mail. Her phone was off. Bruno forced himself to stay positive as he walked back down the street. He was on maintenance duty tonight. There was a leaky sink in the men's bathroom. He knew it wasn't going to take him long, so he had planned in his mind other projects he could do to occupy his time. He wanted to know where she lived, but he hadn't even gotten her last name.

Nina had spent most of the day in bed. Lorraine brought her cream of chicken soup and a sandwich for lunch. It was wrapped in foil on the nightstand. It was still warm. She sat up and bit into the sandwich. Dipping it into the soup, she had a few more bites and returned it to the stand. She was feeling better, focused. She wanted to go outside; to breathe the fresh air that was far from present in her congested room where its dampness seemed thick and sticky.

Stepping out of bed, she threw on her robe and went downstairs. Lorraine was in the backyard. The flower garden she had created over the years required constant maintenance.

She had tried to be a part of the upkeep with her grandmother, but Lorraine wanted no part of her assistance.

"You won't do it right. There is a specific way to tend a garden, and I don't see green thumbs on those hands of yours."

Nina despised her lack of faith in her. She had been raised to believe that she couldn't do anything right. She spied through the curtains debating on making an appearance. She didn't want her to see her. To see she was feeling better. Grabbing a water bottle from the fridge, she headed upstairs. Entering the bathroom, Nina bent over the tub and cranked the hot tap full blast. She wanted to wash away all the negativity. She could feel that something wasn't right. Not normal. Not explainable.

She had to see him. The need for more was all too consuming. As she lay in the tub letting the bubbles grow up around her body, Nina felt good again. She was going to sneak out and find him. Knowing she was sick; her grandmother would more than likely not check on her. This also being viable as she would probably be worried about getting sick herself. She also liked knowing Nina was in her room alone, stored away from the world like a princess in a stone castle.

She pulled the plug and stepped out of the porcelain tub. Pinching her cheeks, she wanted to look flushed and fevered still. Putting on her robe, she opened the back door and called to Lorraine.

"Grandma, I'm still not feeling well. I had some lunch you brought me and a bath, but I'm still exhausted. I'm going to crawl back into bed."

It was 7:00 PM when Nina went downstairs to ensure a good night's visit with Lorraine.

"You still look pale, probably low on iron. You never eat enough eggs."

"You're right, grandma, I don't. Why don't you make me some for breakfast? Over easy so I can dip the yolk."

"You will get what I make, and you will enjoy it."

Lorraine focused her attention back on the blanket she had been crocheting. She had felt a draft in the front room, which seemed to leave her with chills.

"Good night, Nina," Lorraine said in a tone that meant business.

She said good night and climbed the steps. With each stair, her smile grew bigger. Her plan was going to work. She had escaped out of her bedroom window before and was borderline professional at it. She knew the drill. She would have to stay in bed until the first visit. She hoped it wouldn't be long as she prepared the outfit to replace the pj's when able.

At 7:30, Lorraine brought a plate of steamed salmon on rice with a side of lemon as Nina liked it and a hot chai tea.

"You really should eat, Nina. You're looking thin, and I don't want people thinking that I don't feed you. It will fill your belly, and the tea will help you sleep. You need to get your iron up."

"Ok, I will, for you. You're right; the tea will do wonders. Thank you for the meal, grandma."

She was kind of hungry, so she ate most of the plate and sipped down the tea. Lorraine waited until she finished and took the tray. Closing the door behind her, Nina heard the lock on the outside click. This was to be a form of punishment, but Nina found her ways around it.

Nina prepared her pillows under the blankets and placed the hair extensions she used for Halloween on her pillow. She changed out of her pyjamas and brushed her hair.

It was 8:30 when she ventured her way out the window and down the trellis. Bent over with a light foot, she tiptoed out of the yard. Feeling safe from Lorraine's sights, she stood up straight and picked up her pace down the street.

She waited at the corner stop and boarded the bus. Flashing her student pass at the driver, Nina took a seat. The Nectar Night Club on 3rd had a bus stop across the street.

'Sweet,' she thought. Being alone at night in this neighbourhood made her feel a bit uneasy. She always carried deodorant spray in her bag as a form of protection.

They were a few blocks away when the adrenaline started to kick in. She slowly exited the bus and waited for it to rumble by before crossing the street. The neon sign flashed OPEN. How was she going to get in? She spotted a payphone and rushed to the booth. She had memorized the number as she played it in her mind that day. Feeling confident, she dialed.

"Hi, you've reached The Nectar. How can I make your night sweeter?"

Nina paused and thought of Bruno.

"Can you put Bruno on the phone, please?"

"Sure. Who's calling?"

Nina froze. She stuttered, "Umm just an old friend in town."

"That voice sounds to me like maybe more than just an old friend," he chuckled, "Hold on, I'll look."

Nina curled her fingers around the cord and placed her head against the glass. Scanning the walls in the booth, she noticed old markings of graffiti plastering the walls. A poster was taped to the back window looking for a lost dog. She wondered to herself as she waited if the pet had ever been returned to its owners.

"Sorry Miss looks like he's tied up at the moment. We got a couple of rowdies in here. Ol' Bruno is working on removing them from the property. Can I take a message? Can I get your name?"

Without letting him finish, Nina hung up the receiver and stepped out of the booth. She sat on the curb and rummaged through her bag. She was sure there was a packet of Kleenex inside.

The metal bang that echoed behind her made Nina jump. She was on her feet and investigating the crash. Three men stood at the front entrance. Two of them were clearly intoxicated, the other one clearly Bruno. Her eyes lit up. She stared hard. She was watching him throw his authority around, and it excited her. As he reached for the front handle, he was still hollering at the now barred customers. He turned his head and stopped.

"Bruno!!!!" Nina cried out after him.

Letting the metal handle slip from his fingers, he turned to face her. She was closer now. So close, he could almost smell the vanilla aroma she possessed.

"I can't believe you're here. I never heard from you. I went by your school."

"You did?"

"Yes, I'm sorry if that sounds weird. I just really wanted to see you again. I wanted to go by your house. I would have if I knew where you lived."

"You can't do that."

"Why not?"

"Well, my grandmother Lorraine would not approve especially now. Especially since I'm grounded, and I just snuck out to see you."

"Wow! All that for me? I thought you were ignoring me. These things happen, you know."

"What things?"

"You meet someone you really like, and they never want to see you or associate with you again."

"Those people are stupid."

They both laughed.

"My grandma took my phone away, and this was the only way I knew how to reach you. I hope you're not upset I came down."

"Upset? Are you kidding me? I'm pumped. Wait here. I'm going to grab my jacket and let them know I'm leaving."

"Ok," Nina blushed.

Bruno ran inside and was back out within minutes.

"So, what would you like to do?"

Nina looked up at the sky and back at him. "Anything with you."

Bruno placed his hand in hers and led her down the street.

Chapter 13

It had been five months since the two had met and were secretly seeing each other. They had grown extremely close physically and emotionally. Despite their age difference, they were truly, madly, and deeply in love. They would talk about moving away and starting their future together when they were with each other. Nina had never imagined she would meet someone so devoted to her. The only thing she had ever experienced in her life was abandonment, and the fact that Bruno had stayed so true gave her hope, a reason to be happy.

On a Wednesday evening, Lorraine confronted Nina at the dinner table.

"I noticed you haven't been using any sanitary napkins. I heard you getting sick in the bathroom. Are you pregnant? Tell me what is going on, Nina. Tell me who he is."

The tone of her voice rose into anger with each word she spoke. Nina stared at her grandmother with fear in her eyes. She had taken a pregnancy test with Bruno when she missed her period. They had both stared at the stick with anticipation. They wanted it to be positive. The idea of starting a family together excited them. They wanted so badly to be loving parents to a child that was produced out of love. Bruno knew that it wasn't going to be easy. Supporting them and making ends meet wasn't going to be hard; the hard part would be telling Lorraine. She knew nothing of his existence in her life, and they both knew that she would not consent to their situation. No matter what the outcome, they had decided together to stay together.

Lorraine was still repeating herself. Waving her arms in the air and pointing at Nina.

"Hello, Nina, come back to earth, Nina. I know you are pregnant. Who is the father? You tell me this instant young lady. You will not be going through with this. I refuse to raise you and another brat. What will people think?"

"You don't have to support me. You don't have to do anything for me ever again," Nina snapped back at her. "Yes, I am pregnant, and yes, I am going to keep the baby."

She pushed her chair back as she stood up knocking it to the floor. Her head started to spin. The ringing in her ears got louder as she ran down the hallway and out the front door. As she turned the corner, relief seemed to set in. She had no idea how she would tell her grandmother she was expecting, and now the truth was out. She had to tell Bruno.

Bruno couldn't help but eye the clock. He was distracted by the absence of her call. His arms followed the beat of the song and emitted emotion with every bang of the drumsticks on the musical barrel. When the song ended, he placed the sticks down and looked up at the front door. A smile crossed his face as he saw the love of his life standing there staring back at him. Bruno rushed off the stage toward her.

"Hi, honey," he said as he held out his arms.

Nina wrapped her arms around him and began to cry.

"Nina, what's wrong?" Bruno asked with wide eyes as he held open the front door and stepped her outside.

"Grandma knows," she cried. "I'm scared. I have dreaded this day. She is going to ruin this for us. I don't want to go back there. I want to be with you."

"Hey, hey, don't cry. Everything is going to be fine. We are in this together remember. Nothing is ruined. I promised you that I would take care of you, and that is what I am going to do. Maybe now is the right time to confront your grandmother and let her see that we have a plan."

"No, we can't go there now. She is livid. She would probably kill you if she saw you right now."

"Honey, you need to calm down. It's not healthy for the baby for you to be in this state. Let's get you somewhere warm and relax. Are you hungry?"

Nina grabbed his hand hard and shook her head no.

"You wait right here. I'm going to grab my things and take you back to my place."

Nina stood under the moonlight and waited impatiently for the man she loved to return. She placed her hands on her belly as the anxiety crept up inside of her. Knowing that Lorraine would not give her up so easy; she took a few deep breaths and closed her eyes, letting the cool breeze blow the hair from her face.

The door opened as Bruno stepped out. They crossed the street to the bus stop and boarded.

"I think you should stay with me tonight, Nina."

"No, I can't. There is nothing in the world I want more right now than to be with you, but I need to go back home. It is the right thing to do. I know my grandma. She will have a missing person report on me if I don't get back soon. I'll be ok. I just needed to see you and tell you she knows. Please understand. I'm sorry."

"You have nothing to be sorry about. I love you, Nina Gallaway. You are the smartest, bravest girl I know and I'm not ever going to let you go. I want you to go home to bed and get some rest. I'm hoping that she has calmed down some and will let you be for the night."

Nina laid her head on his shoulder and sighed. She was exhausted. The emotions and symptoms of the pregnancy were taking their toll on her. All she wanted now was to curl up in bed. The bus stopped up the street from her house. The two got off and stood on the sidewalk. Bruno leaned down and kissed her forehead.

"Are you sure you will be okay?"

"Yes," she replied, kicking a stone with her shoe.

"Ok, but I am going to sit out here and wait until I know for sure. Wave at me from your bedroom window before you crawl in, so I know you're safe."

Nina hugged him tight. "I will, and I love you, Brett Mazuno. I don't know what I would do without you."

"Well, babe, that will never happen. I'm yours now and forever."

She let her hand slide along his arm as she turned toward the house.

Chapter 14

Lorraine stormed into the police station. The force of her entry slammed the doors against the walls that held them in place. Heads turned to watch the older woman throwing a temper tantrum like a five-year-old wanting candy at an amusement park. Her dress billowed up around her knees as she spun around.

"I want him charged!! He cannot get away with this. He is a grown man having sexual relations with a young girl. This is an outrage. He should be locked up."

An officer confronted Lorraine and motioned her into a nearby office.

"Now, you need to calm down and tell me what is going on."

"Calm down; I can't calm down. I try hard to keep my granddaughter safe from lurking, horny men, and this is the thanks I get, a knocked-up teenager. He forced her to do it. I know it. How many others has he taken advantage of? I want him arrested."

Lorraine eyed the silver-plated name tag on the left front pocket of the man.

"Sgt. Drake, is it? Is it not your duty to serve and protect the people in this community?"

"Yes, ma'am it is. I'm sorry I didn't get your name. Why don't you sit down and start from the beginning? Would you like something to drink?"

"No, I don't want anything. I want you to make sure that man pays for what he has done."

"I can't help you until I know the situation. I urge you to have a seat."

He motioned to the fabric-covered chair. Lorraine took a few deep breaths and sat down.

"My name is Lorraine Mayfield. My granddaughter is fifteen years old. She is just a child. I thought I had raised her to have more respect for herself. She has gotten knocked up, and the man who is responsible is in his twenties, maybe even thirties, who knows, a grown man fooling around with a young girl. It's sick. I can't even bear to think about it."

Lorraine was beside herself. The officer pulled his notebook from his side pocket and started taking notes.

"Did your granddaughter come to you about this? Was she harmed physically in any way? Is rape a factor? Do you know who the father is without a doubt? We must tread lightly with cases such as these, Ms. Mayfield. I hope you understand."

"I understand that he is a pedophile. She has been sneaking around behind my back and gotten herself into a situation with an older man who has no right to defile her innocence. Nina has issues. He persuaded her to perform sexual acts."

"I know how hard this is for you to deal with right now, but these things happen with young girls these days. No one uses protection anymore. Sex isn't sacred. Is she going to keep the baby? Do you know the relationship between the two?"

"I'm sure they have had lots of relations. My granddaughter, a whore."

"Ms. Mayfield, I would really like to speak with your granddaughter. If this man has pressured her in any way, we will make sure justice is served. Firstly, we can't go arresting innocent people without evidence. You seem like a proper woman, and I feel you're very upset, but we need to cover all the bases. When can we meet with her? Nina, is it?"

"Yes, Nina Gallaway. She will be home from school this afternoon. I would appreciate it if you sent someone over then."

Lorraine gave Sgt. Drake the address and phone number and left the station.

When Nina got home, she noticed a patrol car parked out front. At first, she thought it must be for the neighbour, and then her mind wandered to Lorraine. What if she fell? Maybe she's hurt. Nina ran to the front door and rushed inside.

"Grandma, grandma, are you ok?" she yelled while looking around.

"Yes, Nina I'm fine. Join me in the den, won't you?"

Nina hung her backpack on the steps and slowly made her way into the den. Anxiety crept along with her. She stood in the entryway; gaze fixed on the officer.

Lorraine glared at Nina. "Have a seat."

She stood there frozen. She forced the noises in her head silent and breathed deep. Keeping her eyes on the officer, she placed herself in the brown corduroy recliner and crossed her arms.

"What seems to be the trouble?" she asked.

"Hi Nina, my name is Sgt. Drake. I would like to ask you a few questions if that is ok with you?"

"What kind of questions?" she replied, fidgeting in the chair as she leaned back.

"Well, your grandmother has informed me that you may be pregnant. Have you taken a test yet?"

She shot a look at Lorraine. "Yes, I have, and yes I am. Am I in trouble?"

"No, no, you're not in trouble. I'm here because if by what your grandmother tells us is true, the man involved may be."

"What?? He didn't do anything wrong. He loves me. I love him. We are happy. He would never hurt me. What has she told you?"

Nina could feel her pulse rise. Her hands grew clammy as she started to sweat.

"She's just jealous because I have someone in my life who truly loves me. She hates me. She has never wanted me to be loved. She has never loved me."

"Nina, you stop that this instant. I have always cared for you and provided for you when no one else would. You are just like your mother. Getting knocked-up and ruining your life. Believing an older man wants to support you is absurd. He will abandon you and that bastard baby just like your father did."

"Now, hold on a minute, Lorraine. There is no need to talk to her like that."

"See, see what I mean. She hates me. She locks me upstairs and tries to hide me away from the world like some dirty secret."

"Is that true, Lorraine?"

Before she answered, Lorraine thought for a moment. "Yes, I have a lock on her door. It is for her protection. Nina has had psychotic episodes, and I worry about her safety as well as mine."

"Psychotic episodes? Can you explain this?"

"We have been monitoring her. She is being diagnosed as schizophrenic. She attacked a girl at school, and I have noticed some strange behavior. Now she is pregnant. How is she going to take care of a child when she can't even take care of herself?"

"Where are your parents, Nina?"

She sat silently in the chair with her eyes to the floor. Looking up, a tear rolled down her cheek.

"My mother took her life when I was eight, and my father left me here shortly after. I never did anything wrong. All I've ever wanted was to be loved. And I am. He proposed to me. We plan on getting married after the baby is born and I finish school."

Nina pointed at Lorraine. "She is just angry because she thinks this baby is one more burden for her. She is wrong though. I won't be living here much longer. He wants me to move in so we can start planning for this pregnancy. He has promised me that he will do the right thing. He wants to. He wants the baby, and he wants me."

Nina was crying now. Drake stood from his chair and grabbed a Kleenex box from the end table.

"Here now, dry your eyes. I don't want to upset you. It is important not to get too worked up in the early stages of pregnancy. Your grandmother has informed me that the father is quite a few years older than you, Nina, and in the eyes of the law, he could face charges for having intercourse with a minor. Do you understand that this is against the law?"

"I understand that she is trying to destroy my life. She has no idea the love that we share for each other. She has no one, and she wants me to have the same."

"This is a grave accusation, Nina. Do you know for sure who the father is?"

"Of course, I know. Despite what she has told you, I'm a good girl. I wanted to wait until I fell in love to be with anyone, and I did. You can't control love. It can happen when you least expect it, sometimes when you need it most. We can't always choose this."

"Well, young lady, you sure made a choice to have unprotected sex with an experienced man. I will not let you go through with this. I have spoken with faculty members from the school. No one has any leads on who the father is, which leads me to believe that he does not go to your school. I will find out, Nina. All your secrets and lies will be revealed, and he will pay for what he has done to you. He doesn't love you."

"He hasn't done anything. He gives me hope and a reason to live. I don't want to be locked up under your roof anymore, wasting my life away. You can't keep me trapped here forever. You should be thrilled that I'm moving out, so you can be alone the way you've always wanted to be."

Feeling the tension, Sgt. Drake asked Lorraine to excuse herself from further questioning for the day. She stood up and stormed out of the room.

"Nina, I am going to give you my business card. I strongly urge you to contact me regarding your situation. I can't help you if you don't help me. You are very young, and a pregnancy at this age needs to be handled with extreme care. Stress can affect the health of the baby. I sense some issues are going on between you and your grandma, but I believe she has your best interest at heart."

"She just wants to control me," Nina uttered. "Are we done?"

"Yes, for today," Drake answered while holding out his business card.

Nina grabbed the card and slid it into her back pocket.

Lorraine walked into the station and directly into Sgt. Drake's office. He was on the phone in what seemed to be a rather heated conversation. He looked up at her with dismay.

"I'll call you back."

He hung up the phone and grunted, "What can I do for you Ms. Mayfield?"

She threw the telephone bill on his desk.

"There's his number. I want to know who he is by the end of the day."

She spun around on her red leather heel and slammed the door. Drake traced the number. It belonged to Brett Mazuno. He ran the name in the system. The search produced no results.

"Kid's clean," he said aloud.

"What was that, Sir?" A Rookie poked his head into the office.

"Oh, nothing," Drake replied, looking back at his desk.

"Hey Marty, come back in here," he hollered to the officer.

"Ya, Boss?"

"I need you to look into this for me. I want all the information you can get on this guy, background, where he works, where he lives," Drake instructed as he waved his hands in circles in the air. "And I need it ASAP."

Marty grabbed the paper from him and folded it in half.

"No problem, I'll get right on it."

"Oh, and Marty, close the door."

It was 5:15 PM when Sgt. Drake got a call. It was Lorraine.

"And what have we found out? Or do I need to start taking matters into my own hands?" she snarled on the other end of the line.

"Ms. Mayfield, we are doing what we can. I have an officer pulling up files as we speak."

Drake rolled his eyes feeling rather annoyed with the persistent woman who insisted on demeaning him. Just as she started to speak, Marty knocked on the door.

"Come in," Drake urged him.

"Lorraine, I will call you back. We may have a lead."

Disconnecting the speakerphone, he wiped his eyes.

"You better have what I asked for."

"I do, Sir. It's all there. No past convictions of any kind. Researching him, I've found him to be quite an honorable citizen in the community. Can I ask what this is regarding?"

He stood there waiting for an answer.

"Honorable or not, he may have gotten an underage girl pregnant, and that is against the law. The girl's grandmother is highly respected, embarrassed, and appalled with the situation. Thank you for your time on this Marty, you can finish up your shift and go home."

Drake opened the file on his desk and began to read. Skimming over the report, he focused on the character of the man whose information sat before him. His history shows that Brett graduated with Honors. He has been working at the Nectar Night Club, where he holds employment as a Drummer, and the main Maintenance man. Previous Volunteer Service at the Salvation Army soup kitchen, as well as the Recycling Depot. Brett donates blood to the Red Cross, drives a '97 Chevy, tutored band students after school, and applied to be a Block Parent.

"Hmm, red flag, this guy is a Saint or truly is a predator."

Drake remembered Lorraine mentioning that Nina had spent a lot of time at Plymouth Pond. According to the report, Brett had started a petition for the place. He jotted down some notes and checked the phone number listed in the report. Drake picked up the phone and dialed the number.

"Hello," the voice on the other end answered.

"Hi, this is Sgt. Drake from the Berkley Police Station. I am looking to speak with Mr. Brett Mazuno."

"This is Brett speaking. How may I help you Officer?"

"Well, we have had some events take place at Plymouth Pond. It has been brought to my attention that you started an Environmental Petition for the place. Is this correct?"

"Yes, I am trying to collect enough signatures to put an end to the cutting of the trees there."

"Your petition for the Pond, did you get any signatures?"

"Yes, I got a few."

"Can I see that list?"

"Of course."

"Would you mind bringing it down to the station for me now?"

"No, it's no trouble at all, Officer. I will be down there shortly."

"Great," Drake replied as he hung up the receiver.

Wanting to get a better feel for the accused, Drake decided to call The Nectar.

"Hello, this is Sgt. Drake. I'm calling regarding an employee of your establishment. Could I speak to the Manager?"

"Yes, sure, please hold the line."

"This is Jason Rundle; how can I help you? Sgt, is it?"

"Yes, Drake is fine. I'm inquiring about an employee there, Mr. Brett Mazuno."

"Oh, Bruno, yes, he works here. Is he in any kind of trouble?"

"Let me ask the questions. How long has Brett been employed there?"

"Umm, Bruno's been around here since he was eighteen, so three or four years. Great kid, super enthusiastic. He drums for the bands and does most of the maintenance on this old place. Couldn't find better help."

"Does he have a girlfriend?"

"I know he has been seeing someone lately, but I've never met her. She may be from out of town. Seems serious between the two, as far as I can see. What is it that you're after, Sgt?"

"Routine check. We received a complaint, just following up."

"Oh, wow, I've never met anyone to complain about Brett; he's a respectable guy. A gentleman, if you will. I hope it's nothing serious, really hate to lose him around here."

"That is all I needed to know. Thank you for your time."

Brett entered the station and stopped at the front counter.

"I'm looking for Sgt. Drake."

"Is he expecting you?" the woman asked while looking him up and down.

"Yes."

The counter attendant waved at the standing officer, "Please take this man to Drake's office."

Motioning him on with a nod, Brett followed him down the wide corridor. The man in front stepped toward a wooden door and turned. Brett noticed the golden plaque mounted on the door with SGT. DRAKE engraved. The officer knocked twice, "Visitor."

"Send him in."

Drake stood up as Brett entered the room. "Please have a seat, Mr. Mazuno, I presume."

He watched him closely as he took the chair. Looking around the room, he rubbed the jeans covering his thighs.

"I brought the petition you requested."

Brett handed him the envelope and leaned back in his chair. Opening the flap, Drake let the papers slide out into his fingertips. Placing the envelope on the desk, he scanned the document.

"I see here that Nina Gallaway has signed the petition." His eyes jolted at Brett, burning a hole right through him.

"Yes, she did. She is the tree hugger type. I believe she spends a lot of time at Plymouth Pond taking photos and escaping the bustle of town. Lots of kids from school have signed it."

"Kids, eh. Being as she is only fifteen, that would put her in that category."

Drake leaned back in his chair, causing the squeak to echo around the room.

"Do you know Nina on a personal level, Mr. Mazuno?"

Brett paused before he answered. "Yes, I have grown to know her quite well over the past while. Is she in any kind of trouble?"

Drake sat forward and tapped his pen on the desk. "No, she's not, but you may be."

Brett's eyebrows rose at the sound of this. He rubbed his now clammy hands on his jeans once again.

"We have been informed that she is pregnant. Checking her phone records, it outlines quite the connection between the two of you. How old are you, son?"

"I will be twenty-two next month."

"Do you know the age of the young girl in question?"

"Yes, I believe she is fifteen."

"Are you aware that having sexual relations with this girl would be punishable by law?"

Brett breathed in deep. He prayed it would never come to this. He knew that Lorraine was behind it. He thought of Nina before he answered.

"Well, Sir, I guess in the eyes of the law, yes, it could be."

"Are you the father of the child?"

"Yes."

"Do you love her?"

"Yes, very much so."

"Well, her grandmother Lorraine sees the situation as unacceptable, and with complaints like these, we have to abide by the law and take all steps necessary to protect minors and serve the community to the best of our ability. Would you be willing to take a lie detector test?"

"Do I have a choice?"

"Well, yes and no. If you cooperate, things may result in your favor. If you deny it, we can't do any more to help you. That woman wants you locked up, and considering the circumstances, I don't believe you will find a judge to think otherwise. I have done a background check on you, and your past is clean, quite an asset to the Berkley community in fact. One thing I noticed was that you applied to be a Block Parent. Why is that Mr. Mazuno?"

"Well, Sir, my brother was killed by a drunk driver when I was sixteen. Hit and run. Driver was never found or charged. He had bled to death in the street. There was no one to help him. People get weird when these things happen. Scared to help. Scared for their own safety. I told myself after that if I couldn't save him, there may be other chances to save someone else."

"You seem like a responsible ladies' man. Why her?"

"She is wonderful. She has been wronged by everyone her whole life. The moment I laid eyes on her, I wanted to know more. She wasn't like the other girls. She fascinated me, so strong-willed like she could beat all odds. I fell in love with her. We've discussed the age difference, and it won't be too long before she is legal. I couldn't imagine my life without her or the baby."

Drake could hear the sincerity in his voice.

"Well, son, I need you to prepare for the idea that the life you dream of may not be in your cards. We are all dealt a hand, and how you choose to play those cards results in a win or a loss. I believe that you love this girl, and your history may help you in this case. Lorraine is a very powerful woman, and she won't give up without a fight. She has made herself believe that you forced yourself upon her granddaughter. After speaking with the both of you, I see that this is untrue. Were you aware that Nina has schizophrenic tendencies?"

"Well, I know that she has been struggling with a few things. Voices and uncertainties. She is seeking counselling for this. I keep telling her that she is fine and it's the stress. I worry about her and the baby. She needs me, Officer. Her grandmother locks her up like a rabid dog. Now you tell me that isn't against the law."

"This has been brought to my attention, but being as she is a minor and there are no signs of physical abuse, we can't get involved with that. Women from an earlier time believe that time out help a child. Keep them safe and out of trouble."

"She is just mad that this was out of her control, our control. It happened. We fell in love. Age has no relevancy. Honestly Sir, Nina and I don't look at our situation as a curse but a blessing. We came into each other's lives exactly when we needed to, and I'm not abandoning her now."

Brett was getting angry. He slammed his fist on the desk.

"Whoa, Mr. Mazuno, you need to control that temper of yours if you expect me to assist you with this further. I will need to set up a detector test and ask you a few questions that Lorraine wants answers to."

He checked the calendar on his desk. "Can you come in for the poly tomorrow? I'd like to proceed as soon as we can before the whole town gets their gossip around. You need to be very careful who you discuss this relationship with. If people didn't know, they will now. You seem like a well-rounded young man who can handle the media when they get a hold of this story. I advise you to keep to yourself. I have booked you in tomorrow at ten AM. Will that work for you?"

Brett thought for a minute. "Yes, I will have to call the Nectar and let them know that I will be late, but it can be arranged."

Drake stood up and shook his hand. "We have all kinds of creeps and pedophiles come through here, but this is a delicate case. I am under the impression now that this was a mutual decision between you and the girl, but it's up to the Judge to decide. Go home and get some rest. I appreciate your honesty and cooperation Brett. See you at ten. Thank you for your time."

Brett left the station and headed to the Nectar. He had to speak to Jason. He saw him sitting at the bar cheering on the game when he walked in. Brett pulled a stool beside him and ordered a beer.

"Brett buddy, what's happening? You ok? The cops called here asking about you. You in trouble?"

"I don't know yet, maybe. I'm going to be a little late tomorrow. Got some things to do."

"What things? I'm your bro man, you can tell me."

"Ya, it's best to keep to myself until I know what's going to transpire. You know how people love to gossip around here."

"Are you going to be ok?"

"I hope so. Gonna head home to bed. I'll see you in the morning."

Brett threw a five on the counter and walked out. His phone rang as he reached the first step leading up to his porch.

"Hi, Babe, it's Nina. Are you ok? What happened? I tried you earlier."

"Yes, love, I'm fine. Seems your grandma doesn't think so though. I'm booked for a poly test in the morning. The officer I spoke with about you seems to be on our side, but Lorraine may be a difficult one to beat in a Court of Law. How are you feeling today? How's the baby? I'm sorry I missed your appointment."

"Everything's fine. We're fine. I just miss you. I feel the baby does to. She's been kicking a lot. She does that when you're not around."

"Nina Gallaway, I love you, and I promise I will always be around. We are going to fight this together. I want you to get a good sleep tonight. I have to be at the station in the morning, but I will let you know how it goes. Don't give up hope. Don't give up on us. We are meant to be together, and no one is going to stop us. Sweet dreams, my girl."

Nina held back the tears as she said goodbye to the man she loved. Hanging up the phone, she crawled into bed and fell asleep.

Knock, Knock. It was Lorraine. The door opened as she stood staring in at her.

"How are you feeling today, Nina? I made you breakfast. Get yourself dressed and come down and join me."

Lorraine closed the door behind her while Nina listened to her retreat down the stairs. At the table was silence. Nina picked through the eggs on her plate and checked the clock. Grabbing her backpack, she left out the front door.

The first class was unbearable. Thoughts of Brett at the station filled her mind. She couldn't wait to know the results. By 11:45 the lunch bell rang, and she hurried outside in hopes he would be waiting for her. He was parked out front with the windows down. She climbed in.

"Let's get out of here."

Brett threw the truck in drive and wheeled out onto the street.

"So, tell me everything. What did the Officers do?"

"Well, they hooked me up to the lie detector test. The main reason was to find out if I had pressured you in any way. I never took advantage of you, Nina. Please believe me."

"I do, Babe. I do. You have been nothing but a gentleman to me. I am so angry at her for putting us in this situation. I don't want you to be charged or punished. Maybe it's not too late to change it. I could say that I had been raped one night, and you felt sorry for me."

"Honey, that's not an option. They know that I'm the father. We just have to play this hand."

Nina started to cry. "I can't do this without you. I can't lose you. I could have an abortion. Maybe she would stop the charges if we agreed to go our separate ways in life."

"I appreciate what you are trying to do, Nina, but I want this baby, and I want you. It's too late. I committed the crime getting into a relationship with you when I knew you were a minor. Now we just wait and find out our fate."

He grabbed her hand and pressed his lips on the back of her palm. "Good things come to those who wait, and we are good people. Don't you ever forget that."

PART 4

July 19, 2008

Chapter 15

It was the summer of '08, July 19th on a Tuesday. The train was leaving Berkley at 10:45 PM, heading to Sherwood Lane. This was the closest flight terminal. Hunter Roberts had to go out of town for business for a couple of weeks. He was a pilot. He was a family man, and since he had been dating Shelly Swanson, he couldn't wait to start one with her. His love for athletics helped him maintain a steady work-out routine. Hunter gave up smoking when he got the job three years ago, but found himself lighting up after the loss of his dad. He kept a pack under the loose board in the closet for those times when he needed a little relief.

He was dating Shelly Swanson, a Registered Nurse at the O'Hanagan Psychiatric Hospital. She had worked at the asylum for ten years. In it were people of all ages, primarily women. Some older and suffering from dementia so bad they had to be institutionalized, others younger and jaded, either by genetics or lost loves. Shelly liked helping people, and the hospital gave her a sense of purpose, that feeling to be needed. The building itself scared her. She always felt uneasy walking through the doors, long corridors and spiralling steps, floors of people with problems. Despite the eeriness of the building, she felt safe. She could understand the patients more so sometimes than your typical community of people.

They awoke that day with the sun and took a long walk down the valley and through the West Side Park. They watched the birds and lay together in the grass, knowing their time together would soon be ending. Hunter made turkey wraps and Greek salad for lunch. After eating, they resided to the bedroom to spend their last hours together.

Hunter grabbed Shelly's hand and pulled her close. His arms wrapped around her, and she could feel the steady beat of his heart against her cheek as she careened her face against his chest. He looked down at her with his sparkling blue eyes. Their eyes met, and he placed a hand on the back of her neck and tilted her head. She indulged herself and kissed his sweet soft lips that felt like satin and tasted of strawberries and a hint of whiskey. Shelly felt a smile cross her face and realized that she was in complete ecstasy. His hands caressed her, unbuttoning her shirt. He placed her on the bed and watched as shadows from the candles flickered around the room. She leaned back against the pillows as he climbed on top of her. Hunter kissed her neck and gently nibbled on her ear lobe. Shelly wrapped her arms around his muscular body and whispered, "I love you," in his ear.

They woke up in each other's arms. Hunter glanced at the clock. He had two hours before his train left. Shelly had to work at 11:00, so she would drop him off on her way. They showered together and finished packing Hunter's suitcase. Shelly put on her uniform and made a lunch to take to work.

They left for the station a little bit early. It was 10:26 when they arrived, and they still had some time to spare. They made their way into the station deli. Shelly ordered two coffees and a couple of doughnuts and sat down in the booth with Hunter. She looked into his eyes and tried hard not to let the tears swell up in her own. Hunter took a sip of his steaming coffee and placed the mug on the ceramic table.

"It's only a couple of weeks, three tops," Hunter said as he stared at Shelly, knowing she was torn up inside that he was leaving.

"I know, but I'm going to miss you, and you know I don't like being alone right now," Shelly replied as she squeezed his hand. The conversation turned minimal, and Shelly found herself counting the minutes till he was gone.

"All aboard for passengers heading west to Stineback, Mertinville and Shadow Lane," the conductor yelled. Passengers collected their belongings and boarded the train. Shelly walked Hunter out and kissed him goodbye. The train departed, and Shelly climbed into her car. She turned up the volume on the radio. A new song by her favorite band was playing. She backed out and drove to work.

The lighthouse that shone through the windows as it made its rounds was soothing, something constant, never changing. Shelly could always rely on this light which would span across the ocean and be seen for up to twenty-three miles, a light of hope and rescue, aiding sailors to shore. She loved it. It was one of the few things she loved at her job. This was her thirteenth shift in a row. They had been short-staffed since the cutbacks, and she always offered to fill in. She hadn't been sleeping well, and the nightmares she lived with her whole life had been intensifying. She wasn't feeling well, and knowing Hunter would be gone devastated her. She prayed it would be an uneventful night.

Down to the staff room, she placed her belongings in her locker and spun the lock.

"We've got a wild one on five," one of the residents relayed to Shelly as they passed each other in the hall.

"Great," she replied and took a deep breath. She had gotten close with the patients over the years and was usually the one called on to diffuse erratic situations. Shelly got in the elevator and pushed the button labeled five. When the door opened, she stepped out and looked around. She could hear loud voices coming down the hall. Shelly picked up the pace and followed the sound. Into a room, she found Nina, one of the patients, backed into a corner. Two residents were trying to restrain her.

"What is going on?" Shelly asked.

The shorter nurse looked back at Shelly. "She didn't take her meds again. We found them under the mattress. She has been going on about a warning, but that's all she will say. We are trying to restrain her, to sedate her for the night before she hurts herself or someone else."

Shelly stepped in front of Nina. "Honey, it's going to be ok. We are going to get you back into your bed and give you something to calm you down, ok." Nina stared at Shelly and nodded yes. Shelly grabbed her elbow and led her to her bed. Nina sat down and lifted her legs. Shelly pulled the sheet over her and administered the tranquilizer into her arm. Within minutes, her eyes were drooping and soon closed. Her breathing was deep. She was asleep for now.

Shelly stood in front of the desk and questioned the nurses. They explained to her that Nina must have had a bad dream. Nina had been in the hospital for three years now. She didn't speak much, and when she did it was usually rants about the devil. She had warmed up to Shelly over the past year. Most of the patients did. She did her rounds and made sure everyone was medicated and asleep. At the desk, she filled out her time sheet. Nausea started to set in.

"I'm going to go on my break now, Donna." Shelly put the file in the drawer and got in the elevator.

Chapter 16

Her hair was blowing in the wind, long and blonde with a slight curl in the ends. She was sitting in the sandbox facing the garage. The five by four-foot wooden box contained only sand and the girl. Who was she talking to? Who was she?

Shelly opened her eyes. She placed her hands on her belly and looked around. She must have dozed off. It was silent in the staff room except for the tick of the clock. She read the time. 4:15 AM. The plate and knife she had used for toast were still on the table. Shelly rinsed them in the sink. Down the hall and up the stairs, she went to finish her shift.

The dreams she had been having lately bothered her. This was the fourth dream in the last two weeks that hosted a little girl. Although Shelly had never seen her face in the dreams, there was something familiar about her. She had lost a child before and worried about her current pregnancy. She was 14 weeks along. The first trimester had passed with no complications, but the trepidation still stood. She had been dating Hunter for three years. He had proposed, but the idea of marriage frightened Shelly. Things change once you tie the knot. She feared that the legal commitment would ruin their relationship. Was it her child she was dreaming about? The idea of the little girl being the one she was carrying at a later age comforted her in a way. If it was her, then she must have a successful pregnancy. She wished that Hunter was home to talk to him about it. She always confided in him the dreams she would have that would upset her. He was delighted that she was pregnant. Hunter was eager to be a father. He had already started a pregnancy plan book with lists of names he wanted. She loved how happy he was. Shelly had spent many years alone before she met him, and it took her a while to let him into her life. Her trust in people had diminished after numerous experiences that had left her somewhat jaded. This was different though. He loved her, and she knew it.

Morning came, and her shift was over. Shelly collected her things out of her locker. She caught a glimpse of herself in the mirror and straightened out her hair. Purse in hand, she left the building.

It was a beautiful sunny day. The birds were out, and it was still early enough that the wind was still calm. Shelly climbed into her car and headed downtown. There was a little bistro on 5th street that made the most amazing bagels. She pictured the menu on the wall that showcased the flavored choices. Jalapeno and cheese, sun dried tomato, blueberry, and a handful of cream cheese toppings. Shelly heard her stomach growl. It was a short drive, and she was soon parked out front.

She watched the paper boy fill the newspaper stand and decided to buy one. She waited until he was done and got out of the car. Her hand shuffled along the bottom of her purse until she felt a quarter in her fingers. She pulled it out and stuck it in the slot. With the door open, Shelly reached down and picked up a paper. She went inside and ordered a sun-dried tomato bagel with butter and a steeped tea. The cup was warm as she lifted it to her nose and breathed it in. There was a two-seater table by the window. Shelly made her way over and sat down. She took a bite of the bagel and went straight to the back page. She always enjoyed the Sunday Tribune as it contained a column for your weekly horoscope. Shelly wasn't sure if she really believed they were true, but she still looked forward to reading it.

Her tea to her lips, she skimmed the page. Her stomach felt uneasy, and Shelly thought she might have to get sick. She shoved the paper into her purse and left the cafe.

When she got home, she filled the tub with hot water and climbed in. The candles that she had lit around the bathroom flickered and danced. The water felt good. It relaxed her. Her nausea had dissipated and all she felt now was exhaustion. She closed her eyes. Her breathing started to slow as she drifted off.

She could see the girl in the distance, that same blonde hair blowing in the wind. She was standing by the water; only a few trees stood by, the tall grass climbing up to her knees.

She was pointing. What was she pointing at? Something was splashing in the water. A crow swooped down. She dodged it and started walking toward the little girl. Every step she took, she seemed to get farther away. She picked up the pace and was running now. The same crow swooped in her face.

Shelly grabbed the side of the tub and let out a cry. The water was cold. She must have fallen asleep. 'How long have I been in here?' she wondered. She reached for the chain on the plug and released it. As the water drained, she wiped her eyes. Shelly stood up and dried herself off. Her robe around her shoulders, she crossed the hall and into her bedroom. The clock was flashing 9:18. The power must have gone out. She slipped into her nightgown and walked to the kitchen. Her cell phone was on the counter. She picked it up and flipped it open. It was 12:46 PM. Shelly poured a glass of orange juice and crawled into bed. She set the time on the clock and double-checked the alarm.

A few hours later, Shelly sat up in bed. She heard something. The storm that raged outside brought the rain pelting down on the side of the house. Thunder cracked loudly again. She slipped her feet into her slippers and tip-toed to the window. Outside she could see cars parked and streetlights beginning to dim. She looked at the clock. It was 8:00 PM.

"Wow! I sure slept this afternoon." Shelly rubbed her eyes and yawned. She had the night off work and considered popcorn and a movie. She went to the kitchen and opened the fridge. She needed groceries, she thought. The cupboards held about as much as the fridge. Feeling hungry, she slipped on a pair of jeans and a sweater. She collected her things in her purse and headed to the All-Night Market.

It was slow in the store. Shelly was glad. She walked the aisles, looking for items she needed. The basket was half full, and she was satisfied enough to pay and leave. She rented a thriller movie. Probably not the best choice since she was alone, but it had been a while since she watched one.

When Shelly reached her house, she looked up as she pulled into the driveway, and realized she didn't want to be home alone. She put her car in reverse and backed onto the road. With the car in drive, Shelly sped down the street. She thought to herself where she wanted to be and who she wanted to be with. Nobody seemed to interest her, so she drove to a little lounge on the outskirts of town called 'The Mystic Temple.'

This is where she had met Hunter and thought it might bring some comfort to be there. New owners had bought it a couple of years ago, and she heard that the place had really gone downhill. The building and everything around it looked rather dingy, and she questioned whether she wanted to venture in. With her wits about her, she climbed out of the car and locked the door. She wondered who all would be in tonight. Regulars, she assumed. She reached for the front door and pulled it open. Shelly walked in and looked around. An old jukebox in the corner of the room seemed to be the only means of comfort. A couple of cowboys were sitting at a table in the corner arguing about which beer is better. 'Looks like they have had enough already,' Shelly thought to herself. She approached the bartender and asked for a Virgin Mary. The bartender studied her and proceeded to mix her drink. Shelly pulled out her wallet to pay the man.

"Here, this one is on the house. It looks to me like you could use it."

Realizing that she must look like a mess, Shelly blushed and thanked the man. The smell of rye lingering in the air from behind the bar smelled so good to her. It carried her away and made her think of all the times she had turned to alcohol for support. She downed the drink and ordered another one. She couldn't have any booze, but she could pretend. Letting her imagination run, she started dreaming about Hunter and how his body felt so warm and safe. What she wouldn't give to hold it right now. She took a sip of her drink and sighed. Shelly looked into her glass and pushed it to the edge of the bar. She threw a five on the counter and walked out.

The night air seemed to send shivers up her spine. It was so cool and crisp against her skin. Shelly took a deep breath and got into her car. A smile crossed her face. She was happy that she had given up the drink. If she weren't pregnant right now, she would have stayed only to find herself too drunk to make it home alone, crying and wishing for a way out. She didn't need her old friends, the Captain and Jack anymore. This pleased Shelly. She had conquered many things in her life, and alcohol was only one of them.

The drive home soothed her even more, and she was soon back in the driveway. Shelly popped the trunk and grabbed her groceries. Into the house, she went into the kitchen and emptied the bags. Filling the kettle, she plugged it in, and proceeded to make a bowl of Caesar salad. Cutting up the pre-cooked chicken breast to throw on top. Shelly opened her purse and pulled out the newspaper. She hadn't got to read her horoscope yet and wanted to know what the stars predicted for the week. She laid the paper out flat and took a bite of salad. One more bite in, she chewed as she looked down at the front page.

A former Willows Cove resident, Mr. Calvin Gibbons, has been released from prison. He was sentenced twenty years ago for sex crimes which took the life of his daughter. This murder also resulted in the suicide of his wife, Mrs. Kathy Gibbons. The law states that anyone convicted of a crime against a child shall not reside within a certain distance of school zones, etc. He has been placed at the Meadowlands Facility, where all the residents of the community who have been released after serving time in prison for sex related crimes, are placed. There is a curfew and routine checks performed by 24-hour on-site security. Mr. Gibbons will not be allowed to leave the village unless accompanied by a member of the authorities. It is the right of the people to know when these kinds of criminals are no longer behind bars. We, the city, strongly encourage parents to go over all safety precautions with their children. It is important they know not to ever go with strangers, be it male or female. If your child must walk home from school,

plan them a route where there is more traffic. Teach them about block parents and how to identify one. These members are there to help protect our children.

The tea kettle whistled like a locomotive engine speeding down the tracks. The steam exploded out of the spout spewing drops of scalding hot water on the floor with the water churning and bubbling inside.

Shelly leapt from the chair, knocking it to the floor. The sound of the bang scared her even more, causing her to jump and nearly fall over. She lunged at the kettle to stop the high-pitched squeal. Her heart raced inside her chest. Both hands on the countertop, she took a few deep breaths. The column she had just read made her feel sick to her stomach again. Shelly poured the hot water into a mug and threw a green tea bag in to steep.

She couldn't believe what she just read. A man who took a child's life gets to live in a community that allows freedom from confinement. A sex-crazed village housing men who have raped and molested women and children actually exists. The thought of this made her gag. Shelly ran to the sink and turned on the tap. The salad she had just eaten left her body before it had time to digest. Shelly washed out the sink and headed into the living room. She popped open the DVD case and slid the disk into the player. Onto the couch, she snuggled under a blanket and pressed play. Shelly didn't want to think anymore today. She just wanted to indulge in the movie and escape reality.

Chapter 17

Calvin had been transported to Meadowlands with a smile upon his face. Now being away from the torture and abuse excited him. So many years, he had yearned to be free of that prison cell. Sitting with his thoughts, fending for himself inside walls of criminals who fucked with him every chance they got. He had been raped several times. Once it was so bad, he was taken to the nursing station for stitches. The other inmates despised him for what he had done to his daughter. He endured beatings of the guards on a weekly basis. His meals were taken from him, or spit on and from this, Calvin had lost a substantial amount of weight, thus making it even easier for them to have their way. He shared a cell with a man for a few years that would masturbate and ejaculate on him in the night.

He was placed in a two-bedroom home with a man who had served time for molesting children. His name was Bill Brady. He had been a gym teacher. He was in his seventies and couldn't hear well anymore. He was grey on top but still had a full head of hair. He would threaten the kids if they told anyone what was going on in the change rooms. Another member of the faculty walked in on him touching a boy's genitals, and immediately called the police. Once he was caught, students started coming forward with stories.

On the second night, Bill confided in him what he had done. How he couldn't help himself. The sounds of the children's laughter thrilled him. Watching them run and play so full of life turned him on. He told Calvin about the first time he had done it. How it wasn't even the molesting that got him off, but knowing he got away with it. This stimulated him, and he craved the risk and the secrets. He had to do it again. It seemed like a drug to him now, always needing that fix. He preferred the boys but had touched a couple of girls with short hair over the years. He had videotaped some of the incidents, and these tapes had been recovered from his home when he was arrested. The family of the boy that he had in his possession the day he was caught sued him. Once other families were aware of the happenings with their own children, a list was created to pay them a small compensation. His house and all its belongings were sold off. His family had disowned him, and he was now going to die alone.

The houses were small, but it was a mansion to Calvin compared to the cement cell he was used to. He could now sleep at night, knowing he wouldn't be bothered. The idea of this kind of freedom made him want more. He and Bill had sat on the back porch and talked the first day he moved in. It had been years since Calvin had any sort of conversation with anyone. They talked about the community, and Calvin asked lots of questions about the security. There was a fence around the property, and he could see the trees rowed together on the other side. His bedroom window faced these trees, and he had spent the first few nights standing in the dark staring into them, calling him to reach them. He started thinking about Bill's stories with the children, thinking about the little girls skipping around the playground and swinging in their dresses. He had pleasured himself several times since he had moved in. Something he couldn't do in the prison. The more he did it now, the more he wanted to. Remembering how good it felt provoked him.

He had watched the custodians at Meadowlands closely. The times they came and how they did their rounds. He wanted so badly to leave the only boundaries he was permitted. He had laid awake thinking about a way to escape. Calvin's family owned a small acreage outside Hampton. It had belonged to his grandfather, who had passed away a few years ago. He knew it would be vacant. Calvin climbed into bed and closed his eyes.

Chapter 18

Nancy stood at the kitchen sink peeling potatoes. It was her birthday. Her husband had wanted to take her out for supper to celebrate, but she was in no mood to get dressed up and go out. She liked the idea of staying in. Nancy had changed after that dreadful night so many years ago when she had lost her sister. She always blamed herself for not doing anything sooner. She knew from the start that Calvin was bad news. When he had lost his job, her husband, Steve, had tried to find him one, but Calvin turned it down. Why wouldn't he? He was getting money from the government to stay home and do nothing, to stay home and get drunk. She hated the way he had treated Kathy. Nancy knew that he would get drunk and beat her. She lied about a black eye a few times. Calvin had always acted like Dr. Jekyll and Mr. Hyde with his split personalities. She found it strange that he wouldn't bathe his daughter. Kathy had told her that he said he felt uncomfortable, as if people would accuse him of touching her. Nancy had heard him yelling at Brian one day. She told her son repeatedly to stay away from him.

She opened the cupboard and grabbed the wooden handle attached to the metal pot on the bottom shelf. She placed it in the sink and turned the water on. Half full, she moved it to the element on the stove and turned the knob to medium. She rinsed the potatoes again and dried her hands. The silence in the house was making her overthink. Nancy walked around the island and pressed the power button on the TV that hung on the wall. The Kelly Lou Show was on. It was a talk show that featured topics around the country. She enjoyed watching it, different than most that bring guests on to find out who is the daddy.

She pulled the paring knife out of the block and began chopping up the potatoes to boil. She had put a roast in the slow cooker earlier, and the cake was in the oven. She set the table and poured herself a glass of wine. Steve should be home any minute.

The commercials ended, and the show resumed.

"Hi, this is Kelly Lou, and welcome back. Tonight, we are discussing the impact sexual offenders have on families and communities as a whole. Before the break, we talked about ways you can protect your children. It is so important that they are aware of the dangers of strange men."

"You know Kelly; it isn't always just strangers. People they have known their whole lives can be just as dangerous, if not more because the child has some sort of trust with them. The important thing we need to teach our children is to always come forward if they have experienced anything that made them feel uncomfortable or inappropriate. When these things happen, they can get scared and worry that they may not be believed, or sometimes they even feel like it is their fault. Start talking to your children when they are young. The sooner they feel they can confide in you, the better."

"Thank you so much for that, Patricia. Patricia Wallis is here with us today. She is a renowned psychologist whose main cases have been victims of abuse, working with foster homes, child protective services, and the police."

Nancy's stomach turned. The hair on her neck stood straight out, the memory of it all hitting her hard. What she wouldn't give to have her sister and her niece over for birthday cake. Nancy daydreamed that she was a little girl getting to blow out the candles and make a wish. She would wish that her little sister had never met that monster.

She placed the cut-up potatoes in the now boiling water and rinsed the cutting board. She lifted the wine glass to her lips and closed her eyes. It was her birthday; she was going to have a nice meal with her husband, and she was going to be happy. Nancy walked toward the TV. Surely there was something a little more uplifting to watch.

"It's funny and a little ironic that I was scheduled to be here today, Kelly, as we have found out from the media that a high-risk sex offender, Mr. Calvin Gibbons, is being transferred from the state penitentiary to the Meadowlands facility. He served his twenty-year sentence and is being let out on good behavior."

"I don't know about you, but hearing this makes me think, of course he was let out on good behavior. There are no children in there."

The wine glass that contained the sweet red liquid that was to make her feel better tonight, shattered on the hardwood floor. The wine splashing everywhere made it look like someone had taken a wet paintbrush and flicked the bristles across the kitchen. She choked and sputtered as the wine had got lodged in her throat. Calvin released. She couldn't believe what she was hearing.

Chapter 19

The next day, he awoke to the sound of water running. Bill was filling the bathtub. Calvin got out of bed and got dressed. He stumbled into the kitchen and opened the fridge. He pulled the half-full jug of milk from the top shelf and took a swig. The cold liquid felt good on his dry mouth. He gulped down some more and returned it to its spot. The air conditioner had been running through the night, and it was cold. Calvin turned the dial off and stepped onto the back porch. The sun was warm and bright. He sat on the steps and waited for Bill to finish in the bathroom.

He heard the door open and went inside.

"How you feeling today?" Calvin called to him down the hall.

"Not so good, boy. My bones were aching. I needed a bath. I didn't sleep well. Been hot and cold all night."

"The sun's hot today. Sitting in it may do you some good." Calvin walked toward the bathroom and went inside. He used the toilet and had a shower. When he came out, the house was silent. He peered into Bill's room and saw him lying on the bed. Bill stared at him, "I'm going to try to get some rest. My heart is beatin' like crazy. I'm having trouble catching my breath. Go on and shut the door for me, will ya?"

Calvin pulled the knob and shut the door. He went back to the kitchen to fix something to eat. There was a knock at the door. A guard entered and met him in the kitchen.

"You boys behaving in here?" He eyed Calvin.

"Ya, I'm behaving," Calvin snapped back.

"Where's Bill, that old coot," he asked as he looked into the living room.

"He's not feeling well. He's taking a nap."

The guard strolled down the hall and opened the bedroom door. He checked on Bill and left the room.

"You leave that old man alone now, ya hear," he said to Calvin as he exited the front door.

"Fuckin hot shot thinks he's so good," Calvin muttered to himself as he cracked an egg into the frying pan.

The day went by, and it was time for lights out. Bill had come out of his room for a bite to eat a few hours prior. He looked like shit and still felt that way. The guard made his nightly visit and retired to his watchtower post. It was shortly after this that Calvin crawled into bed.

A few hours passed, and he heard something. It woke him from his sleep. He sat up in bed and listened. Something crashed on the floor. Calvin jumped to his feet and down the hall. He turned on the light in Bill's room. He was on the floor, clutching his chest. Calvin ran over and knelt. Bill's face was red, and he was sweating.

"Hold on Bill, I'll call for help." Calvin darted down the hall to the front entrance. There was an emergency buzzer on the wall. When pressed, it alerted the staff in the watchtower that there was trouble. He pressed the red button and held it in. Down the hall and back into Bill's room, Calvin ran.

"Help is on the way. Can you hear me, Bill?" Calvin placed his hand on Bill's chest. He knew he was having a heart attack. Panic set in, and Calvin's adrenaline raced.

"Don't worry Bill; you're going to be ok."

Calvin heard the front door open, and footsteps came in.

"Who pushed the alarm? What is going on?" The voice and the footsteps entered the bedroom. The guard that had been by earlier stared at the two of them on the floor.

"He's having a heart attack," Calvin yelled.

The guard pushed him out of the way and bent over Bill. "Bill, I'm going to call for an ambulance."

Calvin backed up and stood by the door. His eyes darted down the hall and back at Bill. Calvin knew it was going to be too late. He knew that Bill was going to die. By the time the ambulance shows up, he will have lost so many brain cells he will be a vegetable if he does survive. Calvin stared at the old man lying on the floor on his way out of this world. He had grown fond of him the past week and hoped that he would get to leave in peace.

The guard was on the radio calling 911. He was talking to Bill as he did this. Calvin looked down the hall again. This was his chance. He could leave now and climb that fence that roused him the past nights. He envisioned himself running out of that house and not looking back, running as fast and hard as he could, away from the imprisonment and watchful eyes, real freedom where he could answer to no one.

By the time he realized it, Calvin was already out the door. He was running, not just imagining it, but doing it. He was going to be free. He locked his eyes on the fence and thanked Bill in his mind.

Fingers out, he curled them around the chain links. The fence rattled and clinked as he made his way to the top. Through the barbed wire, he forced his body to the other side. His leg was bleeding, and his chest hurt. He got to his feet and bolted through the trees. The air smelled damp as it filled his nostrils. His mouth had been so dry lately, and it tasted good. He pushed his way through the brush and stumbled upon an old tree trunk downed in his path. He crawled over it and spread himself flat on the ground. He had to catch his breath. He was laughing. 'What a rush,' he thought. He hadn't felt these emotions in years. He felt young again. Like he had just crossed the football field dodging the opposing players as he made the touchdown. He made it. He was free. He pictured the old farmhouse and knew he had to get there. He knew they would be looking for him. He knew they already were.

Back to his feet, Calvin ran. He could hear the whir of the ambulance siren through the trees, the red and yellow lights flashing and spinning in the darkness. He followed the lights that pointed him to the road. The lights passed, and the siren faded out. He was getting close. He could see more lights coming. Calvin wondered for a moment if it was the pigs looking for him. He came too far now to get thrown back in that creepy centre, even worse, thrown back in jail.

He stared at the lights as he listened. It was a diesel engine. Knowing it wasn't any kind of member of authority, Calvin ran to the roadside. He started waving his arms for the vehicle to stop.

The lights crept closer, and the diesel truck pulled over on the side of the road. As it approached Calvin, the window rolled down. A Hound dog stuck its head out the window. The tongue from his mouth, hanging out as it drooled.

"Go on now, get in the back," the driver reached over and opened the passenger door. The dog leapt down and ran to the tailgate that was lying flat. He pounced onto it and licked his lips. The mangy beast waltzed to the cab of the truck and lay down with a yelp.

"What you doin' out here, stranger?" the driver asked Calvin as he leaned against the steering wheel.

"I ran out of gas on a dirt road a couple of miles back. I'm trying to get to Hampton. My brother is there. I got a call that he had been in a bad accident. Can I catch a lift with you? Doesn't matter if you're not going the whole way. If you can take me as far as you're going, I'd really appreciate it," Calvin told the strange man as he stared him down. He was missing a tooth and his skin was almost black. He either works in a coal mine, or he hasn't showered in months. The scent of body odor, wet dog, and liquor drifted from the cab. This was his only chance to escape.

"Please," Calvin begged the man.

"Well, all right, hop in but no funny business you hear. There is a town of weirdos around here. You got any money?" he said to Calvin while rubbing his fingers in the air.

"No, I must have left my wallet in the car." 'Shit,' Calvin thought. 'I don't want to have to kill this guy for his truck.'

"Nobody rides for free," the man said as he grabbed his crotch.

Calvin's eyes went wild as he glared at the man. His mouth dropped open as he began to speak.

"I'm just shitting you, man," the driver slapped Calvin on the arm and let out a laugh. "I got you real good, should've seen the look on your face." He smacked the steering wheel and looked down the road. "I can drop you in Hampton. I'm on my way through there. I hope your brother gonna be ok."

"Me to, and thanks."

"The name's Mac, and that there is Brewster." He pointed to the box. The dog perked his ears and sat up. "He got his name from a beer box. He showed up in the yard one day, and I found him in the cardboard. He somehow managed to pull all the bottles out and climb inside. Darndest thing I ever seen, so I had to keep him. He's a good dog. He keeps the skunks out of the yard. Best friend I ever had. Great hunter to. Ain't much help when we're fishing though. Can't keep him out of the water. We're on our way to the cabin. Nothin' better than cookin' your catch over an open flame. Where you comin' from?"

"I live in Berkley. Been so long since I've been out this way. I forgot there aren't any service stations from there to Hampton. I was in such a rush when I got the call about my brother that I didn't fill up. It's a good thing you stopped Mac. Never know who could've picked me up."

"Well, I believe if you do good, it's gotta come back to ya. Maybe since I giving you a ride, me and Brewster will get to have a good feast."

Calvin looked back at the dog through the window and back at Mac. "I don't know if that's how karma works. You're not supposed to expect anything in return."

"Well, I reckon I could kick you out right here if you figuring it ain't gonna get me nowhere. Brewster hates riding in the back, and you're in his seat."

Calvin started back pedalling. "I didn't mean any harm by it. Fuck, who am I to know how the universe works. I'm not expecting any good cause I've never done much good." Calvin stared out the window at the stars in the sky. The moon shone down at him through the glass. He thought of her now. His daughter and his wife were his life. He died that night along with Jessica when he took hers. He pictured her smiling face giggling on the carpeted floor. She loved to play dress-up with her dolls and made him play with her sometimes. She would be the doctor and pretend he was the patient using a stethoscope to listen to his chest. 'You're sick,' she would tell him and put tic-tacs in his hand. He was sick. He thought about her and Kathy as the truck sped down the Interstate. He wasn't proud of what he had done to the both of them. Their memories he had buried deep inside years ago. He had to, to survive the guilt he had. If only his wife would've pleasured him before she went to work that night, he may not be where he was now. Running from the law, living in fear. As he thought more, he blamed

Kathy. Anything to take the blame off himself made him feel better.

Calvin saw a reflection in the side-view mirror. It was red and blue lights. He could hear the sirens as they neared faster. His heart fell. Calvin started to sweat. They were after him. They were going to catch him and lock him up again. He held his breath.

"Somebody's in trouble, or we're in trouble," Mac said as he started to pull over and slow down.

Calvin was petrified. He was still holding his breath as the cop car sped by the truck. He let it out as his heart started to return to normal. 'That could've been the end of it', he thought. He had to get out of here before it was too late.

The truck drove by the entrance of the Meadowlands community. Calvin gawked in its direction, his eyes losing sight of it as they drove on. He smiled to himself, 'Thanks, Bill.'

A cross hung from the rear-view mirror and swayed back and forth. The blanket on the seat was covered in dog hair. Cigarette butts overflowed in the ashtray protruding from the dash.

"The radio don't work no more, but Brewster can sing for ya." Mac tapped on the window. "Let me hear you roar buddy."

The dog howled at the moon. Calvin was relieved. The last thing he needed was for Mac to hear that a resident had escaped. His leg burned, and he could tell it was deep. The blood had soaked through his pants. His hands ached, and his feet hurt.

"You thirsty?" Mac reached behind the seat and pulled out two cans of beer. He put one between his legs and held the other out towards Calvin. A beer. It had been over twenty years since he had one. He grabbed it and popped the top. The foam appeared as he raised it to his lips. He swallowed hard. It was warm, but it still tasted like heaven. It brought on thoughts of his teenage days cruising with his buddies carefree and wild. Partying every night and checking out chicks. He kept chugging till the can was empty. Calvin lowered it and burped.

Mac burst out laughing, "Geez Louise, you'd think that was your first beer. I'd give you another one, but I only got a couple left."

"I guess I was thirsty," Calvin said with a grin as he crushed the can. He felt a slight buzz and craved another one.

He could see the sign ahead. Hampton 1 Mile.

"Where you wanna get dropped?" the man who helped him escape questioned.

"There's a gas station on the right. That will be fine. They have a payphone, so I can call someone to come get me." Calvin was ecstatic. Bill was right. The thrill of not getting caught does something to a person.

The diesel pulled into the station. "There you go, Mr. Say, I never did get your name."

Calvin pulled on the handle and pushed the door open. "I like the sound of Mr. Thanks again." He stepped out and slammed the door. The truck wheeled by and headed back to the highway.

Calvin looked around. The roadside station was closed. ONE STOP SHOP flashed on a sign that hung on the front of the store. A couple of the letters had burned out, so it looked like ON TOP SHOP. This made him laugh. He was glad that no one was there to see him or Mac's truck. The farm was a few miles away, but he could walk that far.

He approached the front of the building slowly. Calvin looked around as he put his hands on the window and peered in. He was hungry, and he would need some food to survive. Around the side of the building, he looked for something to break the glass with. A shovel was leaning against the wall. "This will do," he said out loud as he wrapped his fingers around the wooden handle.

In front of the door, he raised the shovel and smashed it through the windowpane. Glass shards exploded onto the floor. He stepped over the pieces carefully, reached in and unlocked the door. Calvin pulled a plastic grocery bag off the reel and quickly scanned the two shelves in the middle of the store.

When he came out, he had a loaf of bread, jar of peanut butter, ten packs of cigarettes, matches, beef jerky, a jug of milk, couple cans of soup, a bag of pork rinds, and two rolls of toilet paper that he had taken from the bathroom. The adrenaline rush had his heart racing again. There was still no sign of anyone around, and for this, he was thankful.

He started down the road to his destination. He could still taste the beer. He wondered if he would find any bottles stored away at the farm. His grandfather enjoyed the drink and always had something on hand when he was alive. They pretty much shut the door after he passed and left the items in the house as they were. Calvin prayed that the house was still vacant. The beer had made him want a cigarette. He had eyed the pack of Smith Lights on the dash but couldn't bring himself to ask Mac for one Pulling a pack out of the bag and peeling off the plastic, he shoved a cigarette between his lips and lit a match. He inhaled and flicked the match. Calvin was tired. Dragging his feet down the dirt road, he slapped himself in the face a couple of times to wake himself up. He knew it wasn't much farther.

He had just passed the old McNaughton farm. The three-storey house stood alone in the yard. It was built in 1897. It was used as a bunkhouse for soldiers until a wealthy man from France, Gerald McNaughton bought it for his wife, Elaine. They came here for the land. Mrs. McNaughton wanted a big family. She was already pregnant with her first-born when they arrived. Lucky for her, it was twins. Two boys, they named Samuel and Alexander. Before they were born, Gerald hired a live-in nanny to help Elaine. She desperately wanted a girl, and the following year gave birth to Edith. Elaine became depressed, never seeing her husband, and became distant with the children. The nanny, Sophia, fed them, bathed them, and taught them how to play. The wine cellar soon became a frequent place to visit for Elaine. Gerald was struggling with business and liked to drink as well. He would come home drunk and give her a beating. She was pregnant with their last girl, who was to be named Florence, when she took her own life. She hung herself in the wine cellar when she was eight months along. It was Samuel who found her. Mr. McNaughton sold the house and moved back to France with Sophia and the children.

He had his wife and their unborn buried in the yard behind the house.

Calvin had learned about the property in History class. They had taken a field trip to the farm to study the rooms and the different murals on the walls throughout the house. Some people say there's a secret room where they made whiskey and bootlegged it overseas. They got to see the headstone for Mrs. McNaughton and the baby. The class single file climbed into the attic and onto the roof to see how it had been built flat for the soldiers. The teacher had explained to them how they would lay up there and fight. They had a good advantage being so high above their enemies.

He couldn't remember who it was now, but some of the kids started horsing around on the tour, and he had fallen off the roof. Lucky for him, he had landed in a bunch of shrubbery that braced some of his fall. He broke his ankle, and the class had to end the field trip and go back.

When he was young, Calvin and his younger cousin would go to the farm when they visited their grandpa during holidays. He would always try to scare him with stories about the ghost of Elaine. His cousin would cry and run back to his dad and tell on him. Calvin chuckled to himself as he remembered this.

When he reached the lane of his grandfather's farm, he stared into the yard. There was no sign of anyone. This was good. Calvin walked up to the house. It had really fallen apart. The shingles were missing sporadically on the roof. The paint was almost all peeled off the boards that held the dilapidated building up. The side window to the back porch was broken. It looks like a rock went through it. That or someone broke it to get in. The doors were closed on the barn. Memories flooded Calvin of his times there as a child and his wedding with Kathy. He pictured her standing in her wedding gown with their baby in her belly. 'Jessica, my little girl, I'm so sorry; daddy is so sorry.' Calvin started to cry. He hadn't cried in years. He sat on the front step and bawled. It made him feel good as he released years of toxins built up from years of guilt. He dried his eyes and stood up.

The door was open. He went in and tried the light, nothing. It was too dark to see anything tonight, and he was exhausted. Calvin walked into his grandfather's bedroom and fell on the bed. Dust lifted up and surrounded him. The rusted springs squeaked beneath him and the worn-out mattress as he fell asleep.

The sun shone through the crack in the curtains and directly into Calvin's eyes. He woke up and squinted against the bright light. He could feel the burning sensation in his leg. Calvin reached down and felt the wet spot on his pants. He rolled over and looked around the room. It looked just like he had remembered it. Even the wooden chair in the corner where his grandfather would hang his jacket was still there. He got up and pulled off his pants. The gash was a couple of inches wide and deep. Blood was crusted in the hair. The floorboards creaked under his feet as he stumbled to the bathroom. He checked the medicine cabinet. There was a box of gauze. He pulled it out and wrapped it around the wound. Back into the bedroom, he found a pair of pants and a clean shirt in the closet, along with an old cowboy hat that he placed on his head.

"Looking good, Gibbons," he said to himself in the mirror as he adjusted the hat.

His stomach growled and twisted. He needed something to eat.

Into the kitchen, he pulled the items from his break-in out of the bag and lined them on the counter. 'Not a bad score,' he thought. He ripped open a pack of jerky and gnawed on it as he opened the cupboard doors. There was a can of beans in one cupboard and a bag of rice that the mice had got into. There was mouse shit everywhere. An old iced-tea can sat on the counter. Calvin popped the rubber lid off. Half full. A smile crossed his face. He could almost taste the frothy sweet goodness. Calvin tried the tap. No water.

He went to the basement to check the shut-off valve. It squeaked as he turned it to the left. The pipes rattled and banged as the water slowly entered them. He found the fuse box and flipped the row of switches to ON.

Calvin checked around the basement for any food or supplies he could use. There were glass bottles along the wall. He ran his fingers along them. All empty except one, a twenty-year-old bottle of scotch. He popped the cork and took a swig. It was strong, and it made him cough. He stared down at the dust-covered bottle and remembered his grandfather. He pictured him sitting on the front steps shuffling a deck of cards the way he always did. He returned the cork and took the bottle upstairs.

Out to the porch, he slipped on a pair of his grandfather's slippers and went outside. He opened an old lawn chair that was propped against the house and sat down. He watched a truck drive by. The dust from the grid road drifted through the air. He listened to the silence of the prairie. He heard a dog barking in the distance. Alone with his thoughts, he leaned back in the chair and closed his eyes. Memories of his time in prison sent a shiver down his spine. That cold cell he shared with other inmates for so many years made him claustrophobic with the thought. He breathed in deep and filled his lungs with the fresh air.

Tink, tink, tink. Something chimed and seemed to get louder and closer. 'What is that?' Calvin wondered. He leaned forward in the chair and listened. He could hear whistling. Calvin stood up and walked down the lane to the road. There it was. The sound coming from a small girl on a tricycle. The tassels on the handlebars swaying in the wind. Blue, red, and yellow strings that looked like fingers as the girl pedalled. She was wearing a purple shirt. Calvin could make out the words 'Daddy's little girl' on the front. As soon as the words entered his mind, he was intrigued. Visions of his own daughter played in his head. He could feel his heart pick up pace as he watched her get closer.

She was staring at him now and started to wave. As she lifted her hand off the handlebar to do so, she veered to the right a bit.

"Well, hello there, sunshine. You better keep both hands on that thing while you're riding. You wouldn't want to have an accident," Calvin said to her in a soft voice. "Where are you headed all by yourself?"

"I'm running away from home. My mom told me that I couldn't go to camp this year 'cause we can't afford, it so I'm going to find my own adventure."

"Every little girl should get to go to camp. How about you let me help you? It's going to be dark out soon. I can build you a fort in the basement. I'm sure you must be hungry after your adventure here. I promise I won't tell anyone you're here and you can stay as long as you like. I used to have a girl who looked just like you."

"What happened to her, Mr.?"

"She was a bad girl who never ate her supper, so she had to go away. You don't have to call me Mr."

"What's your name?"

"What would you like it to be?"

"Hmmm, how about Fred? I like Fred. I don't get to watch cartoons anymore since my mom cut the cable."

"Well, I think Fred is just fine. What's your name?"

"Mallory Ann Reynolds."

"Ok, Mallory Ann, let's get you inside. Now you remember that good little girls need to finish all their supper."

Mallory smiled up at him. "I will, Fred."

He walked beside her as she pedalled down the lane. He couldn't take his eyes off her. The need to smell her and feel her skin brought back the urge he knew so many years ago. They reached the front porch and went inside.

The spring on the door slammed it hard behind them. Mallory followed him into the kitchen.

"What are we going to have for supper, Fred?"

"Do you like peanut butter sandwiches?" He asked with curious eyes.

"I sure do. My mom always puts strawberry jam with my peanut butter."

"I'm sorry, I don't have any jam today."

"That's ok. I can bring you some if I come back another day. My mom makes it every year. I get to help her pick the strawberries. She says I'm only allowed to eat one while we are picking, though." Mallory put her head down and looked at the floor.

"Ok, now you just sit right there in that chair until I come back, ok." Calvin grabbed a spoon from the drawer and went to the bathroom. He opened the medicine cabinet and reached for a pill bottle on the shelf. Popping off the top, he dumped two pills in his hand, placed them on the counter and crushed them with the spoon. They were sleeping pills that he noticed had been left behind from his grandfather. He swept the dust into the spoon and went back to the kitchen.

With the spoon on the counter, he took the twist tie off the loaf of bread and pulled out four slices. The peanut butter was on the second shelf in the cupboard. He brought it down and unscrewed the lid, smearing it on two slices. Calvin sprinkled the crushed-up pills on one slice, and covered it. He placed the sandwich on the plate and set it on the table.

"Now you eat all that, ok sweetie," Calvin winked at her and smiled.

She took a bite and licked her lips. He watched her swallow and take another bite.

"Are you going to eat with me, Fred?"

"Sure I will." He buttered another sandwich and sat across from her at the table.

She finished her sandwich and asked him about the fort he was to build for her. He explained to her what he was going to use and how they could have a make-believe fire with marshmallows. She started to yawn and rubbed her eyes.

"You look tired, honey. Do you want to lie down?"

Mallory nodded as her eyes got heavier. Calvin stood up and lifted the girl into his arms. He carried her into the living room and placed her on the couch. He smelled her hair and touched her face. She was out like a light. A smile formed on his lips as he looked down at his new toy.

Calvin went outside and grabbed the tricycle. He wheeled it into the tool shed and found a couple of bags of sand that were on a shelf. A coil of rope hung on the wall. He cut three pieces and attached them to the bags. Everything in hand, he went around back to the dugout. With the bags tied to the bike, he threw it as far as he could. It splashed as it hit the water, and he watched it sink out of sight. Calvin picked up the remaining rope and walked back to the house. His excitement grew with every step. He couldn't wait to have her in his arms. It had been so many years since he had even seen a female, and now he had one in his possession.

He went to the basement and pulled the string on the light in the storage room. The cot that he had slept on as a boy was still there. He knelt and tied the rope to the leg. He flipped the mattress and went back upstairs.

Into the living room, he scooped her up and carried her downstairs. She was sound asleep as he laid her on the tiny bed. He pulled both of her arms behind her back and tied them together. He pulled the ends tight, pinching her skin.

Chapter 20

The wind was blowing. Gusts up to a hundred kilometres blew through the yard. The barn door flapped and clanged against the wooden siding. The rooster that perched on top was leaning as it spun its course. The steady chirp of birds could be heard through the howl. Something squeaked in the distance. Like an old swing with rusty chains linking the leather-bound seat. There was a sign on a post at the end of the road that led out of the yard. The clouds rolled in and brought with it rain. She could smell the dirt as the drops began to saturate the ground. The lightning lit up the sky. She could see the house. She heard a girl scream and started to run. She reached the front porch and put her hand on the doorknob.

Shelly sat up in bed and let out a groan. She was sweating. The sheets were drenched, and her nightgown clung to her skin. She could hear the rain hitting the window. The dream she just had ran vivid in her mind. She lay back down and stared at the ceiling. She focused on the image of the house. The feeling of dread consumed her. There was a little girl in trouble. She could feel it.

Shelly closed her eyes and forced herself back to sleep in hopes of revisiting the current dream.

When she awoke, she immediately thought of the dream she had. She had to talk to Hunter. She had lived with a parasomnia disorder her whole life. It was something she had grown used to. Not so much because she wanted to, but she had to. They had gotten so bad when she was younger that she had to seek medical help. They hooked her up to an EEG machine to test her brain waves. The possibility of a tumor on her temporal lobe had to be ruled out. There was a long list of medications that she had tried to help reduce the dreams. The Dr. had prescribed antipsychotics and sleeping pills. Antipsychotic medication is used to slow thought processes, and he thought they might help put her into a deep enough sleep not to dream. After taking them for a few months, she realized that the dreams lessened somewhat, but she found herself getting up in the night and doing things she wouldn't normally do, as well as things she wouldn't remember doing. This scared Shelly, more so than the dreams themselves, so she stopped taking them. The sleeping pills were another route she tried. They made her fall asleep fast, but she didn't stay asleep, and the side effects were similar to the other meds. Hot baths, tea before bed, going for a run, eating, not eating, alcohol, drugs were all used to experiment with her sleeping behavior.

When she met Hunter, she got the nerve to tell him about this before they had spent the night together. It embarrassed her. She felt stupid. Shelly explained to him that she would walk and talk in her sleep with no control over it. Hunter had laughed and thought it was neat. He was actually curious and wanted to experience an episode. He poked fun and cracked a few jokes. Shelly was bothered by this response and started to cry. She told him how a man in her past had criticized her for it and claimed she was possessed. Hunter felt terrible for making her feel that way and bought her flowers the next day. He assured her that he would be there to support her. When they moved in together, the dreams started happening less. This, and the security she did feel when he was beside her upon waking, made her ecstatic.

She climbed out of bed and found her cell phone. Shelly checked the calendar to see where Hunter would be at that moment and if he would be available to talk. According to his schedule, he should've landed and transferred to his hotel for the night.

She flipped her phone open and dialed the number. It rang a few times. No answer. Shelly closed the phone and started to cry. A feeling of dread came over her. She yanked a Kleenex from the box and laid back down. Ring, Ring. It was Hunter.

"Hello," she said, trying to fight back the tears.

"Hi Sweetie, what's wrong? Sorry I missed your call. I just got back to my room. I went out for supper with a couple of attendants. I left my phone here to charge. Are you ok, my love?"

Shelly quietly wiped her nose. "Yes, everything is fine. I have been having dreams lately that I can't seem to shake off. I just wanted to hear your voice."

"Aww honey, maybe you're having dreams because I'm not there with you."

"I'm sure that may be part of it, but I think there's more to it. I keep seeing a little girl with blonde hair. I don't know what she looks like, but I have the strongest feeling that she is trying to contact me, to show me something, to help her. I am considering going to the police."

"Really, Shelly, that does sound serious. What are the dreams about?" he questioned.

"I don't know for sure. But there is always the girl, and I am in a farmyard. I have a feeling that it's some kind of warning."

"I am always here for you. You know that, don't you? I wish I could be there with you now."

"Me to, babe, me to." Shelly fought back the tears again. "I'm going to let you go now, but I love you and thank you for listening."

Hunter made kissing noises into the phone. "I love you more. Try and have sweet dreams tonight, ok. I will be home before you know it."

Shelly hard boiled a few eggs and placed the wedges on top of her salad. She packed her lunch and stuck it in the fridge. With the sheets ripped off the bed, they were thrown into the wash. She ate her salad and checked her email. When the machine beeped, Shelly tossed the bundle into the dryer and went out the door to work. She couldn't wait to be home in fresh sheets. Something wasn't agreeing with her, and nausea crept in. 'Maybe the eggs,' she thought.

When she got to work and started her shift, the place was in chaos. Patients having fits, nurses yelling to calm them down, the TV from the common room blared in the background. Shelly rushed over to help. A man had been brought in earlier. He was picked up and brought to the hospital. He had years of history with manic depression and drugs. He lived off the streets. One of the residents tried to get him to drink a glass of water.

"You're dehydrated, Joseph. You need to drink this glass."

"NO," he screamed at her. "I want my medicine."

Shelly stepped in between them. "Hi, Joseph, my name is Shelly. I just want to help you feel better and get your medicine okay. I just need you to do what she says first and drink some water okay. Can you do that for me?"

Joseph started to calm down. He reached out for the water. His arm was shaking. He was obviously malnourished. The nurse handed him the glass, and he started to drink. Shelly turned to her, "Will you go and get 10 mg of Ativan please."

The nurse nodded and went for the medication.

"Good job Joseph. I'm glad that you want to co-operate with me."

Joseph passed her the empty cup.

"Now, can you sit with me on the couch and tell me what is going on? The nurse will be right back with your medicine." Shelly placed her hand on the small of his back and guided him to a sofa in the common room. She clicked off the TV and sat beside him.

The nurse showed up and handed Shelly the tiny paper cup that contained the pill. She gave it to Joseph. "Now put this under your tongue, and I promise you will be feeling better in minutes, okay."

Joseph put the pill in his mouth and sat silent.

"Do you want to talk to me now?" Shelly asked him softly. No answer. He sat on the couch and stared at the wall.

Shelly stood up. "I will be right back, Joseph."

She walked to the desk and found his file. She opened the brown pages and read the report. It stated that Joseph had been picked up outside PINOCCHIO'S PAWN. He was high on something and was flashing a gun around threatening to shoot. When questioned, he said he had got the gun from Jepedo in his workshop. The police had confiscated the weapon and brought him to O'Hanagan.

When Shelly went back to the common room, Joseph was asleep. She went to the linen closet and retrieved a blanket. She swung his legs up on the sofa and covered him up.

"Keep your eye on him, please. I'm going to do my rounds. He will probably be out for a while, but let's monitor it closely."

"Sure thing Shelly, and thank you for your assistance earlier. You certainly have a knack with the patients." Shelly smiled at the nurse and found her chart.

A couple of hours had passed, and Shelly still wasn't feeling very well. She plunked some change into the vending machine and pressed B7. The can of ginger ale rolled down the chamber. She was hoping the carbonation would ease her stomach a bit. PSSSTT! She pulled the tab on the top and let it fizz. She downed half the can and let out a burp.

Nina was next on her round. Shelly quietly made her way back down the hall. Peering into her room, she noticed she was awake. Nina was sitting up in bed with her knees pulled up. Shelly slowly moved toward the bed to see what she was doing. Nina's eyes shot straight at her. She must not have noticed her walk in. There was a book on her lap.

"What are you drawing Nina, can I see?" Shelly reached for it. Nina pulled away and shoved the book under the blanket.

"Sweetie, you know it's past your bedtime. I can't let you stay up all night. Why don't you give me the book and I will set it on the dresser for you? In the morning, you can have it back after breakfast."

Nina stared at her with wild eyes. Whatever she was writing in the book had upset her. She reached under the blanket and handed Shelly the notepad with restraint. Shelly yanked it from her fingers. She flipped it open and scanned the pages. There was a drawing of a little girl riding her bike down a gravel road. A hot air balloon was in the distance. Shelly's heart skipped a beat. She couldn't help but think of her dreams. The long blonde hair looked so familiar.

"Who is this, Nina?" Shelly snapped at her.

Nina shook her head and covered her eyes. She started rocking back and forth.

"Hey, I'm sorry. Do you know this girl? Is this you?" Shelly questioned her for answers.

Nina leaned back and pulled the covers over her head. Shelly set the book on the dresser and left the room. She checked on Joseph once more. He was still fast asleep.

It was 3 AM. She still had four hours left.

"I think I have to go home, Jeanette. I am really starting to feel under the weather. I've been trying to fight it off, but if it is the flu, I don't want to be responsible for making anyone else sick."

"It's fine, girl. Everyone is asleep. We will be just fine without you. You go home and get to bed. I'll keep my eye on the new one and make sure that he is looked after when he wakes up."

"Thank you so much. You have a good evening." Shelly gathered her belongings from her locker and headed home.

She tossed a couple of ENO tablets into a glass of water and set it on her nightstand to fizzle. She turned the dryer on for ten minutes to heat up the sheets. The timer dinged, and out they came. They smelled so good. Tucking them under the mattress nice and tight, she crawled in and downed the bubbly mixture. Shelly felt better already. With the lamp clicked off, she drifted off to sleep.

The sky was dark. She was out in the country. The surroundings felt familiar. She followed the path with her eyes until they reached the end. The wooden post in the ground standing three feet high looked to be glowing. The sign that was nailed to the other side called to her. She stepped in front and looked down. There were numbers burned into the wood. She read them aloud and repeated them.

Shelly sat up fast in bed, the numbers playing in her mind. She started saying them to herself as she clicked on the bedside table lamp. It was 5:13 AM. The top drawer contained a pen and pad of paper. Quickly, she pulled them out and wrote the numbers down. She wrote them again. What does it mean? She wondered. She gazed at them for a few minutes and returned the pad to the nightstand. Shelly clicked off the lamp and pulled the covers over her head.

It was 9:30 AM when Shelly got out of bed. She pulled the pad out and reread the numbers. She called the hospital. Margaret, the resident on duty, answered the phone, "Hi, you've reached the O'Hanagan Psychiatric Hospital. This is Margaret speaking. How may I assist you?"

"Hi, Margaret, it's Shelly Swanson. I don't think I'll be able to make it in to work tonight. I went home early last night with an upset stomach, and I think I may be coming down with the flu. Can you see if there is anyone who could cover for me, please?"

Margaret pulled a schedule out of a file in the drawer. "It looks like Lacey is off tonight. I will give her a call and see if she will come in. You just worry about yourself and that little baby of yours. You get some rest, Shelly and let us know how you are feeling, okay."

"Oh, Margaret, you are the best. Thank you so much," Shelly responded before hanging up the phone.

She took a shower and had a bowl of cereal. Shelly decided to go to the police. She needed answers, and she needed help. She got dressed and headed downtown.

Shelly walked into the station with hesitation. The little voice inside herself begged her to pursue the meaning of the dreams. The police headquarters was bustling with officers and citizens. She could feel herself start to sweat. She approached the wicket window. An African American lady sat at the desk. She was on the phone and taking notes. Shelly could smell the coffee on her breath from where she stood, stale and pungent. It reminded her of her school days when the teacher would walk by the desks up and down the rows giving a lecture and breathe on everyone. It was a nasty smell. It was something you never forget.

A man was yelling. Shelly turned around. An officer was escorting him in wearing handcuffs. He looked to be in his early twenties, ripped jeans and sneakers. 'I wonder what he did?' Shelly thought to herself. She must've been staring at him because he noticed. "What the fuck you looking at bitch?" came from his mouth and directed right to her. Shelly quickly looked away and back at the woman behind the desk.

"Can I help you, Ma'am?" she strummed her long-painted nails on the wooden top.

"I need to speak to someone, please," Shelly stuttered the words.

"And what is this regarding? If it's for a parking ticket, we don't deal with those here. You'll have to go to City Hall."

"No, it's not for a ticket. I believe a little girl may be in trouble."

"And you think you can help her? Have a seat, and someone will be out to get you." The phone rang, and the lady was back on the receiver. Shelly took a step back and studied the chairs. There was an empty one by the wall. She made her way over to it and sat down. The chair was plastic and uncomfortable. Her bones dug into the seat as she shifted. She checked the time and waited.

Watching the clock made her feel even more uneasy. Fifteen minutes had passed before an officer approached her.

"Are you the woman who is here to speak to someone about a little girl?" He eyed her.

"Yes," Shelly replied.

He stuck out his hand. "Hi, I am Officer Brock. I work with the Child Services Unit. Would you kindly follow me?"

Shelly shook his hand. "Yes, thank you."

They went up a flight of stairs and into a room labeled Questioning.

"Please have a seat, Miss. I'm sorry I didn't get your name."

"It's Shelly Swanson," she said as she sat at the table.

"Can I get you something to drink? We have coffee or water in the common room."

"I'll take a water, please." Her mouth was dry, and she felt dehydrated.

The officer left the room and returned with a Styrofoam cup. He set it on the table in front of her. He pulled out a pad of paper and sat down.

"So, Shelly, tell me about this little girl."

"I think there's a little girl in trouble somewhere, and she is trying to reach me. I know how this sounds, but it is affecting me enough to want to investigate it. I've been having dreams, and in the last one, I saw a sign with a grid road location on it. I did some research and I know where it is. I know who the property belongs to. Or at least who it used to. I read in the paper that a man was recently transferred from prison to a community for sex offenders. The land deed has his grandfather's name on it.

"You've had some dreams?" He lifted his eyebrow.

"Yes, that's what I said," she glared back.

"Dreams of a girl you've never met?" He scribbled something on the paper.

"I don't know for sure. I don't think I have met her. I have never seen her face just her long blonde hair." Shelly picked at her fingernails while the officer continued to write.

"Do you dream often, Miss Swanson?"

"Well, actually, yes I do, but this is different."

"Are you pregnant, Shelly?" he asked in a calm voice.

"Yes, I am. Why?" She could feel her face get hot.

"Maybe you are just having these dreams because you read in the paper that a sex offender was released, and the hormones that happen during pregnancy probably just brought this on. I noticed you aren't wearing a wedding band. Is the father in the picture?"

Shelly was disturbed by this comment. "Officer Brock, is it? I am a sane woman. I would not have come down here to waste my time or yours if I didn't think it was at least worth considering." Shelly grabbed her purse off her lap and stood up. "Thank you for your time."

She spun around and walked out. She was furious. If the people who were supposed to serve and protect weren't going to believe her, she would have to take matters into her own hands. She would need some kind of protection to go about it alone. She wanted to phone Hunter and tell him what had happened and how they had treated her. She knew that if she did, she would break down and upset them both. She had to be strong.

She drove home and went inside. Shelly made a sandwich for the road and threw it in a lunch bag with an apple and a bottle of water. The pad of paper in her nightstand went into her purse. She locked the house and backed out of the driveway.

She stopped at the bank and withdrew five hundred dollars. From what she read in Joseph's file, there was a pawn shop in China Town that supposedly sold firearms, and Shelly needed a gun.

Shelly turned onto Bourbon Street. Garbage littered the sidewalks. There were metal bars on the windows of the shops. Neon lights flashed. Homeless people wandered around everywhere. She hit the lock button and rolled the windows up tight.

The pawnshop was a few blocks up. She could see the billboard sign mounted on the roof. 'PINOCCHIO'S PAWN.' She read that the owner called his illegal business 'Jepedo's Workshop.'

Shelly had never seen a gun before, and she certainly didn't know how to use one. Locals stared at her as she drove down the street. An older man with a grey beard banged on her car door at the stop sign. He was wearing a garbage bag for a vest. Shelly jumped in her seat, making her foot press hard on the accelerator. He swung his arms in the air as she squealed past.

She veered into the parking lot and got as close as she could to the front entrance. She held her purse in front of her for dear life, got out, and locked the car door.

The bells that hung from the door chimed. She stepped in and looked around. A sign that read 'YOU BREAK IT, IT's SOLD' was taped to the cash register on the counter.

A tall man who looked rather shady moved the beaded doorway back with his two hands and entered the store. He was wearing glasses that had been taped together in the middle. His arms were covered in tattoos. Shelly could see the piercing in his tongue as he smiled. His shirt was ripped along the bottom. It read 'surf's up.'

Shelly could smell the incense burning that barely masked the scent of marijuana. Hearing the Reggae music playing throughout the store made her think of a poster on her wall when she was in high school. This made her chuckle to herself. She slowly reached the counter and looked the man in the eye.

"I'm looking for Jepedo," she said as she clung tight to her purse. She was sweating, and she could feel his eyes burning through her. Panic and paranoia set in. He just stood there staring blankly at her.

"I'm sorry, I must have the wrong place," she turned around and headed for the door. 'What am I doing here? I don't know how to use a gun. This is crazy.' A hundred thoughts went through her head in the few steps she took.

"Wait, wait, wait, I am Jepedo."

Shelly froze. She swallowed hard and faced him.

"Come here now. What can I help you with? Let me guess, you like the cocaine. Such a pretty thing shouldn't be in these parts all alone. You're a brave woman coming down here."

Shelly couldn't help but blush. She sat her purse on the counter and pulled out the wad of bills. "No, I don't want drugs. I need a gun, and I need it now." Her eyes fixed on him. He was right; she was brave or stupid. The fear she had was gone. She stood up straight and held out the money. "So, can you help me?"

The man who called himself Jepedo started to laugh. "You come with me to the workshop. Now, what is it you are looking for? I have AK47, N16, 38, and Colt 45. What type of damage you want to do?"

"I don't know how to use it, and I don't want to have to use it, but I need it for protection. I don't have much time. A life is at stake. I need you to sell me this one and show me how to use it." She pointed to the Snub nose .38 in a red velvet case.

"So, you want to buy bullets to? That will cost you extra."

Shelly checked her wallet. There was no more cash.

"Will you take this?" She undid her watch and handed it to him. It had been a gift from Hunter last Christmas. She was so excited when she opened it and put it on. It was the most expensive gift she had ever received. It made her smile, looking at it every day, knowing the man who loved her had gotten it for her. He would be so angry if he knew where she was and what she was doing right now. Shelly had wanted to tell him, but she knew he would be furious if he knew she was putting her and their baby's life in danger.

He held it up close to his face and examined it. He placed it next to his ear and listened.

"Okay, okay, I take this." He lifted the revolver out of the case and cocked the hammer. He opened a drawer on the desk and removed a few bullets from a plastic tin. Spinning the chamber, he loaded them in. "We got out back, and I show you how to shoot."

They walked into the alley. "See that garbage bin, that is your target. You hold the gun up like this, you aim with your eyes, and you pull the trigger." He made the motions as he spoke. He handed the gun to Shelly. It was cold in her hands, and heavy, heavier than it looked. She rubbed her fingers along the barrel. She got in position and lifted the gun. She stood there for a minute. Holding the gun in her hands scared her. She had never imagined herself in an alley getting instructions on how to shoot a firearm. She wanted to drop it and run. She wanted to be safe at home, but Shelly knew she had to do this.

"This take too long," he huffed.

The sound of his voice angered her. Shelly pulled the trigger and fired. She wasn't braced for the impact, and it blew her back a couple of steps. She giggled with excitement. What a rush! She could smell the gun powder linger in the air. The faint scent of cordite filled her nose.

"There, see, you master already." Jepedo smiled as he held the door open.

Shelly passed by him and stepped back inside.

"Now remember, you know nothing of Jepedo, and if you get caught with that, you did not buy it here."

"No worries, and thank you," she said as she placed the handgun in her purse and left the store. She felt safe. She felt ready.

Chapter 21

His greasy fingers reached into the half-torn bag, pulling out a few pork rinds as he shoved them past his lips, and licked them. Salt crystals collected around the corner of his mouth and under his fingernails. The VHS tape that was left in the VCR came to a stop. The women in their bikinis on the beach in the movie had excited him.

He could hear her screams from the basement, throughout the house, and in his head. The girl's shrill voice echoed off the walls and sent a chill up his spine. He thought of her body sprawled across the pull-out cot in the corner with stains on the sheets and blood on the walls. Strands of blonde hair covered the rug on the floor. It excited him. It made him feel powerful. Her body now his trophy as if he won some competition. So many nights, he had laid in that cell fantasising about his daughter and the way she smelled. The soft murmurs she made as he had watched her sleep. About Kathy and all the times they had been intimate.

He got up and went into the basement. He stared at Mallory's tiny body breathing on the cot. Memories of Jessica's bedroom where pink butterflies were painted on the wall and teddy bears poked out from underneath the blanket flooded his mind. Night after night, he would enter her room, sit on the corner of her bed, and listen to her breathing. He had never meant for it to go that far, but that made it even more of a thrill. He had a secret from his wife.

When Mallory woke up, she started screaming. She had been tied to a bed with the strange man sitting next to her.

"Hush now, sweetie, we're going to play for a bit. Remember now; you promised you were going to be a good girl," Calvin whispered to her as he tied a handkerchief around her mouth. She closed her lips tight and pulled her head away. All he had wanted to do was touch her. Feel her soft skin under his fingers and against his palm. The sweat dripped off his nose and down his cheek. Her voice excited him, so innocent.

"You don't want to make me mad, do you?" he said in a stern voice.

Mallory shook her head and blinked through the tears.

By the time he had finished, she had no fight left. Her body ached and bled. Calvin put on his pants and untied the gag around her face. It was soaked, and her teeth had cut a hole in it.

Mallory was barely breathing as he left her there to die.

The bottle of scotch he had found was near empty, and he was drunk. His eyes started to get heavy. He lit a smoke and leaned back in the recliner, taking a few drags as he closed his eyes. The cigarette burned down to the filter. The couple inches of ash that started building on the end held its place as Calvin passed out in the chair.

Chapter 22

Hunter had landed the plane on the runway at the Yorkville airport. He couldn't wait to call Shelly and see how she was doing. The conversation they had bothered him. He hated hearing her upset and wanted to be with her. He knew that the combination of her dreams and the hormones weren't easy for her to deal with.

He had found a crib online that he had purchased to surprise her. It should be arriving before he got home. He knew this would excite her. It was a little pricey, but he wanted her to have it. It was a 4-in-1 convertible crib and change table ensemble. It had a sleek modern look crafted from natural wood. He was going to paint the nursery on his next days off so Shelly could start decorating the way she wanted.

After the passengers exited the aircraft, Hunter got his things and hurried inside. He caught a cab to his hotel and checked in. First, he wanted to shower and get settled in bed, so he could talk to her before falling asleep. He knew that she would be close to her break time at work.

The phone rang until it went to voice mail.

"Hi Sweetie, I'm just calling to make sure you are feeling ok and to tell you that I love you. Call me back when you get this, ok." Hunter hung up the phone and turned on the TV. The news was on. He pressed the volume button up a few notches.

A six-year-old Hampton girl has been reported missing from her family home. The mother phoned, in saying they had gotten into an argument. She is wearing a long-sleeved purple cotton shirt with a sequin crest that says, 'Daddy's Little Girl,' white leggings and, black strap shoes. Her backpack is orange with a hot air balloon logo on the front pocket. Her tricycle is missing from the home as well, which her mother believes her to be riding. It is red with tassels on the handlebars. If anyone knows the whereabouts of this girl, please contact the Hampton Police Department. If you see anything strange, please don't hesitate to call. The 24-hour emergency line is 1-800-555-2369. Again, 1-800-555-2369. Police are also searching for Calvin Gibbons, a high-risk sex offender who had been transferred to Meadowlands. He escaped from the yard during a medical emergency involving his house mate in the unit. We have reason to believe the two may be together. Be on the lookout for a 6'1 man weighing 160 lbs with brown hair. He was last seen wearing a button-up denim shirt and dark jeans.

Hunter clicked off the TV. He immediately thought of Shelly's dreams and had to talk to her. She had said she was going to the police, and he hadn't spoken to her in awhile. He tried her cell again. No answer. He couldn't help but be alarmed. Hunter called 411 and got the number for the Psychiatric Hospital. Dialing the number, he waited.

"Hello, thank you for calling the O'Hanagan Psychiatric Hospital; this is Lacey speaking. How may I direct your call?"

"Hi, this is Hunter Roberts phoning. I am trying to reach Shelly Swanson. May I please speak with her?"

"Mr. Roberts, Shelly called in sick today. I am filling in for her shift. She went home early last night with the flu. Can I take a message for her?"

"No, that's fine. Thank you." Hunter hung up and tried her cell again. He was beyond worried about her now, and all he could do was sit and wait for her to return his call. As he watched the numbers on the clock roll by, he surfed through the channels looking for something to occupy his mind. He craved a cigarette. He had to have one.

Hunter got dressed and took the elevator down to the Lobby. He had noticed a 24-hour convenience store across the street when he arrived. He stopped at the ATM at the entrance and withdrew some cash.

The damp air outside sent a chill up his spine. He hurried across the road and up to the store. The doors slid open and chimed as he entered. He approached the counter and waited. An old woman was checking her lottery tickets. She appeared to be homeless. Wearing layers of clothing that were tattered and torn. He could smell the body odor wafting off her as she moved her arms. Hunter gazed at her and zoned out, wondering where she got the money to buy the tickets, and thought it was crazy how instead of buying a necessity, she chose to try her luck gambling. The look on her face was so full of hope as the teller scanned the bar codes. He hoped she would win something. No luck. The lady put her head down and walked out of the store. Hunter was still staring at her.

"Excuse me, Sir, do you want to buy something?" The dark-skinned man behind the counter snapped his fingers toward Hunter.

"Oh, yes, I need a pack of Ocean Red," he stammered back, realizing he was still watching the old woman.

"That will be $10.50," the teller said as he handed him the pack of cigarettes. "Would you like matches?"

"Yes, please." Hunter reached in his pocket and pulled out a bill to pay him. Putting the change away, he left the store. Outside, he lit a smoke and inhaled it quickly while walking back to the hotel. He didn't want to go back to the room. All he could think about was Shelly. There was a lounge inside that might still be open. He checked the directory and headed in its direction. The doors were open. He could hear jazz music coming down the hall.

Up to the bar, Hunter scanned the room. The band played in one corner and a few customers sat around tables in front watching. He pulled out a stool and sat down.

"What's your poison," the man behind the counter asked while wiping out a mug from the sink.

"Spiced rum on the rocks, heavy on the ice."

The bartender set the glass on the rubber mat and made the drink. He slid it across the bar towards Hunter. He placed his hands around it and swirled the ice.

Pulling his cell phone from his pocket, he checked the screen. He tried to be positive that everything was fine, telling himself that if Shelly went home sick, maybe she was in bed sleeping. His mind wandered as he drank the rum.

"Well, hello stranger," a female voice cooed in his direction. Hunter turned to the voice.

Her name was Miranda. Her flight attendant number was 9729. She had been flying international airlines for years. She was beautiful, and she knew it. Her long dark hair and big brown eyes could and did make men crumble at the sight of her. She was the envy of every woman. Frequent flyers often booked flights based on her schedule. She was wanted by men all over the world. But Miranda only wanted one man, Hunter Roberts. And here he was, sitting all alone in a bar.

"Hi," Hunter said, looking at her and back at the counter.

Miranda pulled out a stool and sat beside him. "I'll have a martini," she waved at the bartender. "You look like you could use some company."

"I could use a phone call," he muttered under his breath.

"Troubles with the ball and chain?" she asked with eyes raised.

"No, Miranda."

She pouted her lips, chugged back her drink, and motioned for another. "You know Hunter; it can get lonely being on the road all the time. A man like you shouldn't have to go without pleasure." She stroked his arm with her eyes fixated on him.

"I am in love with Shelly, Miranda. And I would never disrespect her or you in that manner. I have a baby on the way, and how dare you try to seduce me. We work together, and nothing more," Hunter lashed at her.

"I don't see a ring on that finger," she snapped back.

Hunter threw a bill on the counter and pushed his chair back.

"Have a good night." His words were angry. He was angry now, mad at Miranda for trying to put him in a position and angry at Shelly for not returning his calls.

Up the elevator, he went back to his room to try to unwind.

Chapter 23

"Coffy, you by?" A voice called over the radio.

Greg picked up the receiver. "This is Coffy. Go ahead."

"We just got a call from Mr. Mulligan. He owns the roadside station in Hampton. The store had been broken into last night. He went to work this morning to find the front window smashed in. There was no money reported missing. He checked the inventory and seemed to be cigarettes and some grocery items unaccounted for. Whoever broke in wasn't after cash; they were looking for supplies. Sounds like Gibbons is written all over it."

"I'm on my way to the property of Charles Gibbons right now. I recommend you send some backup."

Shelly had been driving down the Interstate for forty-five minutes when her cell phone rang. It was vibrating on the seat next to her. Shelly picked it up and hit the talk button.

"Hello, Miss Swanson, this is Greg Coffy. My dad was the officer on duty the night Mr. Gibbons was arrested.

I work for the Willow's Cove Police Department. I am sorry that Officer Brock didn't get back to you sooner. You have to understand how it looks from our end when a person claims to know things because they had a dream. We have been informed that Calvin has escaped from Meadowlands. I read your report concerning your suspicions. It says in the file that you think you know where this farmyard is. This has turned into a very serious matter. It has come to our attention this afternoon, that a young girl has been reported missing in that area. I hate to think the worst, but if he somehow got her in his possession, we may be too late. I am getting in my car now. Can you give me the location, please?"

"It is Range Road 43 and junction 11. I am on my way there now," Shelly informed the officer.

Sgt. Coffy punched the coordinates into his GPS system. "We don't know what he is capable of. Being in prison for that long can do any number of things to a man. It is in your best interest to hang back until I get there."

"A little girl is in danger. You guys have wasted enough time already." Shelly hit the end key and tossed her phone on the seat. She sped up as the conversation she just had infuriated her. She is thankful someone believed her and wanted to investigate further but she was still so angry that she was treated in such an unprofessional manner in the beginning. Maybe if they had taken the directions down, they could have been on their way sooner.

"Miss Swanson," Officer Coffy yelled into the phone. "Shit!" Greg replaced the handset and turned on his sirens.

He knew he had to hurry. The cop car peeled onto the highway and sped towards Hampton.

Shelly could see the farm from the road. Knowing it had to be the one, she slowed down, and pulled into an approach, shutting off the car. She lifted her purse from the floor to the seat and opened the zipper. Her fingers wrapped around the handle of the revolver and removed it. Opening the chamber, she spun it, watching the bullets swing around. Closing it, she pushed the door open and climbed out. As she repeated the numbers in her head, she advanced the wooden sign and read it aloud. With the gun shoved in the back of her pants, she headed down the lane and toward the house. It was getting dark, and she hoped it was enough to keep her hidden. She passed the garden and a small well as she grew closer. She tiptoed along the side until she reached a window. Slowly, she lifted herself until she could see inside.

Calvin was passed out in a chair. A shiver ran down her spine as she snuck around the back. There was a small window that sat an inch off the ground, propped open. Down on her knees, she crawled up and looked in. There she was, lying on the cot in the corner of the room. Her hair was tangled. It lay on the bed and down her back. Shelly scanned the room. The fluorescent bulb that buzzed from the ceiling was just bright enough to light the cellar. Milk crates were piled up in one corner. Empty glass bottles lined the shelves on the wall. There was a rug on the floor that may have been white once. A

TV tray sat beside the cot. A bucket that was missing its handle had been placed underneath. The rope binding her tiny hands, was tied to the leg of the cot that had been bolted to the floor.

She watched her for a minute to see if she was breathing. There was no movement coming from the tiny body. Shelly prayed she was alive. The wind howled behind her. Her adrenaline kicked in as she lowered herself through the window to the floor. It was barely big enough for her to squeeze through. She held onto it as she climbed down to ease it back in place.

The wind was blowing more robust now. The trees swayed back and forth, barely keeping their roots in the ground. Dust blew across the lane and into the field. The rooster could be heard clanging and banging on the barn roof. A strong gust knocked a branch against the house and startled Calvin. He sat forward in the recliner and looked around. He took a minute to realize where he was. It was dark now, and the TV was the only thing lighting up the room. He reached for the scotch and took a swig. It burned his chest as he ingested the last swallow. Leaning back in the chair, he struck a match and puffed on a cigarette. The playboy channel was still on. Calvin watched the girls on the screen and tried for another drink. Empty. He went to the bathroom and pissed in the toilet.

Shelly crept across the floor on her tiptoes. When she reached the cot, she knelt and put her hand on Mallory's arm. The little girl turned her head towards Shelly. With her finger against her lips, she motioned for Mallory to be quiet. She started crying at the sight of her. She had been saved. Shelly hushed her as she untied the knots in the rope that bound her.

"Shhh, it's going to be okay. I'm going to get you out of here. I need you to be a big strong girl okay," Shelly whispered in her ear as she pulled on the rope.

Mallory nodded as the tears streamed down her face. There was a bruise on her cheek, and her wrists were bleeding. Shelly stopped suddenly and wrapped her arms around the girl. The floorboards creaked above them. Calvin was awake. Shelly knew that he would be down any minute, and she had to hurry.

The water ran through the pipes as he flushed the toilet. Shelly looked at the ceiling and back at the knots in the rope. She was trying hard not to panic. If Mallory sensed she was upset, it would upset her even more. The creaking from above continued. It was going straight for the top of the stairs. A couple more pulls of the rope, and Mallory would be free. Shelly hushed her as the footsteps came down the stairs.

The door flew open, and there he was, standing in the doorway. Swaying back and forth like a drunken sailor on a rocky ship. Shelly jumped to her feet and pulled the gun from her pants. She stood beside the bed and pointed it at him. At the man she had married. The man who had killed their daughter all those years ago and was about to take the life of another innocent child.

Calvin focused his eyes and stood straight. "Kathy?? Is that you??"

The tears started to fall as she stared at him. "Yes, Calvin, it's me. I never wanted to see your face or hear about you again. You took my baby away from me. They should have locked you up and thrown away the key. You should've lost your life like she did, like I did. I should've killed you myself that night." She was shaking and screaming at him with the gun in the air.

"I thought you were dead. I thought you loved me, Kathy. You made me touch her. You were never around. I know you were out cheating on me with every fuck in town. You phoned the cops like the stupid bitch you were."

Calvin lunged at Kathy, knocking the gun from her hands. He hit her in the face, and down she went. He was on top of her, with his hands around her neck, choking her as she gasped for air.

"Kathy, you fucking whore, I'm going to kill you. I'm going to rape you like I did the night of prom, and then I'm going to strangle you until you lay lifeless like Jessica." He was spitting on her, one hand holding down her neck, the other working the buttons on the crotch of her pants. Kathy struggled for air beneath him, squirming on the floor. He lay on top of her and pulled down his pants.

Chapter 24

The GPS directed Greg to the farm. He saw a car parked off the road and knew it must be Shelly's. He saw the wooden sign and compared the numbers. Yep, this was it all right. He turned down the lane and parked in front of the house. It was dark inside. The sound of the wind whistling was all he could hear. He stepped out of the car and unbuckled his holster. Greg fingered his gun and prepared himself to enter the house. He prayed that Shelly and the little girl she had dreamt about were okay. Using his free hand, he pushed the door open and looked inside. Greg could hear sounds coming from the TV. The front door creaked behind him as he stepped in. Gun in the air, he poked it around the corner and looked around the room. It was empty.

BAM!!! A gunshot had been fired. It came from the basement. Greg followed the sound and ran down the stairs with his gun aimed and ready. He reached the bottom and entered the room.

There she was, standing four feet tall. Arms raised, with a gun in her hands. She was shaking. Greg's eyes darted to the floor. Calvin lay lifeless on top of Kathy.

She was crying hysterically and gulping for the air to fill her lungs. Officer Coffy lowered his revolver and ran to the little girl. He pulled the steel weapon from her tiny fingers and placed it on the floor. Over to Kathy, he pushed Calvin off her. Mallory had shot him in the side of the head. Blood poured out of the wound and formed a puddle on the floor. Putting his arms around Kathy, Greg lifted her onto the cot.

"Shelly, it's Greg Coffy here. Calvin is dead. Can you hear me? Are you ok?"

She put her arms around him and cried. She cried for Jessica, for the man she once loved, for Mallory, for her unborn baby, and for herself. The painful memory of the night that changed her life was happening all over again, the same pain in her heart that she had tried to forget about all those years. She had never wanted to hurt Nancy by disappearing. She felt she had no choice. She tried to jump from the bridge that night, but she couldn't bring herself to do it. She knew that Jessica wouldn't want her to die that way. She was scared that if she took her own life, she would end up in limbo, never seeing Jessica again. Too scared to face her own guilt, she ran from it. She ran from the life she knew, and she never looked back. She buried Kathy and Jessica Gibbons deep down inside and moved on with her life, with her new life as Shelly Swanson.

Hearing Calvin call her Kathy, woke something up inside. The girl she once was, a girl so full of despair and denial. As she stared at the man she had given her life to lay in a pool of blood with his pants down, she knew it was over. His life had now been taken by a victim of his own dangerous and unholy addiction. The man that so violently murdered her daughter was dead, and the emptiness she had felt as Kathy wanted to be whole again.

Mallory walked to the cot and put her arms around Kathy. She climbed into her lap and wept against her chest. The two held each other and rocked slowly. Officer Coffy stood up and grabbed his radio.

"This is Coffy. I am at the Gibbons property. Calvin Gibbons is dead. Shelly Swanson and Mallory Reynolds are alive. We will need an ambulance to transport them to the hospital. Please phone the girl's mother and let her know she will be on her way there."

The three of them waited in the basement until the ambulances arrived. Two stretchers were brought down. Kathy and Mallory lay on one as the paramedics carried them out of the house and into the back. Lights and sirens on, it sped out of the yard and to the Hospital Emergency where medical staff was awaiting their arrival.

They placed Calvin's body on the other and covered him with a sheet. Officer Brock walked down the stairs and stepped aside as they passed him.

"Looks like we owe a lot to that woman for saving that little girl's life," he said to Coffy.

"Looks like you owe her an apology, Brock." Greg sneered as he went upstairs and exited the house. He turned his lights on and headed to the hospital.

Chapter 25

She was lying on the bed gazing out the window. The sun shone through, reflecting itself off the walls and lit up the room. She could taste the sweet salt from her tears as she licked her lips. The events that had unfolded left Kathy paralyzed. Seeing Calvin again, the man who had taken her life from her, was overwhelming. She thought of Mallory.

"Mallory!!" Kathy cried out.

She sat up and wrapped her arms around her knees. Kathy could hear footsteps coming down the hall. They were getting louder and closer. They stopped. Kathy lifted her head and looked at the man she loved holding a bouquet of flowers in the doorway.

"Hi baby, how are you doing? It's so good to see you. I never want to lose you again," Hunter started to cry as he placed the flowers on the night table and crawled onto the twin-size stretcher beside her.

"They said that the baby is doing fine. They will keep you in for a few days to monitor you. You saved a girl's life. You are a hero. I love you so much."

Kathy cuddled up to him as tears streamed down her face. Hunter got off the bed and knelt. He pulled out a little velvet box and opened it.

"Shelly... Or Kathy ... Whoever you want to be called... will you do me the honor of being my wife? Will you let me love you for the rest of my life? Please say yes."

Hunter stared into her eyes and waited anxiously for her reply.

She removed the ring from the box and slid it on her finger. "Yes, I will marry you. I love you. I will always love you."

Hunter stroked her hair and smiled. He stood up and hugged his fiancé.

Kathy leaned back and fixed her eyes on his.

"I would like to be Kathy again. I have lived a lie for so long that it's time to be me. My name is Kathleen Rae Crane. I had a daughter, Jessica Dawn. I am so sorry I hid all this from you and everyone else in my life. I was a coward. I ran. I'm ready to face it all now. Let go and move on with my life, with you. I have never loved a man the way I love you, Hunter."

"Kathleen Rae," he whispered in her ear. "I like the sound of that," he said while placing his hand on her belly.

Chapter 26

Kathy wrapped her fingers around the handle of the drawer on the old oak desk and pulled it open. She played through her mind all the things she wanted to say; all the things she had wanted to say for a very long time. She never wanted to hurt Nancy when she disappeared. The phone call she was about to make had been one she never imagined she would get to do. She was excited and scared to hear her sister's voice on the other end. It felt like going home after coming from a war; a war where pain, suffering, and deceit had plagued her. She found the phone book and flipped through the pages.

Steven Spencer 555-387-4773. Kathy stared at the number and forced back the tears. She prayed someone would answer.

Receiver in hand, she dialed. With each press of the numbered button, Kathy's heart beat a little faster. The line was connected. The long monotone ringing in her ear stopped and started. Her finger twirled itself around the cord, getting tighter with every ring. She let it ring six times. No answer. Kathy placed the receiver back onto the telephone base. She sat there for a minute, slightly relieved that no one answered. 'Was a phone call the way she wanted to reunite with her sister after twenty years?' Kathy thought to herself.

She stood up and made her way into the bedroom. Kathy rummaged through the closet and pulled out a small backpack. She placed a change of clothes in the bottom and tossed it onto the bed. Into the bathroom, she filled her travel makeup bag with cosmetics and her toothbrush. She had to see Nancy in person. It was time to put all the pieces of her life back together again. With her bag packed, Kathy walked down the hall to the kitchen. She grabbed an apple from the fruit bowl that sat in the middle of the table. Along with a bottle of water from the fridge, the items went into her purse.

Kathy picked up the handset again and dialed Hunter. She knew that he would be in flight but wanted to leave him a message in case he landed and tried her at home. It went straight to his voicemail, "Hi, you've reached Hunter Roberts. I am in the air or away from the phone, so please leave your name and number, so I can return your call as soon as I am able."

Kathy waited for the beep.

"Hi honey, I tried to call Nancy, but there was no answer. I have decided that I need to confront her in person. I am going to head out right away. I love you. I will call you later this evening."

She hung up the phone and fingered the items in her purse, making sure she had her keys. She pulled her wallet out and unzipped the side pocket. Sliding her fingers in, she felt the laminating of the photo. Kathy stared down at the picture she had stashed away for so many years. Nancy was sitting on a rock beside the lake. She was eleven then. Their father had taken them camping to teach them how to fish. Kathy had always loved that picture, Nancy with a smile a mile wide and the sun reflecting off the water in the background. She returned it to its place in the pocket and zipped it close. Kathy slung the backpack over her shoulder and locked the front door as she stepped outside.

One quick stop at the Speedy gas station to fill up, and she was on the road. Kathy tuned the radio into an oldies station, "*Tonight you're mine completely. You give your love so sweetly. Tonight, the light of love is in your eyes. But will you love me tomorrow?*"

The sound of the girl band played through the speakers and all around the car. Kathy cranked the volume and started to sing. The music took her back to when she was a little girl, a little girl with Nancy, dancing around the kitchen while their mother made shortbread cookies and shooed them into the living room. The closeness they shared made them almost one with each other, sisters, best friends, family. She remembered the smiles and giggles as they held hands and twirled around the coffee table and onto the couch. She wondered, 'Would Nancy still love her? Would she forgive her?' She knew that it was silly to think this way. She cracked the window a bit. The sound of the tires on the pavement and the wind against the car relaxed her.

Kathy sat in her car and stared at the house. She envisioned the address from the phone book and knew this was this place. The path leading from the sidewalk up to the house had been lined with flowers. Pinks and blues surrounded by yellow and white petals. The grass had been recently mowed as she could still see the lines from the lawnmower left from the up and down passes. A birdhouse hung from a thick branch on the farthest tree in the yard. The driveway housed a black Envoy. She read the licence plate, HRG 753. The numbers and letters played over in her mind. Her palms were clammy. She shook her hands in the air and took a deep breath. Kathy placed her keys in her purse and clutched the leather strap. With the driver door open, she stepped onto the street. Each step closer to the house seemed to take a lifetime, as if time had stood still, waiting for her to be in this exact place at that exact time.

"*If I leave here tomorrow, would you still remember me?*"

A red convertible sped past blaring music from the stereo. Kathy jumped a little and glanced at the birdhouse in the tree. It was true. Birds really are free. Free to fly wherever their instinct took them. The ones that were lucky enough to find a home always knew where it was and how to get back there. Kathy knew that Nancy was her home. And here she was, back to her true nest.

She climbed the wooden steps up to the front porch. The warm breeze made its way through her hair and made the hair on the back of her neck stand straight up. The creaking of the two-seater swing at the far end paralyzed her. The constant repetition of the metal rubbing against itself as the wind moved it back and forth soothed her. She remembered when she was a little girl and shared a room with Nancy at her father's house. Her grandmother had given her a soundbox. There were three different buttons. One was a rainforest that had random birds chirping at a high-pitched tone. The second was a heartbeat, which

Kathy enjoyed, but it beat too fast for her to fall asleep. The third was the sound of the ocean waves crashing against the shore. The steady shoo sound cleared her mind and gave her something else to focus on besides her thoughts. Nancy hated it. It had the opposite effect on her, so Kathy stopped using it.

She took a step closer to the front door and lifted her finger to the bell. She paused a moment before pressing it. She held her breath and pushed it in.

DINNNG! DONNNG! The long rhythms made way to the sound of footsteps coming closer.

Nancy opened the door and stared at the woman in front of her. The eyes that stared back at her pierced her soul. She breathed in deep and reached out her hand. Her fingers ran along the cheek of her sister, who she yearned for all these years. She couldn't believe what she was seeing. She pulled her hand away and paused.

"Kathy!!" she cried out.

Nancy pulled her hand back a bit farther and thrust it forward. Her palm made contact as she slapped Kathy across the face.

Kathy let out a cry as she cupped her cheek in her hand. "I'm so sorry, Nancy."

She grabbed her sister and pulled her close. She wrapped her arms around her and squeezed. They were both crying in desperation, Nancy desperate for answers, Kathy for forgiveness.

The two women stood there for seven minutes. No words, just embracing each other as if scared to let go.

"Nancy, who is it?" Steve approached them. His jaw dropped, and his eyes grew big.

"Kathy, is that really you?" He put his arms around them both and started to laugh. He was crying now with them, as the joy he felt overwhelmed him. Kathy had been like a sister to him, and seeing her now made a piece of his heart feel whole again.

"Come in, come in. Are you hungry or thirsty? Let me make a pot of tea."

Steve ran into the kitchen and grabbed the kettle. His heart was beating fast. The girls joined him and sat at the table.

"Oh my god, Kathy!! A part of me always knew that you were alive. I could feel you sometimes. It is an absolute blessing to see you." Nancy squeezed her sister's hand on the table.

"I'm speechless. I honestly don't know what to say other than I'm sorry. I have played it over for so many years but seeing you now makes all of it seem ridiculous. I can't imagine the pain I have caused you. I left you alone to deal with the tragedies of my life. I'm sorry, Nancy. I pray that you can forgive me and give me a chance to make it up to you."

"Forgive you? Of course I forgive you, Kathy. I am just happy that you are alive and have returned to me. I heard on TV that Calvin was released from prison and transferred to a facility. It made me sick, and I cried for you all over again, you and Jessica."

"Calvin is dead." Kathy looked at the floor and gagged.

"Dead? How do you know?" Nancy eyed her sister.

"He escaped from the Meadowlands facility. I had dreams about a little girl. At first, I thought she was

Jessica. A part of me also thought maybe it was the child I am carrying now."

"You're pregnant!" Nancy's eyes lit up.

"Yes, I am," she smiled at her and Steve. "But then I dreamt one night of Calvin's grandpa's property. I read in the paper right before this that he had been moved. I knew in my gut that there was a little girl in trouble and that she was in his possession. I went straight to the police for help. I was mocked and demeaned by an officer there, so I took matters into my own hands. I bought a gun for protection, and I went to the old farm. I was right, Nancy. Everything I had been dreaming about led me to a little girl that he had tied in the basement. Her name is Mallory. She is six years old, and she saved my life. We saved each other. I had just got her untied when Calvin came down the stairs and attacked me. She pulled the trigger. She ended the life of a man who was going to end hers. The police showed up shortly after. It's all over now, Nancy. When he called me Kathy, it took me back to my real life. The one I had eliminated so that I could keep on living. I changed my name to Shelly Swanson, and I buried my past. I know it was the wrong thing to do. It all happened so fast. I had to live with the choices I made. Now all I want is to have you and Steve and Brian back in my life. I am engaged to the most amazing man, and we are very excited to have this baby. He is going to be so excited to meet you, Nancy."

"None of it matters now. It is what it is, and we are very excited to have you back as well," Nancy said while glancing at Steve.

No one could help but to hug again.

"Can I use the washroom?" Kathy asked.

"Yes, honey, it's just down the hall to the right."

Kathy's legs felt like Jell-O. She slowly exited the kitchen and down the hall. She pushed open the wooden bathroom door and stepped in. It smelled like coconut oil. The pink on the walls exploded around the room. A small black vanity sat against one wall, the marble top showcasing a bowl of rings and hairpins. The mirror on top was tilted. Kathy looked at her reflection. She could see Nancy in her face, the same round eyes and eyelashes that stretched a mile. The tears that filled them streamed down her cheeks. She could still feel her sister's arms around her. Kathy blinked and looked down. The tiny drawer on the front that held a woman's secrets was open. Pill bottles lined the bottom. Plastic containers robed in prescriptions. The white tops played off the blue bottles. Kathy sighed and tilted her head. She felt guilty for snooping, but she had to see what they contained. She had a fairly good idea knowing it was a mood stabilizer of some sort.

She reached her hand inside the drawer and gently eased it open. Her fingers ran across them and pulled one out. It was Amitriptyline. It was an anti-depressant used to treat insomnia. Kathy saw the tiny round pills and knew before she read the label. She felt sad for Nancy that she needed to take these meds. It was her fault. Disappearing and abandoning her to grieve her loss and her niece. Kathy breathed in deep and tried to fight the knots tightening up in her stomach. She would have to learn to forgive herself for the choices she made. It was their chance to gain back all the lost years.

She replaced the bottle and used the toilet. Kathy washed her hands and looked in the mirror. She wiped the smudged mascara off her cheek and returned to the kitchen.

"Kathy, would you like to visit Jessica's grave in the cemetery?"

Nancy stood up from the table and grabbed her sister's hand.

"Yes, I would like that very much," she replied as the tears filled her eyes.

"Steve, can you start the car, please?"

"Yes, of course," he said while turning quickly to the front door.

The two girls hugged again and made their way outside.

Parking the car along the side of the road facing the front gates, Kathy and Nancy undid their seatbelts.

"I'll wait here, honey. You two go ahead," he said, smiling at his wife.

They climbed out of the car, and Nancy wrapped her arm around Kathy. She led her to the resting place of her daughter and their mother. Nancy could see the tree's branches she had planted for Kathy, swaying in the breeze. The necklace with the charms she had placed there so many years ago still hung around the bark.

Kathy fell to her knees beside the plot. She cried hard and loud. The pain was almost unbearable. Swaying back and forth, she ran her fingers through the grass. Nancy knelt beside her and ran her hand along Kathy's back.

"I'm so sorry. I'm so sorry." Kathy cried and repeated it over and over.

"Shhhhh. It's ok, honey. Just let it out."

They sat in each other's arms and let their emotions run.

"I had the tree planted in memory of you, Kathy. I wanted you to be with Jessica and mom. I wanted it as a place to visit you as well."

Kathy smiled at her sister. "Thank you, Nancy, thank you for everything. I love you."

Chapter 27

The stories were out. News reports about Kathy being alive and the events that had taken place twenty years prior were on every TV station and newspaper across the country. Every news reporter and talk show host wanted her on air. Officer Brock made a public apology and asked for Kathy's assistance in other missing children's cases. Mallory's family sued the Meadowlands Facility for breaching security measures during Bill's heart attack.

Kathy and Nancy started a petition that went viral around the country. People from all over joined them to protest.

"We can't protect all the children in the world all the time, but we can try to eliminate future abuse with stricter laws and suitable sentencing. A man with a sick sexual desire does not outgrow it. He should do the time that fits the crime. Good behavior laws allow and enable these diseased minds to do it again. These acts of violence affect the victims for the rest of their lives. The people should have a say. How does this type of thing happen? These types of communities need to be reassessed."

Kathy didn't try to fight her dreams anymore. She had spent so much time trying to block them out that once she started accepting them for what they were, she realized they weren't all that bad. She set aside a journal and kept in touch with the Police Departments Special Victims Unit.

Kathy had taken some time off from O'Hanagan's and was ready to return to work. She had been thinking about Nina a lot and wanted to see her again. She had a few dreams while away and needed to check in on her.

Her first night back, she went straight to her room.

"Nina, honey, if you are having dreams or feelings of any kind, I encourage you to talk to me about it. I'm going to let you in on a little secret. I have lived with dreams of my own, and it wasn't until recently that I started accepting them. I kept track of the things I saw, and soon realized that they were more than just dreams. They were guidance. I followed the information that was given to me, and I pursued it. I even went to the police for help. Regardless of their lack of involvement, I carried forward to investigate on my own. The result concluded in me saving a small girl's life from a very troubled and mentally diseased man. The same man who destroyed my life years ago. I felt that I needed to run away from that life and start fresh. My real name is Kathy, and you can call me that if you like. I understand that it may be a change for you, so if you want to call me Shelly, I will understand."

Nina stared at her with eyes that moved back and forth like an old typewriter jotting down the information.

"I believe we have gifts in life, some more spiritual than others. I believe that you may have this gift as well, Nina. You don't have to be scared or feel alone. I am here for you. I will let you think about what I have said, and you let me know when you are ready to confide in me."

The next day, Nina was very anxious to see Kathy. Her drawings were ready, stacked neatly in the top drawer of her nightstand. When Kathy entered the room, she pulled them out and placed them on the bed. Kathy sat next to her and slowly fingered through. There was a little girl in everyone. The main theme of most seemed to be the beach. There was lots of sand and toys around.

"Did you dream of taking your little girl to the beach, Nina?"

She shook her head. "It's not a beach."

Flashes of the dream Kathy had prior of the same thing, flooded her memory. She stared at it hard and wondered what it meant.

"Is that you as a child?"

"No."

"Is she someone you know?"

"I never knew her then. That's how I see her now," Nina said softly, while chewing on her fingernail.

"Nina, sweetie, I have read your reports. I know that you lost your newborn at a very young age. That must have been very difficult to deal with."

"Yes," she replied with tears in her eyes.

"Nina, the file is very inconclusive. What happened to her? There was no funeral?"

Nina crawled under the sheets and cried louder. She sniffed and whimpered into her pillow.

"I think that's enough for today. I will bring your meds and let you rest for the night. I am on night shift tonight, so if you wake up and feel the need to talk or feel scared, no matter what it is, you just ring your buzzer, and I will be here ok, honey. To make progress with the healing, we need to accept the challenges we are faced with to move on. I know you are a strong girl, and I have faith in you. It may take some time, but we will get through this."

Nina didn't move. Kathy went to the front counter for her prescription and brought it back with a glass of water.

"Take this honey, and you will sleep soundly. Remember what I said. I'm just down the hall. Good night."

With that, she swept the bangs across the young girl's forehead and backed out of the room.

Kathy did her rounds with the other patients and resided to the chair at the front desk. Fingering the mouse, she clicked open the archives folder and began her search. She needed to know more about Nina's past. She vaguely remembered her being admitted and at the time, didn't think too much about it. Cecil Brimley was the head nurse who had spent more time with Nina than anyone in the Ward. A heart attack took her life, and Kathy knew this had also affected Nina.

Scrolling through the years of prescriptions, counselling sessions, and treatments, she found what she was looking for. Kathy read the report in its entirety. Her previous address was listed as well as her guardian, Lorraine Mayfield. According to the report, Lorraine had come home one night and found Nina in the rocking chair with her arms cradled in her lap as if holding an infant. There was no child in her arms. She was just singing and rocking herself. They had searched the entire house with no sign of the baby. She said in her statement that she was just trying to make her stop crying. That she had tried everything, and it kept getting louder. The voices told her that it was the only way. The remains had never been located, but Nina mentioned that she had suffocated the child with a shower cap. She was still a minor and couldn't be tried as an adult. When evaluated by the medical board, she was placed in O'Hanagan.

The father, Brett Mazuno had been charged as a registered sexual offender and placed in the Meadowlands Facility before the child was born.

"Oh, my god," Kathy gasped as she read the words on the screen.

Kathy had to know more. Where was the baby? Where was Lorraine? Who was Brett to Nina? Was she raped? Kathy needed answers. None of it felt right. She jotted down the address of the residence and slid the folded-up piece of paper into her pocket.

Kathy got up the next day and made coffee. She pulled out the map and found directions to the previous residence of Nina. She prayed that Lorraine was still there and could give her more background on the events that had taken place. She put together a lunch and drove to the corner gas station.

With the tank full and the feeling of an adventure waiting, she headed for her destination. It was a beautiful day, and it felt good to just drive. Kathy cranked the tunes and put the windows down. She double-checked the map and hung a right at the lights. The car slowly crept down the street. She eyed the numbers on the homes, searching for the one she prayed would lead her to answers. There it was, peering above the others on the street. Her heart sunk as she focused on the Realtor sign swaying on the front lawn. She put the car in park and jumped out. Running across the street with her eyes fixed on the board dangling on its chains, she couldn't believe what she was seeing. It was Nancy's Realtor Sign. The disappointment of the vacancy diminished and was replaced with hope. Kathy giggled to herself as she fumbled through her purse for her cell phone. She scrolled the N's, found Nancy, and waited impatiently for her sister to pick up.

"Nancy, Nancy, I have to see you."

"Kathy, what's wrong?"

"Everything is good. I am standing in front of a property of yours, and I need to talk to you."

"Ok, I am meeting a client this afternoon. We could get together this evening. Where are you?"

"I am on McIntyre Road. I must work tonight, but I am sure I could find one of the girls to switch shifts. This is very important. I will see what I can arrange and let you know. Thanks, Nancy, I love you."

"I love you, to.'

She closed her phone and dialed the hospital.

"Hi, Margaret, it's Kathy calling. I won't be able to make it in this evening. Something has come up, and it can't wait. I don't have the schedule with me, so I am wondering if you could contact one of the girls and see if they will switch me a shift. I will take whatever you can find."

"Sure, Kathy, I'm sure that won't be a problem. Is everything ok?"

"Yes, everything is just fine. I have a matter to attend to that simply cannot wait. Thank you so much, Margaret. I may have my phone off, so go ahead and leave me a message as soon as you are able."

Kathy walked onto the porch and peered through the windows. Around the side of the house, she unlatched the gate and stepped into the backyard. There it was. As if calling to her, the sandbox from the dream glowing against the lawn. Her stomach turned, and her heart began to race. This has to be the sandbox Nina spent so much time drawing. Her thoughts swirled around, trying to piece it all together. The baby had never been found. Kathy didn't want to believe it, but she already knew. She almost felt relieved. It couldn't be, but it had to. She wanted to start digging. She spun around in the yard, looking for something.

"No, I have to wait. I have to talk to Nancy."

Kathy stared out the window of the Diner, impatiently waiting to see Nancy's headlights pull in. The half-empty cup of coffee in front of her was already cold.

"Would you like more?" the waitress asked, breaking her from her gaze as the young girl stood beside the table swishing the black liquid inside the glass pot.

"Yes, yes, please," she replied while holding the ceramic mug in the air.

She cracked open a creamer. Letting it drip out, changing the color in the cup. Clicking the spoon against the walls, she stared at it. Her thoughts brought her back to the last cup of coffee she had served to the old man, his hands so worn from time, lines that could only be understood through his eyes. The same anxiety she had felt that night returned.

Nancy sat across the booth from her sister.

"Hi Kathy," she smiled at her.

"Oh, Nancy, thank you so much for coming."

"Kathy, what's wrong? Are you ok? Is the baby ok?"

"The baby is fine. I need to ask you some questions about the house that was owned by Lorraine Mayfield. A girl on my ward used to live there. I am just trying to find some answers."

Nancy slid the mug across the table as the waitress returned. She let her fill it, watching the steam rise. The coffee was hot. She needed it to warm her insides as she began to explain.

She told Kathy how she had been trying to sell the property since it went on the market. The house had been in the Mayfield family since being built in 1901. A few years prior, Lorraine abandoned it and all its possessions.

The Town put it up for auction. Nancy had put in a bid and won. She was thrilled that she had an opportunity to make some extra money back on the property.

There didn't seem to be much interest in anyone to purchase the home, so she had allowed a family to move in on a rent to own basis. They cancelled the contract after the first month of residing there. They claimed that the house was haunted. The two young children refused to play in the backyard and stopped sleeping in their bedroom after the first week. The couple were feeling the tension which resulted in a lack of sleep for all members. The youngest girl began having vivid nightmares and insisted that she live with her aunt and uncle.

The homeowners packed their belongings and fled the house. Once word of this got around, the place stayed vacant with no potential buyers interested.

Kathy was in shock. Telling Nancy her story of Nina and the baby suddenly felt easy. She had been scared to tell her, for Nancy to think she was crazy and delusional. She knew that the tiny soul had to be set free.

"Nancy, I know why the house has its energies. There is a young girl at the psychiatric hospital. She is Lorraine Mayfield's granddaughter. She was admitted after losing her baby. She is schizophrenic, and the body was never recovered. When I stopped at the house today, I went into the backyard. There is a sandbox on the lawn, and I am more than certain that she buried her there. I'm sure if you told Steve, he'd want to admit me to my place of employment, but I truly believe there's a lost spirit on that property. I am going to release it one way or another. I just have two questions; do you believe me, and are you with me?"

The tears that welled up in Nancy's eyes streamed down her cheek. Her nose was red, and Kathy could feel that she was speechless, wanting to say something but couldn't as the reality of the situation unfolded itself. The thought of the child's life taken so ruthlessly and inhumane made her think of Jessica.

"You're so strong, Kathy. You had your child stolen from you, punished in such a way by a man who should have been protecting her. You risked your life to save one that wasn't even yours, and now you can free one that isn't even here."

"I am far from strong, Nancy. That's why I ran. I was weak. Too weak to carry on and face the consequences that resulted from the choices I made. I hate myself every day for not following my instincts. I should have never gone to work that night. I should never have stayed. You, Nancy, you're the strongest one. You did what I couldn't. I will never forgive myself fully for abandoning you. But we have a chance to go at this one together."

"Then together we will be."

Kathy searched through her phone for Greg Coffy's number. She knew that he would consider the possibility of the situation and assist her.

"Hello, Officer Coffy here."

"Hi, Greg, it's Kathy Crane calling. I may have located the remains of a child that has been missing for a few years. Would it be possible for you to meet me at the location?"

"For sure, Kathy. Let me grab a pen so I can write the address down."

She gave him the information and hung up.

"He is going to meet us there within the hour," she explained to Nancy. "Let's head over there and wait."

They paid the bill and left the diner. Nancy pulled her car behind Kathy's and followed her to the house.

The patrol cars showed up, and officers began to tape off the property. Yellow caution bands separated the house from the others on the block.

A member of the Excavation Crew, Mr. Flynn, pulled up shortly after. The rumble of the engine on the old three-quarter ton echoed down the street. The driver climbed out and slammed the door. Lowering the tailgate, he slid the shovel across the box.

Officers on the scene had already begun to prepare to remove the wooden boards encasing the plot of land that Kathy knew was an unmarked grave. The moon lit up the sky casting light upon the yard below.

Mr. Flynn dragged the steel shovel across the sidewalk, scraping the cement before slinging it over his shoulder. He hitched up his pants and strolled into the backyard.

"Mr. Flynn, thank you for coming." Officer Coffy greeted him, holding out his hand.

"Not a problem. Ain't nothing on the tube tonight anyhow. A man's gotta have some kind of excitement in his life from time to time. What is it that we are looking for? Treasure I hope," he snickered, showcasing the gold caps crowned upon his teeth.

"We have reason to believe that there may be a child buried in the sandbox."

"Jesus. That sure gives me the willies. I have unearthed many things in my time but never any remains."

Mr. Flynn stepped toward the sandbox and lowered his shovel. Very careful removal of the topsoil was required. Inch by inch, he worked slowly at the dirt.

The sand had been dug away, and the boards that lay on the ground were ready to be removed. Using a pry bar, Mr. Flynn wedged the end of the metal rod under one and leaned back, pulling it away from the others. It cracked as the earth below let go. Tossing it aside, he continued to remove the rest. A layer of soil was spread under the wooden planks. Grabbing a spade, Mr. Flynn carefully tilled back the dirt. The tip of it caught something. Down on his hands and knees, he scraped the wet soil aside. The plastic bag could be seen now. Gently pulling it from the ground, it held the decomposed body of a child, a baby.

Officer Coffy reached for the bag which had just been unearthed. He pulled it close and cradled it in his arms as he slowly opened the bag. There was a shower cap wrapped around its tiny head. Coffy sighed hard. He stared at the remains for a moment.

Kathy slowly made her way to him. Tears in her eyes, she tried to focus on the contents of the bag. She reached her hand toward it and pulled back a flap of the opening.

Something sparkled and caught her eye. There was a gold band around the tiny fingers. Kathy slid the ring off and cupped it in her hand. Gazing down at it, she started to cry.

"May I take this? I know who it belongs to."

Coffy's eyes met hers as he nodded. Covering the face of the small child, he turned away from her and left the yard.

Putting her arm around her sister, Nancy escorted her through the gate and out to the street.

"Do you want to stay with me tonight?" Nancy asked her, hoping she would say yes.

Kathy didn't want to go home alone. She nodded to her sister and headed toward her car. Opening the driver's door, she turned back to her, "I will meet you there."

Chapter 28

Morning came, and Kathy was ready to face the day. She had spent half the night tossing and turning in bed, replaying the events of the evening. She was exhausted but ready for more answers. After joining Nancy and Steve for breakfast, she drove to the police station to meet with Greg.

After recording the incident, they discussed the next steps. Kathy acquired the location of Lorraine and was anxious to track her down. She left the station and followed the directions on the map.

She could see a lane of trees leading to a small yard up the road on the right.

"That must be the place," she said as she turned down the volume on the radio.

Slowing down, she noticed NO TRESPASSING signs posted down the lane. With her wits about her, she turned onto the tiny path and crept into the yard. Smoke billowed out of the chimney perched on the roof. Kathy could almost hear the wood crackling in the stove, producing the heat which warmed the house. Clouds had rolled in, covering the sky with a gloomy haze. It was humid.

And although it had not yet begun to rain, you could see the moisture forming on the leaves. The dampness turned the logs on the cabin a shade darker giving it an eerie appearance. The silence of the country made Kathy uneasy. She was an uninvited visitor and had no idea how her unexpected visit would make Lorraine respond.

She turned the ignition off and waited. Her hands were clammy, and her mouth was dry. She licked her lips that felt cracked and chapped, swallowing hard. The curtain behind the window on the south side of the cottage shifted. Kathy was scared, but she knew that she had to be strong. She opened the car door and stepped onto the gravel road.

As she approached the front porch, the wooden door creaked open.

"Go away from here. Can't you read? No one is allowed on my property. You're a brave woman venturing in. I have a gun, and I know how to use it. I don't take kindly to strangers. Whatever it is you're selling, I don't want it. If you're looking for something, you can't have it."

"Lorraine Mayfield, my name is Kathy Crane. I'm not interested in buying or selling. I'm here regarding your granddaughter, Nina. I work at the O'Hanagan Psychiatric Hospital."

"I don't have a granddaughter. You've made a mistake. Leave me alone."

The door slammed shut, rattling the tiny bells nailed to the front.

Kathy yelled to the old woman inside, "Ms. Mayfield, please. I know what happened to your great-grandchild. With the assistance of the Police Dept, we have uncovered the remains of the newborn. Nina had buried her in the sandbox in the backyard of your home. I really must speak with you."

Lorraine slowly opened the door once again. Kathy stood on the steps and waited. She couldn't see her, but she could hear her begin to sob.

"I don't know the circumstances regarding any of this, but I truly believe that if I can find out, it will help assist me in counselling Nina. She is an extremely troubled girl. She has no one in her life. All I want is a few minutes of your time. Don't you care about her at all?"

"How dare you ask me that? I love her. I removed myself from her life. It was a hard decision I made, but I felt it was the right one."

Kathy could hear her crying now, "Please, Lorraine, will you let me come in and sit down? I can see you are upset, and that was not my intention. I just really need answers. I don't know where else to go. Nina needs me, and I can't help her if you don't help me. I can pay you for your time if you let me."

"I don't want your money. I will allow you to come in, but only because I trust you are here to benefit Nina."

"It's all I care about, Lorraine. Do you mind if I call you that?"

"No, Lorraine is fine."

Kathy stepped up the worn-out boards leading to the cottage as Lorraine held back the door for her to enter. She could smell the faint scent of moth balls over the fire. Lorraine motioned for her to follow. She pointed at the green corduroy sofa.

"Have a seat."

Kathy unzipped her jacket and sat on the couch. She looked around the room while Lorraine threw a couple more logs on the fire. She could hear the raindrops begin to pelt on the asphalt roof. Her feelings of uncertainty were replaced with comfort. Lorraine was going to cooperate. Kathy couldn't wait to hear their story.

"So, you work at O'Hanagan, eh?"

"Yes, I have been there for many years. Nina is a patient on my ward. Her file is very inconclusive. She doesn't say much to anyone. I have gotten her to open up to me a little bit. That is how I came to discover the child. She likes to draw, and the pictures contained many of the same images. I have dreams Lorraine that have enabled me to save a girl's life. I now work with the police when I receive any leads through my dreams."

Lorraine eyed her up and down. Kathy could feel that she thought she was crazy.

"Yes, Lorraine, I know what you must be thinking. It has been a long hard road for me, but I have been given a gift and, I can't deny it any longer. I had a dream one night about a girl in a sandbox, and when I saw Nina's drawings, something clicked. When I tried to research her admittance, the report was very vague. I went to your previous property looking for you. I didn't find you, but I did find the sandbox. My sister owns the house now. We brought in a crew and dug up the sand. The remains were found with a shower cap over the face. I am very sorry for your loss, Ms. Mayfield. I can imagine the pain you had to go through when it happened. Most times, the hardest part for people to deal with, is the not knowing. Blame and regret takes hold. Believe me, Lorraine, I have been in a similar situation. It's difficult to understand what drives a person to take the life of their own child."

"Nina was a very sick girl, mentally ill. I blame myself for leaving her alone. I blame myself for being the one who made her that way. I know he loved her."

Lorraine broke down in tears. She pushed at Kathy, turning her head as she stood up to comfort her.

"Please don't touch me. I don't deserve to be felt sorry for. This is all my fault."

She put her head in her hands and bawled. Kathy sat back on the couch and leaned forward toward her.

"What was your fault, Lorraine? What happened? You said he loved her. Why is he at Meadowlands?"

Lorraine tried to get her composure. She yanked a Kleenex from the pocket on her apron and blew her nose.

"She was only fifteen. She had her whole life ahead of her. I know she didn't have many friends growing up. Her mother took her life, and her father abandoned her. When he came along, I thought he was trying to take advantage of her. He was so much older than her. It wasn't right. I didn't want her to get hurt again. We hadn't been seeing eye to eye for some time. This was my fault as well. I resented her, and I pushed her away. I pushed her right into the arms of another man. He worked at a club. He drummed for a band. Late nights, booze, and drugs are always a part of that scene. I didn't want her to go down that road. She was starting to have episodes, and I locked her up to protect her."

"You locked her up?"

"Yes, I did. It was for her own good. She started sneaking out and lying to me. I was furious when I found out she was pregnant. She wouldn't tell me who the father was. This made me even angrier. I couldn't believe he actually loved her. I thought he had brainwashed her to save himself. After it all happened, I found letters he had written to her. Love letters full of hope for the two of them. He wanted that baby. He wanted to be a good dad and husband to her. I had him charged and put away before the baby was born. With Nina in her condition, I know in my heart it was my fault she killed the baby. She couldn't handle it without him, and I couldn't handle her. He never deserved to be punished and placed there. I know now the kind of person he was. Does age really matter when love is at stake? I ruined the lives of the people I loved. That baby, my great-grandchild, could've had a happy life. It was ripped away before it even had a chance. When Nina was admitted, I couldn't handle it. I ran. I could no longer be a part of society. I couldn't be with her. She hates me and has every right to."

"I don't think she hates you, Lorraine. You are the only family she has left. Despite her mental condition, with the medication available and the right resources, she could still live a normal life. There will be a lot of therapy involved, but I'd like to see her live a better one. A life that she deserves outside of closed, confined walls. I believe that the release of the child's body may help Nina snap out of some of the personal demons she struggles with. She doesn't know yet that I have uncovered the remains. I feel strongly that she needs to have closure to move on. I am going to arrange a service, and I need you to be there, Lorraine. This will be very difficult for her. She may insist she can't go through with it. I have studied the grieving process, and we can't grieve until we accept it and learn to let go. Finding the body will be a complete breakthrough for her. I am sure she repressed the events, but the wound needs to be healed. One step is saying goodbye. I urge you to consider joining me at the ceremony. I think it's time for you and Nina to put the pieces of your life back together. Everyone she ever loved has abandoned her in some way."

"I don't know if she will see me?"

"It is going to be her choice, Lorraine. I am going to speak with her regarding our visit. How long has Brett been sentenced to Meadowlands? I would also like to talk to him. To be honest, I had no idea of the relationship between them. It could've been rape which happens more often than not. My ex-husband was transferred to the village, and he deserved to be. Loving someone shouldn't be a reason to be there."

"Miss Crane, thank you for coming here. Thank you for caring enough about my granddaughter to go to these lengths. I will do whatever I can to assist you further."

Kathy stood up and thanked Lorraine for allowing her in.

"I have a lot to do. I must go now. I will come back once I have a plan, that is if I am welcome?"

Lorraine grabbed Kathy's arm and pulled her close. "Yes, you are more than welcome. I will be waiting."

Chapter 29

She pulled her car up to the metal gates that surrounded the village. Kathy peered up through the windshield at the bars that separated her from the world inside, a world full of men who had abused and killed women and children getting to live their lives inside. Calvin entered her mind as the vision of him being there played out like a movie she wished she had never seen. If only she had turned down the tickets handed to her for the late-night matinee. The horror show played out by accepting Calvin's invitation to prom, would not have endured the pain that followed. She imagined him on the doorstep breathing the air he had taken from their child. A shiver ran down her spine that made Kathy shake. She couldn't allow herself to think about them. She was there for a reason, an unselfish act to help another.

The security guard standing on the other side of the gate was stern. He stood there as if frozen. With his eyes locked on hers, Kathy wrapped her woolen sweater tighter around her waist and tied the fabric belt. She was nervous. Swallowing hard, she fingered the satin tie tucked under her shirt, tugging slightly on it as she swept her hair over her shoulder. A Visitor's pass held her picture and ID. Reaching out her hand, Kathy passed her badge through the gate. The guard looked it over.

"You're from O'Hanagan. That lighthouse that shines over there must make it all worth it, eh."

He opened the metal barrier slowly. It creaked like the rusty feature it was. The sound made her hair stand on end as Kathy stepped into the yard. With the gate latched behind her, she looked around.

"Here you go, miss. Maybe you can help one of these people here, sick souls."

"Well, Mr. I didn't get your name. Thank you for that, but I believe I am here because they're not all sick."

She placed the silk ribbon tied to the Visitor badge over her head making it visible to the members of the village.

The community bulletin board stood prominently along the sidewalk in front of the homes. Kathy approached it with hesitation. She was nervous and she couldn't help the fear that started to rise from the bottom of her stomach. Praying that she would get the answers she came for, her eyes scanned the colorful posters pinned to the corkboard under the fibreglass casing. Glancing to the left, she noticed a layout of the village. The homes were numbered, outlining the residents who lived in each one. She placed her finger on the glass and pulled it down slowly until she reached #17. Brett Mazuno. Breathing in deep, Kathy couldn't help but read each name listed. Calvin entered her mind. She imagined the time when his name was on this board. A part of her wanted to know which unit he had resided in. Getting lost in her thoughts, she was brought back to reality by the sound of a male whistle. Kathy turned her head fast and sharp. She looked around in search of the caller. With no one in sight, she clutched her purse under her arm and moved swiftly down the row of homes to #17.

The wind was cool. The once clear sky blanketed itself with eerie grey clouds. That didn't help the shivers that had already ran up and down Kathy's spine. She examined the tiny homes as she passed each one. The lawns had been well maintained. Surely, they pay someone to keep up with the yard. There was a basketball court at the end of the street. A deflated ball leaned against one of the metal goal nets. The Court looked baron. Kathy envisioned young high school and college kids cheering each other on, full of energy and the need to win. The cement pad was vacant. The village itself seemed desolate. She could hear the odd chatter and what sounded like a weed whacker in the distance. The clouds grew in a little thicker, and slight drops could be felt on her face.

Kathy picked up the pace and sprinted to the house's awning she had located. The front porch had two cement steps leading to a small veranda. A bay window from the outside produced a near-empty house. She could see someone moving around inside. Part of her wanted to turn back, go to the car, and drive away. Kathy felt nauseous. She took a few breaths and reassured herself that she had been in these kinds of situations before, and her fear wasn't going to stop her.

With her hand on the rickety metal railing, she pulled herself up the steps with force. Thunder cracked behind her. Kathy jumped and banged on the door. She gasped as she had not been prepared to knock yet. The sound of footsteps inside grew closer. Standing almost as if frozen in time, the door creaked open.

"Hello," the young man said, staring at her with wonder.

"Hi…i.. .i .. i .,." Kathy stuttered.

"Can I help you?" he questioned, opening the door a little wider and peering behind her.

"I'm looking for Brett Mazuno. It states on the village map that he resides in this unit. Is he home?"

"Well, that depends. What is it that you need to see him about?"

His eyes looked her up and down, waiting for a response.

"My name is Kathy Crane. I am investigating an incident that happened a few years ago, and I need his help with the matter. I don't mean any harm or trouble, just looking for answers that could assist in the well-being of a young girl, a patient of mine in Berkley."

His eyes lit up. "Nina?"

Kathy smiled. "You must be Brett? May I come in for a minute and speak with you?"

He hesitated for a moment. The wonder of the visit on Nina's behalf made him invite her in. He was curious and anxious now. Stepping into the dwelling gave Kathy a feeling of relief. She could sense by how he moved that he was a gentle man, surely not the type to be confined to a place like this.

"Come in, sit down. Can I make you some tea or coffee? I'm out of creamer, but I do have sugar. Maybe you prefer it black?"

"Black is fine," Kathy replied while pulling out a wooden chair pushed under the kitchen table.

"Everything ok in here, Miss?" the Guard asked, standing in the doorway.

"Yes, everything is fine. Thank you."

"Ok, I'll be right outside if you need me."

He closed the door directing Kathy's attention back to the kitchen. She watched him make the coffee. He had such grace doing so. Slightly tapping on the rubber lid of the can with two spoons, he hummed to himself.

"So, I hear you are quite the drummer."

"Was," he scoffed. "Sure miss it, the music. The way it can build you up inside and release all anxieties or stress. It's good for the soul. All I have in here is the radio which doesn't produce the same effect. I was really good, played my whole life. Life is a funny thing. One minute you're on top of the world, the next you have to hide from it. I don't belong here, you know. All I did was love someone. The law sees it their way, I guess. Don't get me wrong, I understand that age is a factor when sex is involved, but what about love?"

He turned to face her now. Kathy was speechless. She agreed with him. He pulled two cups out of the cupboard and filled them with the freshly brewed coffee. Kathy stood up to help him.

"I got it, have a seat."

She sat back down. "Thank you, smells good."

The sound of the rain hitting the roof was soothing like it could wash away the pain of the past. Kathy truly believed that the sun would shine for him and Nina again.

Sitting across from her at the table, he stared into the ceramic mug. Kathy unzipped the side pocket of her blouse. The gold-banded ring slid down her long, slender finger as she pulled it out. She held her closed fist on the table. Brett stared at her hand.

With eyebrows raised, he asked, "What is it?"

Kathy slowly turned it over and bared the palm of her hand. Brett gasped as he yanked it from her.

"Where did you get this?"

He turned it in his fingers, eyeing the circle of jewellery. He stopped. Pulling it close while squinting his eyes, there he saw the letters GM engraved.

"This is my mother's ring. Where did you get this, I asked you?"

His eyes were wild now. Kathy could sense he was forcing back the tears.

"I'm very sorry for your loss, Mr. Mazuno. The police removed this item from the remains of your child. Was it Nina's ring? Did you give it to her?"

Brett started to break down. The tears streamed down his cheek as he wiped them with the back of his hand.

"Yes," he shook his head. "I proposed with that ring. I loved her. I wanted to marry her and start our family. Nina is the sincerest person I know. She wanted the baby. It was Lorraine who should take the blame and be the one suffering behind bars. The same way she made her granddaughter. I have wondered where it went. When I saw Nina, she wasn't wearing it. Did she look like she suffered long? My little girl, she was going to be daddy's girl."

Brett held the ring close to his lips and kissed it. "Does Nina know you have it? Does she remember what she did? How is she?"

Kathy could tell by the worry in his voice that he truly loved her.

"I didn't come here to upset you. I came to help you and Nina. You say this is your mother's ring?"

"Yes, she gave it to me when I was eighteen. She said to give it to a girl I thought she would approve of. A gentle soul who is unable of anything but treating me with true love. I thought she loved me."

"Brett, I am sure that Nina loves you very much. I have spoken with Lorraine, who takes full responsibility for everything. She was trying to protect Nina, but realizes it was the biggest mistake of her life having you charged and taken from her. The way she treated her and the lack of faith, she believes, ruined the lives of four people. I am looking for answers to help me treat Nina now."

"I am glad you came here, Miss Crane. Not a day goes by that I don't think of them. I dream about getting out of this place and finding her again. I swore to myself that I would make it happen someday."

"I have faith in that as well. Do you mind if I hold onto the ring? I would like to return it to Nina."

"By all means. It belongs to her."

"Thank you, Brett. And thank you for seeing me. I promise you that you will find your happiness with her again. I will be in touch with you. Until then, I need you to stay strong and keep praying."

Brett placed his hand on his heart and smiled, "I will."

Chapter 30

As the light danced across the ocean, it calmed Kathy. The sound of the waves lightly crashing against the rocks and the fresh air filled her with hope. She walked up the steps along the hospital and leaned out over the ledge. Closing her eyes, she smiled as the breeze blew across her face. She entered the main doors and headed to the ward to start her shift.

Stopping at the reception desk, she chatted with the on-call nurse before making her way to Nina.

Down the hall and into her room, Kathy went. Nina rolled over in bed and looked up at her with anticipation in her eyes. She had been waiting for Kathy to return.

"Hi Nina, how are you feeling today? I missed you."

Nina sat up as Kathy neared the bed. Sitting down beside her, Kathy placed her arm around her shoulder.

"I missed you too," she said softly.

"Honey, I have some amazing news for you. I'm not sure where to begin, and it is going to be a lot to take in. Do you feel well enough to talk right now?"

With eyes full of wonder, Nina squeezed Kathy's hand, "Yes."

"I have a sister. Her name is Nancy, and she owns the house that you lived in with your grandma, Lorraine."

Kathy slowly pulled the gold ring from her pocket and opened her hand.

"Nina, honey, do you know what this is?"

Yanking her hand from Kathy's, Nina placed them both over her face and began to cry. She cried as Kathy pulled her close and held her tight.

"Shhh, sweetie, let it out," Kathy whispered in her ear as she rocked her on the edge of the bed.

"Lily," Nina repeated as she wept for her baby.

"Lily, that's a beautiful name, Nina. She is at peace now. We have recovered the body, and she has been taken to a safe place."

Nina sat forward and gently removed the ring from Kathy's hand. She slid it on her finger and examined it.

"Brett," she whispered as the tears streamed down her face.

"Nina, I am so sorry for all the pain you have had in your life at such a young age. I spoke with your grandmother. She hates herself for what she did to you and your family. She loves you, Nina, and she wants to be a family again. I will be planning a service to allow you the chance to grieve your loss. Would you like that?"

Nina nodded as she held her hands tight.

"Your grandma would also like to be there to see you and support you. Is that something you want?"

"Brett, I want Brett," she whimpered.

"I know you do, sweetheart, and he wants to see you too."

"You saw him?" she questioned.

"Yes, I did. We had a good visit. He is quite a handsome young man, I must say. He has a heart of gold. He loves you Nina and he has never stopped. He is worried about you. I can't promise that he will be able to join you for the service, but I will promise you that I will do whatever I can to try to make it happen."

Nina broke down again. The emotions swirled around inside of her as the memories of her life before flooded her mind and her heart. Years of thoughts that had been trapped inside all alone within herself yearning to be set free. The secret she had held onto for so long, now known to the world and the ones she loved. She turned the ring on her finger. A smile crossed her face as she remembered the day that Brett had given it to her. The weight she had been carrying seemed to lift, replaced with a feeling of hope.

"Thank you," she cried. "Thank you for everything."

"You are very welcome, Nina. It is my job to care for my patients, and I care so much about you. I want you to get some rest now, ok. I am going to see your grandma again soon. I will be back in a couple of days."

Kathy handed her an empty journal. "I brought this for you. You can use it to write down anything you are feeling. Happy thoughts, fears, maybe there is something you would like to say at the service for Lily."

Nina opened the notebook and flipped through the pages. Placing it on the nightstand, she pulled the covers up and laid her head down. She was exhausted, mentally, and emotionally. Kathy tucked the sheet around her and kissed her on the cheek.

"Sweet dreams, love."

Chapter 31

Lorraine stood in the orchard and felt the warm sun on her face. The apples that had fallen from the trees colored the ground red. It had been a long time since she had even wanted to go outside, and it made her feel good.

When Kathy pulled up, she was on her way back to the house with a half-full bucket of bruised fruit. Climbing out of the car, she met her with a smile on her face. Kathy could feel the enlightened aura of the woman who stood before her. She looked years younger and full of life.

"Good morning," Lorraine waved at her.

"Hello Lorraine, you've got quite the orchard out here."

"Yes, there's nothing better than fresh apple pie. I had to get out here and collect the fallen off the trees before the birds got to them. Here try one," she said as she pulled one from the bucket.

Kathy turned the apple in her hand and took a bite.

"Wow! That is delicious, thank you."

"Come on inside. I made fresh-squeezed lemonade this morning. I wasn't sure when you would be back, but it is a pleasure to have you so soon."

Kathy followed her into the cottage, slipping off her sandals as she entered.

"How is my granddaughter?"

"She is doing good, Lorraine. I didn't want to go into too much detail about our meeting and everything else that has taken place, but she knows I was to see you and Brett. I gave her the ring, and explained that Lily has been recovered and asked her about having a service. I believe that this is going to be a huge breakthrough for her and exactly what that young girl needs."

"I want her back in my life Kathy. I want her here with me, her and Brett. She has suffered alone for too long. I have done a lot of thinking since you came to see me. This is my chance to give my granddaughter the life she deserves. I am a wealthy woman, Miss Crane. With wealth comes a certain degree of loneliness. You learn to lose trust in people. You seclude yourself from others. I spent a lot of years of my life believing I was better than those less fortunate. I realize that the financial stature has no relevance to the nature of the individual. I understand that Nina has a very serious illness, but she doesn't belong in that place. I need to know what it would take to have her released into my care."

"I appreciate your eagerness to reconnect with your granddaughter, Lorraine. An outpatient treatment plan consisting of medication, social skills training, and vocational and recreational support would have to be obtained. I could apply for custody on your behalf as long as you are completely aware of the responsibilities that would go along with this. I will speak with Nina first to see how she feels about it before I approach the Medical Board."

Lorraine put her head down and closed her eyes. "Would you mind if I asked her?"

Kathy gazed at the woman standing in the tiny kitchen so full of hope and the need for acceptance. Before she could answer, Lorraine lifted her head and opened her eyes. Kathy could see that she was fighting back her tears.

"I think that is a great idea. You need to regain your relationship with her before she can commit to trusting you. She has spent multiple years behind closed walls, behind closed eyes. You need to prepare yourself for any kind of rejection she may give you. It is a big decision, and it may take her some time to forgive you before she decides."

Lorraine walked to the china cabinet in the hall and pulled open the top drawer. Reaching inside, she pulled out an envelope. Returning to the kitchen and across from Kathy, she handed it.

"What is this?" Kathy asked her with curious eyes.

"Go ahead, read it."

Lifting the flap, Kathy removed the letter and exposed the woman's handwriting on the lined piece of paper.

Criminal Division of the Dept of Justice
78390 Grand Manor Way
Berkley, NH 3057-82972

Dear Honourable Judge Clayton,

My name is Lorraine Mayfield. I am writing this letter in regarding Mr. Brett Mazuno, a man who resides in the Meadowlands Facility in 2005. He had been dating my granddaughter, Nina Gallaway, which resulted in her becoming pregnant at the age of 15.

I pressed charges against him, and he was found guilty of having sexual relations with a minor. He was listed as a registered sexual offender and placed in the village for a duration of four years. Three years have passed, and I would like the sentencing to be readdressed with a consideration of early release. He was never a predator. The relationship between the two was mutual. He is a non-violent prisoner with no previous criminal charges. Mr. Mazuno was a Volunteer and a Good Samaritan. I believe that it would benefit the public to have him back in society, as well as my granddaughter to have him back in her life.

I am willing to take full responsibility for the convicted sexual assailant under my care at the property in which I reside. Thank you for taking the time to consider this request for early release.

Sincerely,

Ms. Lorraine Mayfield
7465 Range Rd. 222
Berkley, NH 3057-82972

Kathy folded up the letter and placed it back into the envelope.

"You are doing an honorable thing here, Ms. Mayfield. I can't promise that we will see positive results through this letter, but the first step is to try. I am going to deliver it to the Dept personally. If all goes well, I will get a chance to speak to the prosecutor and explain in more detail the situation. I have a good feeling that we are on the right track."

"Thank you so much for all that you have done, Miss Crane. I have something else for you as well," she said, turning back into the hallway. Kathy watched her climb the wooden steps with the corner of her dress held up by one hand, the other on the railing. She disappeared to the top floor, and Kathy stood up, making her way over to the fireplace mantle on the opposite side of the room. Scanning the items lined along the dust-free ledge, she noticed a photograph. Removing it, she turned it over and examined the young girl who sat in the grass.

"That was my Rose," Lorraine stated as she slid the photograph from Kathy's fingers and placed it back on the mantle.

"Oh, I'm sorry, Lorraine, you startled me. I never meant to pry," Kathy blushed.

"Here., I want you to have these," she said as she handed Kathy a stack of envelopes.

"What are they?" Kathy inquired as she ran her fingers along the ribbon that bound them so neatly together.

"They belong to Nina. They are from Brett. I would like for her to have them back," Loraine said as she bowed her head and returned to the chair in the kitchen.

"Oh, ok. I will make sure she gets them. Thank you," Kathy replied. "But I really must get going."

Kathy swallowed what was left in her cup and stepped toward the front door.

"Have yourself a good day, Lorraine, and keep me informed if you receive any information back regarding this letter."

"You do the same, Miss Crane," Lorraine nodded as she watched her walk out.

Lorraine hired the neighbours' son a few miles down the road to remove all the NO TRESPASSING signs posted throughout the yard and down the lane. Tossing them into the burning barrel, she lit a match and watched as the wind forced the flames up from the metal encased hole. She didn't want to be alone anymore.

Retiring to the kitchen to bake a couple of pies, a sense of purpose filled her. Humming to herself as she opened the oven door to put them in, something caught her attention. She could hear the rumble of a vehicle coming down the lane. Lorraine watched out the window as it drove a circle around the house and parked in front. A plump man with a ball cap on his head hopped out and proceeded to the porch. Lorraine watched him closely as she hid behind the curtain. He was carrying a brown manila envelope.

The rustic antique frame of the black metal mailbox stood on the worn-out wooden front porch, Lowering the tiny door, the man placed the letter inside. He rounded the truck, jumped in, and drove away.

She stood there for a moment and watched him until the brown boxed truck was out of sight. Wiping her hands on her apron, she untied the string and hung it on the lattice back chair. Lorraine knew what it was. She wanted so desperately to open it, but she was scared; scared of the contents it contained. Her granddaughters' future lay amongst the words tucked inside the tiny box. She wished that Kathy was there to read it to her, to support her. Lorraine knew it was time to visit them both at O'Hanagan's.

She went upstairs to the bathroom and turned the taps on the porcelain claw tub. Lorraine placed her best Sunday dress and a pair of garments on the bed. Stepping into the hot water, it cleansed her. She leaned back and let the water absorb around her. She had waited for this day for a long time, a chance to redeem herself to the world and her granddaughter.

The old Eldorado had resumed its place in the barn shed for the past couple of years. Lorraine prayed it would start up right away. Opening the wooden doors, there it sat. The blue tarp that had been tied over it to preserve it, was covered in dust. Looking at the car she once cherished more than life, more than her granddaughter's life, had no deep connection to her now. She daydreamed about bringing Nina home as she carefully lifted the tarp from the classic car. 'Maybe she could teach Nina how to drive it,' she thought to herself.

The steel door handle sent her shivers as she pulled up and out. Climbing in, she turned the key and listened to the old car fire up as if it had waited for this day. Lorraine inched it out of the shed and up to the house.

She bustled around collecting the pies, her purse, and the letter. Lorraine stepped on the gas and headed to town with excitement running through her veins. She felt alive as she turned down the windows and upped the volume on the radio. She was on a mission; a mission to rebuild the relationship lost and to create a new one. She forced all the negative thoughts that began to creep into her mind and replaced them with positive life-changing ones. Nina had to forgive her.

The lighthouse was breathtaking. Lorraine peered out over the ocean and filled her lungs with the fresh ocean air. The brick walls of the hospital were the only thing separating her from her granddaughter inside. Lorraine said a silent prayer before entering. The sealed letter burned a hole in her pocket as she wondered what it said. She felt safe in the company of Kathy and needed to read it with her.

The Receptionist at the front desk was talking into a headset when Loraine approached her. She smiled as her fingers moved swiftly across the keyboard before saying goodbye.

"How may I help you?" the lady asked her.

"I am looking for Miss Kathy Crane."

"Kathy works on the fifth floor. Take the elevator to your left. Once there, hang a right, and there you will see the Nurse's station. They should be able to help you locate her there."

“Thank you so very much,” Lorraine nodded as she proceeded to the elevator.

The aroma from the pie filled her senses. The tin was still warm against her palm. The anticipation built up inside of her as she stood in the elevator and watched the numbers rise. She couldn’t wait to see Nina and prayed that their reuniting would go well.

The doors chimed as they slid open. Lorraine stepped out, nearly dropping the pie as she resumed her composure. Following the directions she was given, she was soon standing at the Nurse’s station. She set the pie on the counter and looked around. There was no one at the desk. She heard footsteps behind her and spun around. It was Kathy.

“Lorraine!” Kathy squealed. “What a pleasant surprise.”

“Oh, Kathy, I am so happy I found you here. I baked a pie that I thought you and Nina could enjoy. I also received a letter in the mailbox today, and I just couldn’t open it alone. Would you read it with me?”

“Yes, of course, Lorraine. Thank you for the pie. It smells amazing. I am sure that Nina will be thrilled to taste her grandmothers’ pie again.”

“My nerves are a bit rattled over seeing her, Kathy. I don’t know how she is going to respond. I would like to read the letter beforehand.”

“No one can predict how she will act. We can only pray for the best. There is a meeting room down the hall. Let’s go in there and sit down.”

Lorraine followed her into the tiny room and took a seat at the table by the window. Taking a deep breath, she placed the envelope face down and slid it to Kathy.

"I want you to open it."

"Are you sure, Lorraine?"

"Yes, please read it to me."

Both women stared at it, looking back at each other.

"No matter what this contains, I want you to know that I am proud of you, Lorraine."

Kathy placed her hand on hers and picked up the envelope. With the paper unfolded in front of her, she began to read:

Dear Ms. Mayfield,

I have received your letter regarding Mr. Brett Mazuno. It is a rare occurrence when the party responsible for the conviction renders a plea for early release.

Considering this matter, we see that he was indeed an asset to the community. He has a long list of worthy and unselfish acts in his past. His intentions with your granddaughter were in no way based on criminal intent. This young man assisted with the renovation of three units in the village that had substantial foundation damage from flooding. His time spent at the Meadowlands Facility was fulfilled by him in a very professional manner. He meets the criteria for early release as defined in the Bureau policy. He will need to complete the follow-up treatment assigned to him. Failure to comply will constitute an automatic return to the Meadowlands Facility, which could also result in an extended stay period.

After careful consideration, I hereby grant full custody of the accused to Ms. Lorraine Mayfield. Upon acknowledgement of this letter, the court will release him into your care where you reside.

Yours Truly,

Judge Clayton
Criminal Division of the Dept of Justice
78390 Grand Manor Way
Berkley, NH 3057-82972

Lorraine burst out in tears. She could not believe what she had just heard. The joy overwhelmed her. Clasping her hands, she slowly rocked in her chair, looking up, "Thank you, thank you."

Seeing the woman across from her in such elation brought tears to Kathy's eyes. All she had ever wanted to do was help people, and she had. The bringing together of this family was more than Kathy could have ever hoped. She pulled a tissue from her coat pocket and gave it to Lorraine.

"This is wonderful news, Lorraine. I have spoken with the Chairman of the Medical Board, and he has agreed to allow Nina back into your care. I will be appointed as her outpatient nurse until I go on maternity leave. The women here are all very caring, and I know that whoever fills my position will have Nina's best interests at heart. I truly believe that having you and Brett back in her life will be the positive outcome you all need and deserve."

"I want to see Nina now. Please take me to her."

Lorraine stood up and threw her purse over her shoulder. Placing the envelope inside, she zipped it closed.

Kathy knew that Nina was doing group therapy. She showed Lorraine to her room and asked her to wait there.

"I will be right back with your granddaughter, Ms. Mayfield," Kathy said with excitement as she closed the door behind her.

Lorraine sat on the edge of the bed and looked around the room. She remembered all the times she had locked her up and felt terrible inside. That type of life for a young girl, as well as the confinement of the room she now sat in, was no life for a child. She checked her watch and waited anxiously for the door to open.

She was staring out the window when she heard it. Spinning around, her eyes met Nina's. She looked beautiful, just like her daughter, Rose, when she was her age. Time seemed to stand still as the two stood on opposite sides of the room, locked in a gaze.

"Nina," Lorraine whispered, beginning to cry.

Nina looked at Kathy and back at Lorraine.

"This must be a huge shock for you, sweetie. Why don't you have a seat on the bed," Kathy said while escorting her there.

Nina sat down and placed her hands in her lap. She twirled the golden ring on her finger and looked up at Lorraine. "They found Lily," she said softly.

"I know they did, honey," Lorraine said as she knelt in front of her granddaughter and placed her own hands on hers.

"They are going to have a service, grandma," Nina explained. "I wish that her dad could come."

Lorraine slid forward and put her arms around her. She hugged her tighter than she ever had before. She didn't want to let go. The two both started to cry as Lorraine whispered in her ear, "He can."

Nina pulled away and looked up at Kathy. Kathy nodded with a smile.

Lorraine sat next to her on the bed and grabbed her hand. Kathy pulled the wooden chair from the corner of the room to face the two.

"Nina, I have some wonderful things to tell you. I would like you to come back and live with me. Kathy will make arrangements so that you can still get the care you need, but you can be free from these confined walls."

Nina sat in silence.

"But you won't be living in my house," Lorraine paused.

Nina turned to face her with wonder.

"I have written a letter asking for custody of Brett. They have agreed to release him into my care. I want to give you two back the life that you both deserve. A life together to rekindle the love you both share for each other."

Nina's eyes lit up. The joy in her face could move mountains. She couldn't believe what she was hearing. The overwhelming excitement she felt filled her heart. Her heart that had been so empty and hollow for years, felt as if it would burst right out of her chest.

The three women stood up and embraced each other. All the wrongs in their lives were finally going to be made right.

Kathy phoned the Meadowlands Facility and arranged an appointment for Brett and Lorraine. On Tuesday morning, the El Dorado picked her up, and off they went. The two women discussed the outcome that may lie before them. Kathy believed that he would jump at the chance to be free from there and back with Nina.

"People change Kathy. He may not hold the same feelings for her as he before the sentencing. I know how badly he wanted the baby, and he may hold a lot of resentment toward her for doing what she did."

"Well, Lorraine, after speaking with him, I suspect he will be thrilled to have another chance to be with her despite the events that took place in the past. I can tell he loves her just as much today as the day they met. Forgiveness takes time, but when that's all you have behind confined walls, you realize the good more than the bad. He doesn't blame Nina. He blames you. That is going to be our most difficult task to overcome. I explained to him how you feel and once he knows you are the cause of his release, I'm certain he will be able to forgive you to. Letting go of the past can be a difficult process, but putting faith in a concrete future can allow this to happen."

"I wanted to talk to Nina first and see how she felt about the idea. I am thrilled that she accepted my offer. I am just praying he will do the same. I am a changed woman, Miss Crane. I wasn't able to save my daughter or my great-granddaughter, but I will die trying to save Nina."

The car pulled up to the gates, and the previous guard leaned into the open window and eyed Kathy.

"Back again, eh."

"Yes, we are here to see Mazuno in #17."

He kicked at the dirt toward the metal gates. Opening them, he allowed the car to drive through. They crept down the street and parked in front of the house.

"Are you ready?" Kathy questioned Lorraine.

The look on her face said no, but she answered back, "Yes."

"Everything will be fine, Lorraine. Don't worry. Brett is a remarkable young man. He only wants what's best for Nina. As you and I both believe that the two of them reconnecting is the best, I can't imagine him turning down your offer. If there are hateful words said by him, I need you to remain calm and let him express himself. You took away his life and his dreams. Seeing you here is going to bring back a lot of hate and revenge for him. I need you to be prepared and on your best behavior if we are going to make this work. We are here for Nina. Would you like me to go in first?"

"No, I am a strong woman. I can handle this."

One of the guards strolled onto the front porch and stood with his arms crossed. The two women got out of the car and approached him.

"Good day, ladies. Brett is a respectable young man. I don't believe you will have any trouble with him, but I will be out here for your protection."

"Thank you," Lorraine nodded, clutching her purse.

Kathy knocked and waited. The same footsteps neared the door, but this time gave her a sense of reassurance. She wasn't frightened. She was confident. Lorraine took a couple of steps back. Kathy grabbed her hand. "It's ok," she assured her.

Taking a deep breath, Lorraine squeezed her hand hard as the door opened.

Standing in the doorway was the man she had put away. His face turned pale as he recognized the woman before him.

"What is she doing here? You never told me she was coming. Where's Nina?"

"Brett, I understand the feelings you are going through right now. Nina is fine. She is safe at the hospital. I have come here with Lorraine as she has some wonderful and life-changing news for you."

"I think she has done enough to change my life already," Brett replied in an angry tone while rolling his eyes.

"May we come in? I'd like you to give her a chance to explain," Kathy asked with urgency in her voice.

Brett stood in the doorway, staring at the two women. He could feel the anger creeping in and forced himself to control it. He was curious what she came all this way to see him was regarding.

"Yes, come in." He held the door open for them, closing it behind.

Lorraine gazed around the tiny home. It was small, but tidy.

"I made iced tea if you would like a glass."

"Yes, please," they both responded.

They sat at the table while he poured the drinks. Lorraine pulled the letter out of her purse with clammy hands.

"I am removing Nina from O'Hanagan. She doesn't belong behind barred walls anymore, and I don't believe you do either. I have written a letter that I would like you to read."

Lorraine unfolded it and handed it to him. Before looking at it, Brett sat in silence. He could only imagine what he was about to learn.

"I hope you consider the option before making your decision."

He gave her a look of uncertainty and began to read the letter.

Once done, he folded it up and handed it back to her. "Now you want us to be together, after everything you put us through? We are to move as if nothing happened. Sweep it under the rug until the next time you decide to lock us up again? How does Nina feel about this? Why can't I see her?"

"You can be released and placed in Lorraine's care if you comply with the stipulations. This is a chance for you both," Kathy explained.

Lorraine started to tear up. "I'm truly sorry for the pain I have caused. I want to make it right. I can't give you back the past, but I can help you have a happy future. I plan to move a house onto my yard for you and Nina to share. It will be a good environment for her, lots of trees and walking paths around. I know she enjoys being in nature. I'd like her to start taking photography classes. We can set up a room in the house for that, as well as a music room for you, so that you can get your passion for music back. I'm willing to do whatever it takes to create a healthy home for the two of you. It's not far from town, so you can resume your work at the Nectar if that is something you would enjoy. I also have lots of jobs around the farm, which I would be more than happy to pay you for."

"This is a new start for you and Nina," Kathy pleaded.

Brett turned his head and gazed out the window. He was processing all the information that had just been brought before him, freedom from the village, a life with Nina. There was no way he could say no.

The silence in the room made the clock's ticking sound on the wall echo through the women's ears. Waiting impatiently for him to respond, they both stared at the young man with anticipation.

Brett looked at Lorraine and stared deep into her eyes before responding.

"Ok, I will accept your offer. I don't want to waste another year of my life here. I want to marry your granddaughter. I want us to be the family we were meant to be."

Hearing this, Lorraine pushed back her chair, and leapt to her feet. Grabbing his arm, she pulled Brett out of his chair and hugged him hard. She was laughing now, laughing and crying tears of joy. She couldn't wait to tell Nina. She couldn't wait to reunite them.

"How long will it take you to pack?" Lorraine questioned him with excitement she could barely contain.

"Just have to throw what I got here in a suitcase. I didn't come with much. Won't be leaving with much either."

"Great. We will go to the mayor's office here in the village and start the release papers for your dismissal. Can you meet us there when you are done?" Kathy questioned.

"Sure thing," Brett replied with a smile.

The two women left the home while Brett began to pack up his belongings. He could barely contain himself, imagining Nina in his arms again. So many lonely nights, he yearned for her touch and the smell of her hair. This was his chance to keep the promise he had made to protect her.

With his suitcase full, he removed her picture from the nightstand drawer and slid it into his back pocket. Brett stepped onto the front porch and closed the door. He finally felt alive again. Down the steps and onto the road, he headed to the office. With his head held high, he could taste the freedom that awaited him on the other side of the lonely rout iron gates. He had to bury the hate he felt towards Lorraine for the damage she had caused in his life.

Brett was greeted by an officer and led into the mayor's office. The paperwork was ready for his signature. Lorraine handed him a pen and pointed to the dotted line.

"Go ahead, sign it. You are free now," she said to him with tears in her eyes.

Leaning over the desk, Brett paused. He envisioned all the things he had witnessed while he was confined to the village. He knew that he would never have to cry himself to sleep or worry about the men around him again as he scrawled his name on the document and set down the pen.

"Wonderful!" Lorraine squealed. "Now, let's get you to my granddaughter where you belong."

Wrapping his fingers around the handle of his suitcase, Brett spun it around and walked outside a free man.

Chapter 32

Kathy took the elevator to the second floor. The storage room that contained the patient's lockers was at the end of the hall. Nina's was #222. Sticking the key in the lock and turning the knob, the tiny door opened. Placing her things into a fabric bag, she couldn't help but feel grateful. Everything she had set out to accomplish for the young couple was happening. She thanked the Lord in silent prayer before leaving the room.

Once on her ward, she stopped at the Nurse's station before entering Nina's room.

"So, they decided it was ok for her to leave in her condition?"

Kathy glanced up from the chart she was reading, feeling startled. "Umm, yes, they have. With continued treatment, Nina should do just fine under her grandmothers' custody."

"Well, I know you have taken a lot of time to do what you felt was necessary for that young girl, but what you may have forgotten, Ms. Crane, is it now? That a diseased mind like that of Miss Gallaway's will always be that way. So, don't be surprised when she ends up back in here."

"Excuse me?" Kathy questioned Jeanette in disbelief.

"I knew your husband, Calvin. That was a pretty crazy thing that happened. It's a shame. He was a cute one."

"How did you know that monster?" Kathy snapped.

"I saw him a few times when I was visiting my brother in the slammer. Something about a man behind bars just turns me upside down and sideways. Knowing they broke the law and are being punished makes me feel powerful over them. They would get down on their hands and knees and beg for stuff if they were desperate enough in there. That's the way it should be."

She looked up at Kathy with scandalous eyes. With her hands on the desk, Jeanette pushed herself back in her chair. The seat spun around violently as she stood up and glared at Kathy while exiting the nurse's station.

Kathy's jaw dropped. She couldn't believe what she had just heard, and from Jeanette of all people. Wiping her hand across her forehead, she took a deep breath and blocked out the vision of Calvin in her mind. Clutching her purse straps, Kathy removed it from the desk with the fabric bag and walked to Nina's room.

She was sitting at the desk with her journal.

"Hi Nina, can I ask what you are writing in there?"

Nina looked up at her and handed her the book. "It's a poem for Lily."

Kathy set the fabric bag on the bed and took the journal from her hands. Her fingers felt the binding as she smiled down at her. Her eyes scanned the pin-striped paper as she flipped back the page.

"Oh honey, it's beautiful," Kathy exclaimed.

Nina smiled and stood from the chair. "I never was much of a writer."

"You are one of the most creative girls I know, Nina and you know who else is good at writing?"

"No. Who?" she asked with wondering eyes.

Kathy pulled the clothes from the bag on the bed and handed them to Nina.

"I have a surprise for you. Get changed out of that gown, and I will be back shortly."

Nina ran her hands over the jeans she had worn into the hospital. The feel of the denim against her fingers made her feel whole. She lifted the folded clothes to her face and breathed in deep, the smell of change, the smell of freedom.

Kathy left the room and shut the door. Nina placed the clothes on the bed and ripped off the gown. She threw it on the floor and kicked it under the bed. With her feet in the jeans, she pulled them up and closed the button. They fit the same way they did when she arrived. She checked the pockets, nothing. She raised her arms and let the shirt slink down her arms before tugging it over her head. Nina held the hood of her coat in her fingers and let it spin around before putting it on. She sat down and smiled, waiting for Kathy to return.

The door opened, and Kathy walked toward her with a bundle of letters in her hand.

"Nina, I am so happy that you get to leave this place. You have brought me great pleasure knowing I helped you make it happen. I trust that you will be in safe hands. It is very important that you stay on your medication and continue treatment. I want you to call me anytime you need."

Kathy slid her business card into the side pocket of Nina's jacket.

"Now, I want you to go outside and take a minute to yourself off this ward before we leave."

She handed Nina the stack of envelopes. All the letters Brett had written her were tied together with a yellow ribbon. "These are for you. Take the path up to the lighthouse and enjoy them."

Nina cradled the package and hugged Kathy. "Thank you."

Nina ran past Kathy, past the elevator doors, and straight for the stairs. It had been years since her legs wanted to go as fast as they were moving her now. She was laughing. She was happy. Approaching the front doors, she held out her arms and pushed the metal bar hard, unlatching it as she sped past the frame. Nina stopped sharply and looked around. She was trying to take it all in all at once. The sound of the train lit a fire inside her with the clang of the chains and the rumble that echoed as the tiny metal wheels sped by on the tracks. She was outside. She was walking now, walking alone in street clothes. Free from restricted area nurses and residents. The memory of the Cheese Cake Castle warmed her thoughts. She could still remember how he smelled the first rainy night they met. Nina didn't want to suffer anymore. She knew it was her time in life to move on, to start a new chapter.

She clasped her hands tight around the bundle of letters. It was slightly cool out since the sun had set. The thoughts raced through her mind so fast and so many at once she almost lost her balance. Taking a couple of deep breaths, she strode forward. She could feel the dampness of her armpits as the shirt sleeves caught a breeze. It made her shiver harder. She only perspired when she was nervous or cold. Nina could run a relay race and not break a sweat. She looked down the path toward the massive beam of light in the sky and started to run. The breeze blew through her hair as she laughed. Her legs were pounding the cement as hard as the heartbeat in her chest. The sound of the ocean moved her, moved her up the hill and right into his arms.

The stack of envelopes went up in the air and scattered the cement platform as she reached the top. It was Brett!! She was in his arms. He spun her around and stopped sharp. They stared at each other in silence, eyes scanning each other wildly. He kissed her hard with passion that could light a match. Standing in the moonlight under the stars, they held each other and cried. The light that shone across the ocean symbolized for them both, the bright future they were going to have.

Pulling away slowly, Brett bent down and gathered up all the letters on the ground. He neatly piled them in his hands and handed them to her. Retrieving the yellow ribbon that laid upon the cement floor, he ran it through his fingers and wrapped it around the bundle.

"Put your finger here," he said, motioning to the cross of the strings.

Nina placed her finger on the tiny yellow mound and stared into his eyes. Pulling the string tight, Nina removed her finger and kissed the man she loved.

"Bound by love, just like us," he whispered in her ear.

Brett slid his right hand into the back pocket of his jeans and displayed the picture he pulled out. Nina gasped as she ran her finger across the front of it. It was her. He had taken it one day while they were at Plymouth Pond. She was sitting on a tree stump five-feet wide with her legs crossed. In her lap was the book 'All About Baby.' Her head was placed in her hands, holding it above the pages. Brett had given her a small shallow whistle making her eyes raise towards him. The look on her face that developed gave him butterflies. The kind that flutter around in your belly so fast you think they may find their way out. But they didn't. For him, they stayed there and were awakened every time he laid his eyes on the photograph.

Nina noticed a piece of tape at the top of the picture. Turning it over was the ultrasound photo of Lily.

"You kept it," she cried out, pounding a fist on his chest.

"Of course, I did. I was so excited to be her dad. I wanted to protect her from the world and show her she was loved. I'm sorry I broke that promise to you."

"You have nothing to apologize for. I'm the one to blame. It's my fault our daughter is gone. I took her life. I did it. Our little girl was so precious, so perfect, just like her dad."

Nina began to cry. She sat down on the wooden bench facing the deep, dark ocean that roared as it slammed its way into the rocks. She sobbed louder as she listened. Brett sat beside her and placed his arm around her.

"Tell me what happened that night," he urged her.

"I can't. I'm sorry. I don't really know."

"Nina, soon to be Mrs.Mazuno, if you'll marry me, I demand you tell me what happened. What was so terrible that forced you to take the breath from our child, my child? I have a right to know. I've waited many years to know. I've played it in my mind, but I need to hear it from you. Please, babe."

The cool breeze against her face and through her hair relaxed her. Nina closed her eyes tight and started to breathe in deeply. She squeezed his hand in hers and began to speak.

"It was a Wednesday night. It was the anniversary of my mother's death. I kept seeing her face that day. It wasn't her, but a distorted version of her. Grandma Lorraine tried to act as if the day meant nothing to her, just another day on the calendar for her to cross off. I had lit a candle in the den after I laid Lily down. Lorraine was going bowling. She played in a League. I asked her to stay home with me. I told her I hadn't been feeling well and worried that Lily had a fever. I was scared. Scared I didn't know what to do and scared to be alone. She pranced around the house in her league jersey, telling me if I wanted the baby, it was my responsibility to take care of her. She insisted I grew up and that she wasn't going to allow me to ruin any more events in her life. When she left, the panic set in. Lily started to cry. I tried to cradle her and rock her. I felt dizzy. It was so loud. I wanted her to stop. To stop making me feel as worthless as my grandmother had. My fear turned to anger. I was angry you were taken away and angry she had left me like everyone else. My head started to pound. I was confused. I wasn't thinking clear.

I prayed to God that the voices would stop. Lily's and the ones in my head."

Brett squeezed her hand as he listened anxiously. "You're doing good, Hun. Take your time."

Nina laid her head on his chest as he wiped the tears from her eyes.

"I..I..I don't remember exactly how it all took place. I don't remember getting the shower cap or using it. I remember being told to, and I realized after what I had done. It was too late. It happened so fast. I tried talking to her. Her tiny lips were blue, and she wasn't breathing in my arms. I'm so sorry," Nina cried out.

Brett held her in his arms and rocked her on the bench. "I'm sorry I wasn't there," he stuttered, choking back the tears.

"So many times I wanted to tell someone where she was. She was hidden away, waiting for me to find her again. When I started having the dreams, I enjoyed them. It was my time with her. I knew if she was found I would lose her again. And I did. Her soul is set free. Free to leave this world in peace."

"Nina, sweetie, she deserved to be found. She is in Heaven now, looking down on us, waiting for her mommy and daddy to come home some day. Forgiveness is the first step to overcome any kind of loss. Nina, I forgive you. I forgive myself for not being able to save our little girl. Tell me so we can find the strength to move on. Do you forgive yourself?"

She stared out into the night sky as the stars reflected off the ocean.

"Yes, I have to. It's the only way."

Turning to face him, Nina leaned in and kissed him hard.

"How did I get so lucky to have you and hold onto you after what I did?"

"I'm the lucky one," he said, placing his hand in hers.

Kathy and Lorraine stood on the steps of the hospital entryway and waited for the reunited couple to join them. The positive energy that flowed through them all was intense. Hand in hand, the two lovers, slowly strode down the path, whispering and giggling to each other. They did it. They survived all odds. Their love never died, and the time lost was now just a bad dream to them both.

Lorraine held out her hand to Nina as they approached. "Nina, I am so excited to have you back in my life, you and Brett. I have been looking into the movement of a home for you to be placed in the yard, but until that can happen, you can stay in the spare room. It's not much, but it will do for now. It won't be long, and I hope you won't mind sharing my home with me."

"Grandma, we would love to. We love you and Kathy. I will never be able to repay you enough for the sacrifices you have both made."

Kathy put her arms around Nina, "Just knowing I've helped bless you in your life is all the thanks I need. My purpose in life is to save lost and abused souls."

Chapter 33

Kathy woke from a dream feeling motivated and optimistic. She had been given a vision of the old Mayfield house which Nancy owned. 'Another Choice' had flashed on the sign out front. It was a sign, a visionary one. As she laid there and pictured the house in her mind, she could see the children playing on the swings in the backyard. She knew what she had to do. She crawled out of bed and snuck down to the kitchen.

Hunter had arrived home late the night before, and she wanted to surprise him with breakfast in bed. She fried up his favorite egg and bacon scrambler and placed the plate with fresh coffee and orange juice on the tray. She carried it upstairs and set it on the nightstand. Kissing him awake, he sat up and stretched.

"Good morning, beautiful. It smells amazing in here," he confessed, turning to the tray of food.

"Hunter, I had a dream last night. I need to call Nancy right away. Enjoy your breakfast and come downstairs when you are done. I love you."

Kathy kissed him on the cheek and ran back downstairs to her cell phone. Flipping it open, she dialed her sister and waited impatiently.

"Hi Kathy," Nancy said with cheer in her voice. "It's good to hear you. You're up early."

"Nancy, I had a dream, a vision. I couldn't wait to talk to you about it. I believe that the old Mayfield house should be turned into a multi-family home to assist women who can't afford to leave an abusive situation. I feel so strongly about this that I even have a name, 'Another Choice.' What do you think?"

Kathy paced in the kitchen, waiting for her response.

Nancy had been woken by the call and was playing it out in her mind before she answered. "I think that sounds like a great idea, Kathy. We would have to sit down and go over the expenses and come up with a formal plan, but I like it."

Kathy squealed into the phone. "Oh, thank you, Nancy. Let's get together and start working toward this, together."

Shortly after Nina's release, the gossip began to escalate around town. The uncovering of the baby had left neighbours in shock once again. The years of whispers between people in town consisted of scenarios about what Nina had done with her child. The older women believed she had taken it into the woods. The younger crowd fabricated stories about her chopping it up.

When the word got out that the Crane sisters were renovating the vacant home into a women's shelter, local businesses started making donations to help fund the cause. Mr. Flynn filled in the hole where the sandbox had been and laid new sod in the backyard. The elementary school donated a swing set to Kathy and Nancy, which Brett hauled and assembled in its place. The Nectar helped fill the home with dishes and cooking necessities. Ladies in the neighbourhood brought over knitted quilts and extra linen. Nina had taken some photographs, which she had enlarged and framed to hang throughout the house. Steve built a wooden wind chime and hung it off the awning in the backyard above the dining room window. Kathy's dream was coming true. 'Another Choice' was more than she ever imagined it could be.

The City volunteered to excuse all utility bills to the house in to help the charity home. The Police Department agreed to make routine checks on the house and watch for any kind of suspicious behavior. The sisters set up a hotline for people to call when they felt they needed answers, had suspicions, or needed to talk to someone.

Hunter rotor tilled a garden plot for Kathy against the back fence. The garden she had always dreamed of having as a child. Mallory spent a day with her, learning to till the rows and plant the seeds. They attached lattice to the fence for the peas to grow. All the produce grown was to be kept in the house for the residents. Lorraine had an apple tree planted on the opposite side of the yard. Once a week, she planned on bringing a fresh fruit pie to the families in need.

The basement had been dug, and the cement was poured. The four-level split home which Lorraine purchased for them now sat on top, ready to be lived in. Lorraine had taken Nina shopping to buy all the things they would need. They turned one room into a photo lab for her and the basement into a music room for Brett. He started playing at the Nectar again one night a week. Kathy set up an outpatient treatment plan consisting of medication, social skills training as well as vocational and recreational support. Nina started attending counselling sessions to learn to forgive herself and others and truly accept what she had done.

Brett landscaped an area in the yard for the burial site of his little girl. He put up a ten-by-ten fence with rose bushes and lilies planted all around. The service held for Lily encouraged Kathy to deal with her own inner demons. She used it as a way to say goodbye to Jessica. All the memories, personal betrayal, and blame needed to be set free. Kathy knew she had to forgive and move forward. She never allowed herself to grieve the loss of Jessica. She blocked it so far from her mind and her heart because she couldn't bear the guilt and the pain. Being there with Nina now, watching her, made Kathy feel strong.

Nina stepped forward and knelt, placing a white rose on the tiny mound. She looked up at the sky and let the sun beat down on her face. The beams that made their way through the white clouds gave her a feeling of peace as she opened her journal and began to read.

We gather in silence and hold our heads low.
Our time to say goodbye, our time to let go.
The body so close, the soul so far away,
Tear-filled eyes close as we all start to pray.

I think of your face and your beautiful smile,
There's nothing I wouldn't do just to hold you for awhile.
I had this bottled up feeling inside that needed to be set free,
I felt like my whole world was slowly coming down on me.

My thinking was distorted, reality was lost.
Is there a price on love and how much does it cost?
Doors opened and closed with me locked inside,
My disease took over and forced me to hide.

I lost you forever because of the choices I made,
I listened to the voices. It was you I betrayed.
I will try to move on and hold my head high,
My darling Lily, I'll love you till I die.

Nina closed her journal and began to cry. The events that took place that dreadful night years ago were still nothing more than a foggy blur in her mind. After being admitted, she had sometimes wondered if it had happened. Questioning why she had been committed and taken away from the world as she knew it. She sat in solitude for three years with no visitors and knew it was her punishment for what she had done to her little girl. The same amount of time was spent by the man she loved who never deserved any of it. The guilt that plagued Lorraine for splitting the two forced her to hide from the world the same way Kathy had. Nancy finally had her sister back in her life, and with the baby set free, the healing could begin. Begin for them all.

Chapter 34

The tiny church that stood at the end of the street overflowed with guests. The wedding bells chimed as Kathy walked down the aisle. She looked beautiful wearing her mother's wedding gown that Nancy had stored away, along with a few other personal belongings when they had cleaned out the house after Jessica's death. Nancy stood at the altar with Hunter and smiled at her sister. She had always felt that Kathy was alive. She was so happy to have her back in her life. So many years had been wasted. As she watched her sister walk down the aisle, Nancy could understand why she left the way she did. All the pain she had to deal with, now a memory.

Her unborn child guided her to the altar under her wedding gown. Mallory had been the flower girl, and Kathy followed the path of petals that led her to the man she loved. Once the ceremony was over, the wedding party joined Nina at Plymouth Pond to do the photo-shoot. She had found the perfect spot for them to stand. The trees that swayed slowly in the backdrop produced an essence of eternal life. The pictures held the faces of true love.

Hunter sent them to the limo to wait as he pulled a jack-knife from his pocket. Grabbing his wife's hand, he stood her before an old oak tree that towered twenty some feet above them. Placing the tip of the blade into the bark, he carved the initials H & K. Kathy stood with her hands clasped, watching him etch the letters. Tears swelled in her eyes as he blew on the tip of the knife and replaced it in his pocket.

"Now, let's go have some fun," he whispered in her ear as he pulled her toward the car.

Brett and his band *'Death Star'* played the music for the reception.

"May I have this dance?" Hunter asked his wife.

Kathy's eyes lit up. Those same words that had been asked to her so many years ago rang like an ambulance siren, whirring through her thoughts. She was just a girl then. Kathy stood in silence and remembered all the faces of the young adults dancing and kissing that night of prom as if no one had been watching. She wanted to marry the man of her dreams, and she had.

Looking up at her husband while placing her hands in his, she replied, "Of course, you can."

Kathy knew at that moment that she would never dance with another man again.

Chapter 35

The Newlyweds left that week for their honeymoon. Hunter had booked their flights around Miranda's schedule. He knew her scandalous demeanor and didn't want her causing any uncalled-for suspicion during their flight.

When they boarded the plane, he couldn't believe it. There she was five rows back helping an older man store his carry-on in the overhead compartment. Hunter grabbed Kathy's hand and directed her to their seats through the curtains into the First-Class Section.

"Oh my God!" she gasped as she ran her hand down the back of the seat. "First Class!! Thanks Babe!!"

"Nothing less for my girl," he smiled as he leaned toward her and kissed his wife.

"Have a seat. Want me to fluff your pillow?" he giggled at her.

Kathy sat in the chair and reclined it back. Hunter sat beside her and placed his hand on her belly.

"I can see him kicking."

"He's letting you know he's proud of you for making all this happen for us. Our first family vacation," Kathy spoke softly, placing her hand on his.

"Mr. Roberts, I didn't know you were on this flight," a voice called behind him. It was Miranda. She blushed at him while throwing her long dark hair over her shoulder.

"Yes, Miranda, I also believed you were off this evening," Hunter snapped back at her.

"Well, originally, but Claire got sick. I told her not to eat the calamari from the all-night seafood stand. You couldn't pay me to go near that. Lessons learned the hard way for some," she winked at Hunter.

He could feel his blood begin to boil. Hitting on a married man when he is alone in a bar is bad enough, but watching her flaunt herself in front of his wife disgusted him. He just knew that she had found out and made the arrangements to be on this flight.

"Oh, I heard you two were off on your honeymoon. I will make sure I keep you both satisfied during your trip," Miranda said while batting her eyes. "It's a pleasure to serve the Captain off duty."

Miranda flipped her hair again and turned to the back of the plane. "I'll be right back," she called back, drawing out the words.

"Do you know her well?" Kathy questioned her husband, feeling the tension between them.

"Her name is Miranda. She is one of our top flight attendants. She is an area-code-girl if you know what I mean. She likes to flirt. I promise you that there is nothing to be concerned about. I love you more than anything, Mrs. Roberts."

A smile crossed her face. "I love the sound of that."

Miranda was back within minutes. She stood in front of Hunter, clicking the ice cubes in the glass.

"Spiced rum on the rocks, heavy on the ice," she explained to him as she set it in the cup holder.

"My wife, Kathy, and I aren't drinking on this flight, Miranda. Please take it back. Bottled water is fine."

Pouting her lips, she removed the beverage from the holder and stormed down the aisle.

Kathy couldn't help but eye him in his seat. She was never the jealous type but sensed there was more going on than he had led on.

Returning with non-alcoholic beverages, Miranda placed them in their trays.

"Not much of a vacation when you can't indulge a lit," she whispered to Hunter while eyeing the pregnant belly beside him.

"Excuse me, Miranda, is it? We are going to have an amazing time on our honeymoon; my husband and I, as well as our non-alcoholic child. Thank you for the drinks. We won't need anything else and would appreciate our privacy."

Miranda glared at Kathy. "Kathy, is it? What happened to the last one, Shelly? The one that you claimed to be so in love with?" she said as her eyes darted toward Hunter. "Let me guess. Shelly found out you knocked up this one and left you. She is a silly woman, Mr. Roberts. You know I would have loved to show you a good time."

Kathy could feel her face grow hot. Her emotions started to run wild. Visions of the two played in her mind. Had they had a past? She began to feel nauseous.

She wanted to go to the toilet, but couldn't bring herself to leave them alone. This was her honeymoon, and she trusted her husband. Taking a few deep breaths, Kathy bit her tongue and sat in silence, twirling her wedding band on her finger.

"I have loved this woman for years. Your accusations are very unprofessional, even for you, Miranda. I would like to request a new attendant for the First-Class passengers."

Miranda scoffed and swallowed hard. Pushing the tray of refreshments through the divided curtain, she remained out of sight.

Hunter smiled at his wife and clutched her hand. "I'm sorry you had to deal with that. I promise you she won't be bothering us again."

Kathy had seen the brochure that showcased the suite where they would be staying. When they arrived, the tiny photos of the resort did not compare to the beauty around her. She couldn't wait to see the fireplace, Jacuzzi, and in-room bar, which were waiting for their arrival. The balcony overlooked the beach and the ocean. She had never imagined being spoiled by a man this way, a man who loved her with all his heart, her newly devoted husband.

The Bell Hop grabbed their luggage and escorted them to their room. He opened the door and stepped inside, holding it back for the anxious couple to enter. Kathy squealed and kicked off her sandals. She ran to the king-size bed draped in white goose down. Gripping the wooden post that held the canopy above, Kathy jumped up and spun around.

"Well, I should let you two get settled in and ready for the show," he smiled while bowing and tipping his hat toward Kathy.

Standing on the bed, she blushed and rubbed her belly.

Hunter giggled at the sight of this. He pulled out his wallet to tip the man.

"My name is David. If you need absolutely anything, don't hesitate to call the front desk. There are towels at the pool for use. Our in-room menu is on the desk by the window along with today's newspaper and a list of Eateries in the neighbourhood. If you choose to order from our kitchen, I highly recommend the smoked salmon with lemon citrus salsa. It is served on a bed of whole grain wild rice and a side of steamed veggies. Along with the Focaccia bread, it is simply to die for."

The Bell Hop twisted his hands in front of his chest and looked at the ceiling.

"Mmmmmm," he grinned while daydreaming of the meal he just described.

"Looks to me like we should go with your recommendation," Hunter said as he passed him the creased bills.

"I'll have to have the chicken. I'm craving garlic cream pasta with tomatoes," Kathy piped in, licking her lips.

She noticed the cravings a lot. Weird ones like eggs with mustard on toast. She never had many cravings or symptoms with Jessica. No morning sickness, and the swelling wasn't too bad. She used to sit in the rocking chair and place the speaker from the stereo against her belly to make her kick. Kathy pictured her baby girl dancing inside of her. Long ribbons in her hair and ballerina shoes played off the likeliness of a bun in her hair. Or she would imagine her being in an all-girl rock band. Having fun in the basement with her teenage friends playing instruments they learned in school. Spending hours coming up with lyrics to songs they could sing about, boys in school or on TV, words about the government and woman's rights. Jessica's singing was something she had missed the most. The tiny voice that had serenaded her daily could still be heard when Kathy wanted to listen.

"Thank you, David. Why don't you let the kitchen know we will be ready for our dinner to be served around six-thirty?"

"Sure thing, Mr. Roberts."

Hunter closed the door as the Bell Hop left the room.

"So, Mrs. Roberts, what would you like to do first?"

"I think we should nap," Kathy grinned, holding her arms out to her husband.

Hunter lay on the bed next to her and snuggled up close.

The knocking on the door jolted Hunter to his feet. He looked at the alarm clock on the nightstand. It was 6:27 PM. Kathy was still asleep in the oversized bed. Straightening his shirt, he cleared his throat and opened the door.

"Room service."

The beautiful Japanese woman dressed in white pushed the cart into the suite. Hunter was in awe as he watched her tiny frame place the tray and look up at him with stunning brown eyes.

"Your orders for the chicken and salmon tonight," she spoke while gracefully lifting the stainless-steel lids off the plates to show him their contents.

"Yes, it looks great, thank you," Hunter answered, holding out her tip. She was breathtaking. He was blushing.

She replaced the lids and pocketed the cash. Turning to the door, Hunter called her back.

"Excuse me, Miss, I'm sorry I didn't get your name. We didn't order champagne."

"Oh, let me see." The server pushed the bottle aside in the bucket. Uncovering the tiny envelope placed inside, she pulled it out and handed it to him.

Lifting the flap, Hunter removed the card tucked inside. He looked at the server and down at the note.

'Happy Honeymoon Hunter ... M.'

Replacing it with force, he looked toward Kathy. She was still fast asleep. Shoving it back in the bucket, he lifted the works off the tray.

"Thank you, but we won't be needing this."

"It was a gift," the woman replied. "No charge."

"That's fine. You may dispose of it as you wish."

"Picky man. This bottle alone is worth thousands. It is made exclusively from the Pinot Noir Grape. To receive it as a gift should be an honour. You must have exceptionally high-class taste."

Guiding her to the door, he motioned her into the hall.

"Have a good evening, Miss."

"Tenshi, my name is Tenshi. It means Angel," the beautiful woman said back to him with fire in her eyes.

As he closed the door, he leaned against it, staring at the tray of food. 'Miranda,' he thought, feeling frustrated. He had always known she had a crush on him, the way she would watch him with sinful eyes, always engaging in conversation. What he didn't realize was her crush seemed more like an obsession. The last thing he wanted was Kathy getting upset in her condition, and on their honeymoon. He decided it was best not to tell her about the wine.

"Rise and shine, sleepy bones."

"The food smells amazing," Kathy emphasized as she sat up in bed. "Why don't we enjoy it on the balcony?"

"I thought you would never ask."

Hunter wheeled the cart out to the platform overlooking the ocean. The wind was warm and calm. He placed the trays on the table and lit the candles that had been arranged in the centre.

"Come join me," he called to her.

"One minute."

Hunter filled two glasses with water from the jug and sat down.

"I kind of wanted to wait, but I'd like you to open it now," Kathy explained as she handed him a velvet box.

"Kathy..." he paused while reaching out his hand. "You shouldn't have. How lucky am I being spoiled already?"

Kathy sat across from him and watched him open the box. His eyes lit up.

"It's perfect."

Standing up, he bent over and kissed her on the cheek.

"You can set it to home time. So, no matter where you are, we are together at the same time every day."

Removing it from the box, he slid it on his wrist.

"I love it, and thank you."

"You're welcome. Now let's eat. I'm starving."

The cobbled streets underneath Kathy's shoes made her wobble back and forth. They took a walk around the Resort after their meal to check out the sizzling nightlife. Kathy spotted a tiny flower shop standing alone across the street. Hunter noticed the look on her face.

"Would you like some?" he asked, already knowing the answer.

She smiled as she pulled him toward the stand.

Kathy pointed at different varieties of the stunning flowers with excitement. The merchant followed her gestures, pulling stems from the bins. He tied the bundle of purple Stork's Bill, Buttercups, and Oleanders with a yellow ribbon. Passing it to Kathy, she stuck her nose in and breathed deep.

"It smells like Heaven," she exclaimed.

Hunter paid the man and grabbed her hand. "Are you up for a moonlit walk along the beach?"

"Yes, of course. Thank you for this wonderful evening," Kathy smiled as she held the flowers close.

The couple made their way through the bustle of the crowds and toward the sound of the ocean. Every star shone down and reflected off the water, illuminating the night sky. Kathy removed her shoes and stuck her toes in the sand.

"That feels amazing. You should try it."

Hunter laughed, "I'll leave my shoes on tonight."

Down to the edge of the water, they strolled, holding hands, and enjoying the scenery. There were groups of people along the beach, singing and telling stories.

"Mr. Roberts, is that you?" a soft voice called toward them.

As they turned their heads in the direction of the woman, Kathy's heart sank. She was stunning. Who was she?

Stepping closer, the woman held out a bottle of wine. Hunter could feel his face grow hot.

"Who is this?" Kathy snapped, pulling her hand from his.

"My name is Tenshi," she said, batting her long eyelashes.

Hunter cleared his throat and piped in. "She works at the hotel. She brought our meal to the room."

"Thank you for the wine, Mr. Roberts. Would you like to try some?" Tenshi offered, holding out the bottle.

"What wine?" Kathy asked, staring at him for answers.

"It came with the meal. I sent it back," he answered quickly.

Kathy felt uneasy. The way the woman before her gazed at her husband created a knot in the pit of her stomach. Her emotions started to run wild. Her nose tingled as she tried to fight back the tears. A vision of Miranda appeared in her mind. She had the same feelings now as she did on the plane. Throwing the flowers to the ground, Kathy turned towards the lights of the vacation spot and started to run.

"Kathy!! Wait!" Hunter called after her.

Tenshi bent down and pulled a stem from the bundle. She slid it through her hair and behind her ear.

"I'm sorry for that. I have to go," Hunter apologized.

"Lucky woman," Tenshi replied as she slid her hand into his coat pocket.

Turning towards the Resort, Hunter ran across the beach after his wife. He could see her in the distance and followed her through the streets to the hotel.

"Kathy!!" He called to her as she reached the front doors.

She looked back at him before stepping inside. Picking up his pace, Hunter hurried behind her.

The metal doors slid open. Out of breath, he made it into the elevator beside her as the doors closed behind.

She couldn't look at him. The tears streamed down her cheeks as she fixed her gaze on the floor.

"Honey, why did you run? What's wrong?" Hunter pleaded to his wife.

"I saw the way she was looking at you. It was the same look from the attendant on the plane."

Hunter placed his hand on her chin, pulling her face towards his.

"Kathy, you have nothing to worry about. That woman was drunk."

"I'm tired. I need to go to bed," Kathy said as the elevator doors opened on their floor.

Hunter pulled the room key from his wallet. He pushed the door open as the tiny light turned green. Kathy entered and kicked off her shoes. Lying on the bed, she wrapped her arms around one of the many pillows and closed her eyes, "Good night, Hunter."

Chapter 36

Chapter 36

Kathy could see him standing on the runway. The Boeing 757 towered over him. There was a stewardess pushing a cart towards him. She could see it bumping along the pavement as the tiny wheels carried the tray topped with a covered silver platter. She watched them as the woman approached her husband, coming to a stop. Her long dark hair blew in the breeze, whipping against his cheek. She placed her hand on the lid and wrapped her fingers around the handle. They were talking, but Kathy couldn't make out what they were saying. The whistle of the wind howled through her ears. Gracefully, the woman lifted the lid and stared at Hunter. The tray was empty. Kathy squinted her eyes in hopes to see more. Just then, the wind picked up. Along with it, a tiny card emerged from the tray, dancing in the air. Hunter reached for it with no luck. Kathy's eyes were locked on it as it blew out of sight.

Kathy opened her eyes and looked around the room. Hunter was asleep next to her. She sat on the edge of the bed and rubbed her eyes. She closed them and replayed the dream she just had. What did it mean? Staring out the window, Kathy stood up and tip-toed into the bathroom. Stepping out of her nightgown, she turned on the shower and let the warm water cleanse her. Tears streamed down her cheeks as she remembered the events of the evening. Something wasn't right. She could feel it. She felt betrayed, lost in her thoughts. Kathy turned off the water and reached for a towel. Wrapping it around her body, she crept into the bedroom and opened her suitcase. She could hear Hunter breathing deeply. Glancing at him, she slipped a sun dress over her head and pulled her hair back into a bun.

She craved fresh air. She could feel the baby tossing in her womb. The movements were slowly increasing intensity into cramps. Kathy knew that the stress she was feeling must be affecting the baby. Sliding the top drawer of the desk open, she pulled out a note pad and pen. Tearing off the top sheet, Kathy scribbled a note to Hunter and placed it on his nightstand.

The courtyard was bustling with tourists and employees. The sun was shining bright in the clearest blue sky she had ever seen. The aroma of the Mediterranean style bistro across the cobbled street filled her nose. Kathy's mouth began to water as her hunger pangs crept in.

"Would you like to join us for brunch?"

Kathy spun around to face the voice behind her. A young man dressed in white held out his arm and bowed before her.

"Oh, you startled me," Kathy blushed.

"Let me assist you. I have the perfect table waiting. You look hungry," the man said as he glanced at her belly.

"Yes, we are," Kathy giggled as she placed her arm in his.

"Will it be just the two of you?"

Kathy scanned the crowds before replying. "Yes, just us," she said softly.

The man led her across the path and into the dining area. Making their way to the back of the patio, he pulled out a chair and motioned for her to sit.

"Thank you," Kathy nodded.

"My pleasure Miss. Will you be having the Chef's specialty this morning? Gringo has created a beef and pepper Panini along with a cream of vegetable soup that would satisfy any craving."

"Yes, that sounds lovely. I will have a green tea and a glass of water as well."

"Right away," he nodded while spinning back toward the kitchen.

Kathy stared out at the ocean. The waves lapped at the shore. People littered the beach, playing volleyball and basking in the sun. The reggae music that played in the background made her smile. Her nerves began to settle as she closed her eyes and listened.

"Is this seat taken?"

Kathy opened her eyes and stared at Hunter as he slid the chair from under the table and sat down.

"Why didn't you wake me?" He asked with puppy dog eyes.

"I wasn't feeling well. I just wanted to get some air," Kathy snapped as she turned her head toward the ocean.

Hunter placed his hand on hers. "Honey, I am sorry you are so upset. I promise you that there is no reason to be. This is our honeymoon. That woman was drunk. Aside from that, I find it very unprofessional of her to have kept that bottle of wine. Why don't we have a nice lunch together and take a walk down the beach?"

"Good morning, Sir," the waiter said as he acknowledged Hunter.

"It is a beautiful day, isn't it? Bring me what she is having," he said as he held out a dollar bill for the man.

"As you wish," the man replied, placing the bill in his pocket. "Thank you."

"Kathy, it's not good for you or the baby to get so worked up."

Kathy scoffed as the dream she had played through her mind.

Feeling her tension, Hunter grabbed her hand. "What would you like to do today, my love?"

The waiter returned with both meals and placed them in front of the newlyweds.

"Can I bring you anything else?" he asked.

"No, this looks great. That will be all," Hunter answered as he picked up his spoon to stir the soup that steamed in the tiny bowl.

As soon as the waiter turned away, another man stood in his place.

"Hunter Roberts! I thought that was you!" the man exclaimed.

He was tall and handsome with a mouth full of perfect teeth that formed a smile under his plump lips. He removed his sunglasses and reached out his hand towards Kathy.

"You must be the Mrs. we have all heard so much about."

Kathy glanced at Hunter before responding. "Yes, my name is Kathy."

Shaking her hand with a firm grip, he introduced himself as Captain Caleb Conway.

"A few of us boys flew down to perfect our golf swing," he chuckled. "You should join us," he said as he stared at Hunter.

"No, I am here with my wife on my honeymoon. We are going to..."

"I think that's a great idea," Kathy blurted out, cutting him off mid-sentence.

Hunter's eyes darted toward her as he tilted his head.

"Well, look at that," Caleb grinned. "Looks like you found yourself a keeper."

"Kathy, I wanted to spend the day with you," Hunter insisted as he leaned forward in his chair.

"I'm exhausted. I wouldn't mind reading for a bit in one of the hammocks along the beach. You go have some fun with your friends."

Placing his hands in the air, Hunter shook his head. "All right, all right, I get it. You are sick of your husband already," he laughed while giving her a wink.

"Perfect," Caleb yelled out. "Tee off is at one o'clock. The boys will be surprised to see you. I'll have a round of cold beers waiting to celebrate the tying of the knot."

Caleb adjusted his sunglasses as he turned and walked away.

"Sweetie, you shouldn't have done that. I was looking forward to our day together," Hunter pouted as he bit into his sandwich.

"Go have some fun. I'll be fine," Kathy whispered.

The streets were bustling with tourists. Kathy wandered in and around the souvenir stands lining the walkways. Her fingers brushed along the satin scarves and keychains. The aroma of fresh-baked bread filled her nose and made her mouth water. Rubbing her belly, she whispered, "You aren't hungry already, are you?" Smiling to herself, Kathy stood in front of an old brick building. The thick cedar wood-framed windows grabbed her attention. They were weathered and faded. She had always loved the look of aged wood. So many stories held in the grain, worn out over time. The tiny sign in the window read OPEN. A small boy carrying a balloon in one hand and a book in the other exited the store. The bamboo that hung in the window clinked against the glass. Kathy grabbed the handle before it had a chance to close. She stepped inside and looked around. It was breathtaking. The shelves lining the walls from floor to ceiling showcased thousands of book spines. There were rolling wooden ladders placed throughout the store. A stained-glass window placed in the steeple allowed the sun to shine down, illuminating the shop with all the colors of the rainbow. Kathy giggled as she made her way around the shop.

"My, my, look what we have here. You must be due at any minute. May I help you find anything in particular?"

Kathy turned to face the soft voice. She couldn't help but notice the multiple strands of beads that were wrapped around both of her arms. Her hair was tied back into a bun, making the glasses that sat on her nose appear much larger than her face. She was staring at Kathy now.

"Oh, hello, I'm sorry. I am just browsing. It must be quite soothing to spend your days here," Kathy replied.

The woman eyed her up and down. "Yes, I have been coming here since I was a little girl. My grandfather opened this bookstore moons ago. People don't cherish the pages in a leather-bound nowadays. All this technology has everyone holding devices and so on. I will never understand it. The smell of a new book and the way the pages feel so crisp at your fingertips is half the pleasure."

"Yes, I must agree with you," Kathy blushed.

"So, tell me, Miss, what brings you here today?"

"I am on my honeymoon," Kathy answered as she gazed at the hardwood floor.

The woman looked around the store. "I could have sworn I saw you come in alone."

Kathy sighed and flashed her a smile.

"Okay, okay, I won't pry. You just help yourself to a book of your choosing, and it's on the house. I will let the cashier know I said so. You take care of that baby of yours."

The woman turned and headed into the back before Kathy had a chance to thank her. She felt good. She felt blessed. She felt silly for doubting Hunter. She wasn't going to let any of the recent events ruin her trip. This was the honeymoon she had always dreamed about. The books that surrounded her soothed her. Kathy spent half an hour scanning the titles before she settled on one.

'*Marriage is a garden, Tend to it daily.*' Sounds fitting, she thought and proceeded to the till.

The lady at the cashier pulled the book from Kathy's fingers and slid a bookmark inside. Glancing at the cover, she looked back up at Kathy. "Enjoy the book and your honeymoon," she sneered.

"Thank you," Kathy replied, feeling her cheeks grow red. She placed the book in her purse and left the store.

The beach was a few blocks away. Feeling a bit tired, Kathy boarded a shuttle and let the tiny caravan take her there.

As she stepped out and towards the beach, the music and sounds of people laughing intensified. Children with their tiny shovels were building sandcastles along the shoreline. She thought of Lily and embraced her belly. She watched the sailboats and teams of beach volleyball as she made her way to an empty cabana. Kathy stepped inside and sat on the white linen covered cot. She pulled the book and a bottle of water from her bag. It was hot and humid. She was happy to be out of the direct sunlight. She stared out into the ocean, watching the waves lap the shore. The reflection of the sun off the bright blue water made her squint. She loved the rays and the way they made her feel. 'Ray,' she thought to herself. That's it. Her baby boy was going to be named Ray. Her middle name was Rae, and as Hunter gets the last name, she figured it was only fair she gets the first. A smile formed on her lips as she laid back and closed her eyes.

"Fore!" Caleb yelled as he placed his club on the sod. Stepping back, he bowed and motioned Hunter to step to the tee.

The Beer Cart approached the men. The driver was stunning with her long hair and deep, rich tan. "You boys need a drink," she winked at Hunter mid-swing.

BOOF!! The golf club hit the ground hard, leaving a half-moon divot. The other men burst into laughter and cheer. "That's a stroke, Roberts!"

Scoffing, Hunter took his stance and swung again.

"Nice shot," the woman squealed.

Hunter returned his club to the bag and pulled out his wallet.

"No way, brothers. This one's on me," Caleb laughed as he paid her for the ice-cold beverages. "The ladies just can't resist Hunter, my man. Keep the change and come back soon."

The woman's eyes lit up as she placed the hefty tip in her pouch and drove away.

"Jesus, I still can't believe you actually tied the knot. You of all people," Caleb snickered. "I thought for sure you and 'Miranda the Late-Night Veranda' were going places."

Hunter glared at his buddy. "Look, Caleb, Kathy doesn't know about my past with her, and I am going to keep it that way. There is no point in stirring up muddy water, so you best keep your mouth shut around her. You hear me?"

"Okay, okay, don't get all fired up. Your secret is safe with me," Caleb replied with a wink.

The men loaded the golf cart and sped down the course.

Kathy opened her eyes and sat forward. Realizing she had dozed off, she gathered her things and headed back down the beach. The cool air hit her face as she entered the hotel. She wondered if Hunter was in the room waiting for her. Kathy took the elevator to their floor and hurried toward the room. She stuck the card key in the lock and opened the door.

"Hunter, my love, I'm sorry. I fell asleep," Kathy spoke loudly, as she entered the room and looked toward the balcony. He wasn't there, and there was no sign that he had been. Kathy sighed and set her things on the side table. Sliding the balcony door open, she stepped onto the landing and peered down into the street. It was five o'clock, and could feel the hunger pains as her stomach growled. 'Where was he,' she thought. Kathy turned around, returning to her suite. She thought of the new book and decided to read it while she waited for her husband.

There were extra pillows on the top shelf of the closet. Hunters' jacket was hanging on the tiny knob. As she slid it off and laid it over her arm, a small card cascaded to the floor. Kathy stared at it as if in a trance. The dream she had earlier flooded her mind. She couldn't reach it then, but she could now. Bending forward, she flipped it in her fingers and peeled it off the floor.

Two sides. Two different women. God only knows how many more. She read and re-read each side over and over.

'Happy Honeymoon Hunter...M' on one side. *'Tenshi 687-3867 xoxo'* on the other. Kathy instantly felt sick. She felt betrayed. She felt lost. Her mind spun just as fast as her stomach, tossing and turning. Kathy ran to the toilet and heaved hard. She could feel Ray kicking as she started to cry. She was bawling now. The tears streamed down her face and into the porcelain bowl. She sat on the side of the tub and opened her clenched hand. As badly as she wanted this to all be a dream, it was real. It was right in front of her.

She could hear the lock unlatch in the other room. Kathy's eyes darted toward the door.

"Babe, I'm so sorry I'm so late. Me and the boys..." Hunter trailed off as he stared at his wife in tears on the side of the tub. "Honey, what's wrong? Are you okay?"

"Okay? No, I'm not okay," Kathy screamed at him, flicking the card in his direction. Hunter stepped toward her and reached out his hand.

"Don't touch me," she screamed again. "I trusted you. Who are you? You are not the man I married. The man I thought I knew."

"Sweetie, calm down. It isn't what you think," Hunter pleaded with her as he stumbled against the sink.

"I think I know exactly what this is," Kathy cried as she stood up. "Are you drunk?"

Hunter gained his balance and stepped back. "I had a few with the boys, Kathy. Is that really such a crime? You're the one who insisted I go."

Kathy pushed her way past her husband. "Maybe you should have a few more. Maybe you should go and get a blow job while you're at it." Kathy was furious. She couldn't believe the things she was saying, but she felt them.

"Maybe I will. God knows I won't get one from you."

"How dare you! And on our Honeymoon."

"How dare me, Kathy? I do everything for you. I stood by you when you became this other person you used to be. You lied to me for years, Kathy. You are carrying my child, and I just found out your real name."

Kathy could feel her blood begin to boil. She was hot. She needed air. She needed to run again like she had so many years ago. Grabbing her purse, she bolted through the door and into the elevator.

"Are you all right, Miss?"

Kathy glanced at the elderly man beside her in the enclosed car. She watched the lighted numbers on the panel descend to the main floor. As the doors slid open, Kathy rushed outside. People were staring at her now. She knew she had to calm down. Taking deep breaths as she walked down the street, Kathy began to focus. Fumbling in her purse, she pulled out a tissue. She wiped her eyes and brushed her hands through her hair. None of it made sense to her. The events that had taken place since she was sitting on the plane showcased themselves in her mind. She wanted safety. She wanted Nancy. Kathy thought of the old woman in the bookstore. She was the only familiar thing she had in that moment. Gaining her composure, Kathy headed back toward the shop.

"Falafel, get your falafel! Fresh, hot, and ready to go."

Kathy felt her hunger return as she glanced at the overweight man behind the stand. Pulling her wallet from her purse, she approached him, "I will take one, please."

"Well now, are you sure you wouldn't like two?" He chuckled.

Kathy smiled at him and blushed.

"Yes, she will take two," a voice piped in behind her.

Kathy recognized the voice. 'It couldn't be,' she thought. Swinging around, she was face to face with the last person she wanted to see, expected to see. It was Miranda, looking more stunning than ever. Kathy could feel her face grow hot. She felt ugly next to her with puffy eyes and an extra forty pounds.

"Down here all by yourself, I see. Where is that handsome husband of yours?" Miranda cooed. "Let me guess, something important came up. With work, with play, perhaps. Being the other woman ain't always easy. You learn you don't talk to a man swinging an axe."

Kathy stepped back with fire in her eyes. Her fists were clenched once again. She could feel her fingernails digging into her palms. She wanted to swing. To wipe that self-satisfied look off her face. Ray kicked hard in her womb, causing Kathy to cradle over. Her stomach tightened as she leaned against the brick wall. She felt a moment of relief as she stood up straight. She also felt wet, very wet. Kathy stared at the puddle between her legs. Her water just broke. As she stared at the amniotic fluid running down her calf, she knew she was going into labour.

Chapter 37

Hunter heard a knock at the door. As he made his way towards it, the banging grew louder. Pulling it open, he veered his head to the right to avoid the tiny fist heading straight for him.

"Miranda!? What the hell are you doing here?" Hunter cursed as he laid his eyes on her. "You need to leave right now. You need to leave me the hell alone."

"It's Kathy. She is on her way to the hospital, St. Marks. I called her an ambulance. Her water broke," Miranda explained.

Hunters' eyes grew wild. "What?? Where did this happen? Why were you with my wife?" He was instantly sober. He had to be. He needed to get to her as fast as he could. Letting the door slam behind him, Hunter ran down the hall. He took the stairwell two steps at a time. He was outside and into a cab before he even realized it.

"Take me to St. Mark's hospital!!" Hunter yelled at the driver.

As the Cabbie sped through the streets, Hunter began to panic in the back seat. He felt terrible for not being honest with his wife and not being there for her from the start. 'He was a changed man,' he thought to himself.

The taxi wheeled up to the Emergency entrance. Hunter opened the door and stepped out as it came to a stop. He threw the cash into the front seat and stepped out. "Keep the change."

He ran through the sliding glass doors and approached the front desk. "Maternity, where is Maternity? My life is in labour."

The lady behind the desk looked up and over her glasses. Pointing at the elevator, she mumbled, "Second floor."

The doors chimed and slid open. Hunter raced inside and pressed the button labelled two. His heart was racing. He prayed that he made it in time. He wanted so badly to be there with her through the delivery. To hold her hand and support her. Pushing the doors apart, he hurried to the desk.

"My wife, Kathy Roberts, was brought in by ambulance. Where is she?" Hunter could barely get the words out.

"Down the hall, fourth door on the left," the Nurse directed him.

Hunter sped down the hall and into the room. There she was. There they were. Kathy was propped up in bed, cradling their newborn son.

"Kathy, I'm so sorry. Please forgive me," Hunter pleaded as he approached the bed.

Kathy smiled and motioned him closer. "Shhh, it's alright now. Would you like to hold your son?"

The tears began to stream down his face as he held out his arms. Pulling the baby in close, Hunter leaned down and kissed Kathy on the forehead. "I love you so much."

He stared down at the tiny life in his hands. "I love you too, my son."

"His name is Ray," Kathy whispered.

"Ray Roberts, it's perfect, Kathy," Hunter exclaimed.

Watching the two of them, Kathy finally felt as if she had the perfect family she had always dreamt about as a child. The past and her nightmares that she had tried so hard to forget made her the woman, the wife and the mother she so desperately wanted to be.

Chapter 38

The Roberts' family boarded the plane, making their way to their seats. Hunter had been doting over Kathy since they left the hospital. He promised that he would never allow her to be alone again. He was going to make it up to her for ruining their honeymoon.

"Well, isn't he just the cutest bundle of joy," the stewardess squealed as she handed Kathy a pillow. "I thought you may be needing this."

"Thank you, and yes, he is," Kathy replied as she smiled down at her baby.

"Now you just call if there is anything I can get you on your flight today," the woman remarked as she winked at Hunter. Kathy bit her tongue and pretended not to notice.

Hunter nodded and thanked the woman. The seat belt lights came on. The loudspeaker crackled as the Pilot began to speak. "Good afternoon, and welcome aboard Flight 735. Ladies and Gentlemen, I'd like to direct your attention to the attendants in-aisle who will be demonstrating the safety features on this aircraft."

Kathy watched the lady buckle the seat belt. She glanced at the pamphlet in the pocket in front of her.

Hunter squeezed her thigh and smiled as the plane began to take flight.

The Pilot began to speak again. "We will be arriving at our destination in three hours and fifteen minutes. We are lucky enough to have two of our own with us today, Captain Hunter Roberts and top attendant Miranda Mayfield. Now sit back, relax and enjoy the flight."

Kathy couldn't believe what she had just heard. She glared at Hunter.

Hunter placed Kathy's hand in his. "Honey, I had no idea she was on this flight. Please don't let that upset you. Who cares about her? She means nothing to me."

Kathy stared out the window. She couldn't shake the feeling that something wasn't right. Things didn't add up. She placed the pillow against the window. Reclining her seat, she cradled Ray close and drifted off to sleep.

She could hear the baby crying in the crib beside her. She was almost fully alert when the crying stopped. The silence jolted her awake. Why wasn't he crying anymore? Kathy sat up on the side of the bed and stared toward the baby in her bedroom. She could hear him cooing and laughing. She rubbed her eyes and stared harder. A little girl with long blonde hair stood over him, reaching into the crib. She turned towards Kathy and smiled. It was Jessica. Kathy stood up and reached for her. Jessica walked to the doorway and looked back at her. "I love you, mommy," she said as she disappeared into the light.

"Jessica!!" Kathy yelled as she opened her eyes and sat forward in her seat. She looked around and realized where she was. The lady across the aisle was watching her. Hunter was next to her holding, Ray in his arms.

Rubbing the back of her head, he reassured her. "Honey, it's ok. You had a bad dream. I got Ray here safe, and I got you too." He leaned over and kissed her on the cheek.

Kathy rubbed her eyes and leaned back. She wanted to go back to sleep. She wanted to see her daughter again, to hold her.

She opened her eyes and whispered to her husband, "Where is Jessica?"

Squeezing her hand, he whispered back, "Shhhh, it's alright."

The vibration of the wheels on the runway jolted Kathy awake. They had arrived, and she couldn't be happier to be home. Ray was still fast asleep in Hunter's arms. Looking at him, she said, "You sure have a way with him, Daddy."

Hunter smiled from ear to ear. "How are you feeling, my love? You were out cold. I didn't want to wake you. You need your rest."

"I feel a lot better, thank you."

The plane stopped and the passengers started grabbing their belongings from the overhead compartments as they exited the aircraft.

"Here, let me take him," Kathy said, holding out her arms.

The couple made their way into the airport towards the baggage carousel. The buzzer sounded, forcing the luggage out of the shoot onto the metal tracks. Ray started to fuss as the commotion around them grew louder.

"I'll grab the bags, Kathy. Go ahead and find somewhere to sit and feed him. He must be starving."

Kathy shifted Ray in her arms as she made her way to an empty row of seats by the window. Lifting her blouse, she placed him on her breast, covering herself with a blanket. The release of the pressure felt good. She could hear him sucking harder and faster. Memories of Jessica raced into her mind as she replayed her most recent dream. She watched her husband pulling a suitcase from the carousel. She watched as Miranda crept up behind him, placing a floral lei on his head.

Startled, Hunter turned to face her. "Miranda! What in the hell are you doing?" Grabbing the lei, he threw it on the floor. "I told you to leave me alone!"

"That should be me over there," she sneered, eyeing Kathy. "What in the hell are you doing with a woman like that is the question?"

Pulling the suitcases towards Kathy, Hunter turned his head. "If you continue this behaviour, I will see to it that you are suspended for harassment. You have been warned."

Kathy stared at him. That same feeling crept back up from the bottom of her stomach. She could feel her face get hot. The taste of jealousy filled her mouth. She clenched her teeth, trying not to bite her tongue, yet trying to bite it to keep the angry words from escaping once again. She sat wild-eyed and silent as Hunter approached her.

"Are my two favorite people in this world ready to go home?" he asked while peeking under the blanket to look at his son.

She wanted to ask him what was said. She wanted to know why this woman kept popping up in their life. She wanted to, but she couldn't make out the words. Ray had fallen asleep. Kathy gently pulled him out from under her shirt, wrapping him in the blanket. Standing up, she passed him to Hunter. Standing there as if in a trance, the ringing in her ears became louder. Her eyes fixated on Miranda. She could see the lei on the floor. The colors seemed to enhance, mesmerizing her. Kathy was running now, running towards the flowery strand. Bending down, she scooped it up without stopping. Her grip tightened as she neared Miranda. She was behind her now. She was screaming as she stretched the band over her head and pulled back. Miranda gasped as she fought for air. Placing her fingers under the cord around her neck, she pulled it forward, trying to break free from Kathy's hold.

"Security!!" she cried in despair.

Hunter was beside them now, yelling at Kathy to let her go. Ray wailed as the commotion intensified. Officers were running towards the women. Bystanders stared with confusion and concern. Grabbing Kathy by the arms, they quickly detained her. Miranda dropped to her knees, choking for air. Hunter helped her to her feet. "I'm so sorry," he said while turning to follow the men escorting his wife across the terminal.

Chapter 39

Hunter stared at the wall, listening to the clock tick. He directed his attention to the woman at the reception desk. She was seriously overweight. Hunter watched her sneaking crackers from the drawer. Brushing her hands together, the woman stood up and swallowed fast.

"Dr. Greenfield will see you now," she said as the office door opened.

"You must be Mr. Roberts. Please come in and have a seat," Dr. Greenfield acknowledged as he held the door for him to enter. He was a short, stalky man. He tried to hide the fact that he was balding, combing over the hair that he had left. Hunter sat in the leather-bound chair, rubbing his hands through his hair.

"What happened to my wife?" Hunter questioned with desperation in his voice.

"Mr. Roberts, it seems as though your wife suffered from a form of postpartum psychosis. This is quite rare but can affect women very quickly after childbirth. Hormones, family history of mental illness, and sudden triggers can cause this illness. I understand that your wife,

Kathy holds employment at the O'Hanagan Psychiatric Hospital."

"Yes, that is correct. My wife isn't crazy, Dr. She doesn't belong in there as a patient."

"Mr. Roberts, we believe admitting her is the best solution for everyone at this time. We have her on suicide watch. Women who experience this type of condition are at a very high risk. We do not want her to endanger herself or anyone else. Her delusions that her late daughter, Jessica, is alive is very alarming. Now I have researched her family history and found no reported mental illness. I understand that Kathy went through severe trauma losing her first child. She ran from her life. She created a new one instead of dealing with the loss. Post-traumatic stress can spiral out of control if not managed properly. The woman she attacked has declined to press charges, so at the very least, you have that to be thankful for."

"This is all my fault. I should have been honest with Kathy. Maybe none of this would have happened. She doesn't deserve to be locked up. She should be home with our son."

"We have her on a combination of mood stabilizers for now. The staff in the Ward are going to take special care of Kathy. It is a blessing that she knows them all very well, as this may help her familiarize herself with reality. It is in the best interest of your child that he does not visit her until we can rationalize the situation further. This type of mania may cause Kathy to want to harm the boy. We don't want to take any chances."

Hunter looked at the Dr. with tears in his eyes. "I understand. May I see her now?"

"Yes, that should be fine. Keep the conversation light. Just reassure her that you are going to be with her every step of the way."

"I will. Thank you."

Hunter smelled the roses he had bought for Kathy as he waited for the elevator to reach the fifth floor. Stepping out, he approached the Nurse's Station.

"Hi, I am here to see my wife, Kathy Roberts."

"You must be Hunter. You are as handsome as she declares," the woman blushed while sweeping her hair back. "Congratulations on the birth of your baby boy. I'm sure he must be cute as a button. Kathy is down the hall, the last door on the right. She was out cold when I checked on her during my rounds. Go on in. She will be happy to see you."

Slowly, Hunter made his way down the hall. Drying the tear that ran down his cheek as he wished this was all just a bad dream. He stood outside the door for a few minutes before entering. He wasn't sure what to expect. The guilt that he felt was increasing. Part of him wanted to turn around and run. Run from the hospital, and this new life that he had created. The same one that he had so desperately wanted. This wasn't what it was supposed to be. Taking a deep breath, Hunter pushed the door open and peered in at his wife. She was lying on her side facing the window. He could hear her breathing deeply, and this relieved him. Quietly, he crept to the side of the bed, setting the roses on the side table. He lowered himself into the chair and watched her. She looked so peaceful. She looked sedated.

Twenty minutes had passed before a nurse entered the room. Hunter held his finger against his lips, ushering her to be silent. Standing from the chair, he motioned her into the hall.

"I don't want to wake her. She needs her rest. I would like to leave her a note for when she wakes. Is it possible to get a pen and paper to do so?" Hunter questioned.

"Of course, Mr. Roberts. I will be right back." The nurse headed back down the hall and returned with the items.

"Thank you," he said, creeping back into the room.

He stared at the blank page and tapped the pen. There were so many things that he had wanted to say. He didn't know where to begin or how this all would end.

Dearest Kathy,

You have been my guiding light to the man I always wanted to be. I am a jet-setter, a free bird, the captain of my own ship. I have tried to change. I thought I had. You have changed so much. I feel so overwhelmed, powerless. I used to have so much control over my life. It's not like it used to be. You aren't like you used to be. I miss Shelly, the woman I fell in love with. When the truth came out about your past, I never understood how you could just run from your life, but I do now. I feel that same urge to leave all this craziness behind me. I am to blame for a lot of it. I don't think I can be the man you need me to be to get through it.

You are my wife, the mother of my son and I will always love you, but I'm not sure love is enough anymore. I'm truly sorry...

He stared at the words on the paper. He envisioned her waking to read it. How could he break her heart that way? He thought about the effects it would have while she was in such an emotional state. Folding the paper, he placed it in his pocket and left the room.

Hunter placed the pen on the counter at the station and thanked the nurse. His heart was beating faster as he waited for the elevator to reach the main floor. He was almost running to the front door, to the fresh air outside. It hit his face and shot shivers up his spine. He couldn't think straight. Did he really want to leave his wife and his son? Hunter opened the car door. Climbing into the driver's seat, he broke down in tears. The emotions flowed through him like a rushing river crashing against the shore. He laid his head on the steering wheel, letting it all out.

BRING!!! BRING!!! Hunter jumped in his seat at the sound of his phone in his pocket. It was Nancy. Staring at the screen, he declined the call. He couldn't talk to her in his current state. He had to get his composure. He had to clear his head. Putting the car in reverse, Hunter sped out of the parking lot.

"Need another?" the bartender asked, tilting the empty glass towards Hunter.

He certainly didn't need one, but he wanted one. He wanted so badly to go back in time, back to the days when he had first met Shelly. If he couldn't be with her, he could be with the memory of her. Hunter motioned for the man behind the counter to bring him one more.

He stared at the jukebox in the corner, the tiny machine that changed his life. C18, '*The Traveller*' had blared through the speaker when he first saw her. She was beautiful. There was something mysterious about her, and Hunter knew it. If only he had known to the extent that this was true. Her choice of song intrigued him. He had watched her sway her hips to the sound of the music. He wanted to approach her. He ordered another drink and stood up. He was too late. She was gone. His eyes darted around the room before locking on her once more. She was sitting alone. Now was his chance.

"I knew I would find you here," Steve said as he placed his hand on Hunter's shoulder.

Startled, Hunter turned to face him. "Shit, man, you scared me."

"Not my intention, but you scared my wife. Nancy said she has been trying to reach you. Look, I understand what you must be going through, but you have a little boy at home who needs you more than ever right now."

"You don't know shit," Hunter sneered, spilling his drink as he threw his arms in the air.

"I know you have had too much to drink. Let me take you home."

Hunter gazed at the floor, swaying on his stool, "Fine."

Chapter 40

Three weeks had passed since Kathy had been admitted to the hospital. Along with the meds, he had prescribed a few shock therapy treatments. She had been very cooperative with Dr. Greenfield. She had to be if she wanted to be released. He was convinced that she had returned to an acceptable level of awareness regarding the death of Jessica and allowed her to be released. Hunter arrived shortly after lunch to take her home. Kathy was nervous. She felt ashamed that she had abandoned her baby boy and her husband. Nancy had taken on so much, leaving Kathy forever grateful to her sister. Things were going to be different now. They had to be.

The couple pulled into the driveway and went inside. Nancy was waiting with Ray in her arms. Taking him from her, she kissed his head and whispered, "Thank you."

The chains holding the tiny wooden seat on the swing set creaked in the wind. Winter was fast approaching; Kathy could feel it in the air. The trees that enclosed the yard were still robed in green. How could this be, she wondered to herself. The purple and white striped pyjamas were piled in a heap on the ground. Shadows cast across them as the swing swayed back and forth. She recognized the print. They belonged to Jessica.

Opening her eyes, Kathy sat up in bed. Ray was sleeping in the bassinet. Her husband was gone. She looked around the room, squinting at the sun shining through the window. Quietly, she pulled her robe off the hook and went downstairs. The coffee maker was on. The pot was half full and still warm. Hunter had left a note saying he was attending a meeting and would be home for supper. Kathy took a roast out of the freezer and placed it in the sink to thaw. She was scheduled for an appointment with Dr. Greenfiled at 2:30 PM. He wanted her to check-in and discuss how her first night home had been. Pouring herself a cup of coffee, Kathy checked the time. She couldn't shake the feeling that she had been in that same yard from her dream. Making her way into the bathroom, she turned the taps on full blast to fill the tub. Peeking into the bedroom, she listened for Ray. He was still sound asleep.

Kathy vigorously scrubbed at her skin. She wanted to wash away all the pain that had entered her mind and her body. She had spent half of her life pretending. Pretending to die so long ago, now pretending to have acceptance for all the things she could not. 'Just one look,' she thought to herself. If she hurried, she could follow her instincts to the place so vivid in her mind and still make it back to meet Dr. Greenfield.

She listened to the water swirl down the drain as she dried herself off. Fast and forceful, just like it had been under the bridge on that dreary June night. She couldn't save her daughter then, but maybe she could reach her now.

Ray was awake in the bassinet. His big brown eyes stared up at her as he began to fuss. Kathy pulled on a pair of leggings and an oversized sweatshirt. Lifting him out, she changed his diaper and grabbed a bottle from the fridge.

He was half asleep when they backed out of the driveway. 'Good,' she thought. Kathy didn't want any distractions. Clicking off the radio, she followed the map in her mind.

"Hi, you've reached Hunter Roberts. You know what to do."

He listened to the voicemail recording and waited for the beep. "Good afternoon, Mr. Roberts. This is Dr. Greenfield calling. Kathy didn't show up for her appointment, and I have not been able to reach her. If you could kindly return my call, it would be greatly appreciated. Thank you."

Hunter fumbled for his phone. Listening to the recording, he hung up and returned the call. "Hi, Dr. Greenfield, it's Hunter Roberts calling. I received your message. I just got out of a meeting and was heading home. I haven't spoken with Kathy today. It's not like her to be a no-show. I will try her now."

"Yes, do that. Please keep me informed," Dr. Greenfield replied with concern in his voice.

Hunter ended the call and tried his wife. It went straight to voicemail. Panic began to set in. She had changed so much in the past while. She wasn't the reliable woman she used to be. Hunter could feel his face grow hot. His panic quickly replaced itself with anger. Scrolling his contacts, he found Nancy.

"Hi, Nancy. Have you heard from Kathy today?"

"No, I'm sorry I haven't. I was meaning to call her soon to check-in and confirm that she still wanted me to come to the house in the morning to watch Ray while she took you to the airport. Is everything alright?"

"I'm sure she is fine. She missed her appointment, and her phone is off. I will make sure she calls you when I see her. Thank you. Goodbye."

Hunter was furious. He reached his car in the lot and sped towards home. Her car was gone. Driving past, he circled the block and continued downtown. Up and down the streets, he scanned the businesses for her car. He thought about Ray and tried her cell again. No answer. Hunter tossed the phone on the passenger seat and headed back home.

The house was silent when Kathy walked in. She crept up the stairs avoiding the known creaks in each step. Entering the bedroom, she clicked on the lamp and placed Ray in the bassinet. Pulling the door half-closed, she ventured back down the stairs. She was consumed with guilt. She knew that Hunter would be disappointed. She wanted to turn back around and crawl into bed. Hide under the sheets and avoid the confrontation she was about to have.

Kathy entered the kitchen, going straight for the sink. She could see the light on through the garage window. The roast was completely thawed. The blood had pooled in the corner of the bag and begun to leak. Kathy stood there. She wanted to run outside and tell Hunter how sorry she was. Sorry for letting him down once again. She was playing the words in her mind when the back door opened. Turning to face him, Kathy began to cry.

Glaring at her, Hunter opened the fridge and reached for a beer. He twisted the cap and flung it into the sink. "Stop your bullshit, Kathy. I am in no mood. Do you know how worried I have been? Everyone has been? Where were you? No, you know what. I don't even care. I know where you weren't. You weren't at your appointment, and you certainly weren't here making me supper."

"I lost track of the time. I'm sorry," Kathy stammered, reaching for her husband.

"Don't touch me. You lost track of a lot of things," Hunter yelled before chugging back the bottle of beer. "You better call your sister. She is waiting to hear from you. I will be in the garage ALONE!"

Hunter scooped the roast out of the sink and threw it in the trash. He pulled two more bottles out of the fridge and slammed the back door on his way out.

Kathy gripped the countertop forcing back her tears. She knew she had to be strong. She thought of Calvin. The way he used to get drunk and disrespect her. The same emotions she lived with in the past resurfaced, except this time, she had no one to blame but herself. Kathy bit down hard, breathing in deep. Slowly walking down the hall, she found her purse and rifled inside. She didn't want to call Nancy or anyone. She wanted the man in her backyard. She couldn't help but feel the immense distance that had grown between them. Placing the phone in her pocket, Kathy climbed the stairs to her bedroom.

She sat on the edge of the bed and undressed. Kathy typed the message, 'Hi Nancy, I am home safe and going to bed. I hope you will still watch Ray in the morning. Good night, I love you.' After hitting send, she lifted Ray out of his bed, pulling him close as they snuggled under the sheets.

When Kathy woke, she was alone in bed with Ray. She knew that Hunter must have slept on the couch. Her stomach was in knots. He was leaving today, but it felt like he was already gone. Ray started to fuss just as Hunter entered the room.

"Let me take him," he said as he cradled the baby in his arms.

"Hunter, I…"

"You what, Kathy? Get up and get dressed. We are leaving in an hour."

Hunter took Ray downstairs to feed and change him. Kathy got up and turned on the shower. She wanted to wear something appealing, something to catch his eye. He had never been this angry with her. Feeling lost, Kathy stood in the shower and cried as the water ran down her face. She wanted to stay there. Where it was warm and safe. She closed her eyes and tried to forget, forget about Kathy Crane, and Jessica.

The doorbell rang, jolting her back to reality. She knew it was Nancy. She knew she had to hurry. Hunter would be furious if she was running late. Turning off the taps, Kathy quickly dried off and got dressed. She swept mascara through her lashes and headed downstairs. His briefcase and suitcase were sitting by the door. Her nose tingled as she felt the tears returning. Kathy took a few deep breaths as she entered the kitchen.

"Hi, honey, how did you sleep?" Nancy asked while hugging her sister.

"Fine," Kathy lied. "Thank you for coming."

"Anytime. I love seeing this little man," Nancy exclaimed as she took Ray from Hunters arms.

Kathy stared at her husband. He looked so handsome in his suit. She wanted to wrap her arms around him. To beg him to stay. To redo their last day together before he left for his overseas flights.

"We better get going. The sun is shining now, but I checked the weather, and this just may be the calm before the storm," Hunter said as he kissed his baby boy goodbye.

Kathy pulled a couple of Kleenex out of the box and shoved them in her pocket. The two made their way outside and into the car. Kathy stared out the window.

She wanted to say something. She wanted him to say something. She could see the black clouds forming in the distance.

"It doesn't look good. Maybe they will cancel the flight," Kathy claimed.

Hunter laughed and turned up the radio. Kathy could sense the worst. There was nothing she could say or do to make things better. She prayed that he would miss her while he was gone. The radio was blaring, but the silence was deafening. She couldn't bring herself to speak. Before she was ready, Hunter parked the car. With the trunk open, he grabbed his bags and slammed the lid. Kathy stood there almost lifeless as he passed her the keys. Putting his hand in hers, Hunter squeezed and kissed her on the cheek. "Come on, let's go."

The couple took the elevator down and into the airport. Kathy held on to the warm hand in hers. She always hated when he had to leave, but this time it was different. There was no laughter or smiles. Kathy began to sweat as they moved farther along the terminal.

"This is me," Hunter said, stopping at the pilot entrance.

"I'm so sorry. I love you," Kathy cried as she wrapped her arms around him.

Hunter pulled her forward, looking deep into her eyes. She could see the hurt in his.

"I'm sorry too. I have to go."

Hunter threw his briefcase over his shoulder and placed his hand in his pocket. Pulling it out slowly, he clasped the paper in hers. Removing his hand, he turned around.

As she unfolded the note, her heart began to race.

Dearest Kathy,

You have been my guiding light to the man I always wanted to be. I am a jet-setter, a free bird, the captain of my own ship. I have tried to change. I thought I had. You have changed so much. I feel so overwhelmed, powerless. I used to have so much control over my life. It's not like it used to be. You aren't like you used to be. I miss Shelly, the woman I fell in love with. When the truth came out about your past, I never understood how you could just run from your life, but I do now. I feel that same urge to leave all this craziness behind me. I am to blame for a lot of it. I don't think I can be the man you need me to be to get through it. You are my wife, the mother of my son, and I will always love you, but I'm not sure love is enough anymore. I'm truly sorry...

Kathy broke down in tears. She lowered herself to her knees and wept on the airport floor. She stared at her hands, at the wedding band that symbolized an endless circle of love. That circle and her heart were now broken once again. As Kathy watched her husband walk away and out of her life, she knew what she had to do.

About the Author

Jaymee has been through several lifetimes of adventure and misadventure with her worldwide travel and life experiences. She grew up in Canada as an avid reader and started reading the newspaper to her grandfather at the age of five.

With her debut novel, *Sandbox Secrets*, she would like to continue the lives of these characters and aspires to pursue writing.

Acknowledgement

I would never have gotten this far without my mom. She was my soundboard and my motivation. Thank you for supporting me with this from my first word to the printed ones.